DOCTOR'S ORDERS

WENDY SMITH

Edited by LAUREN CLARKE

Cover Design by SPRINKLES ON TOP STUDIOS

Photography by CJC PHOTOGRAPHY

Cover model MIKE HESLIN

This is a work of fiction. Names, characters, businesses, places, events, and incidents are either the products of the author's imagination or used in a fictitious manner. Any resemblance to actual persons, living or dead, or actual events is purely coincidental. Ariadne Wayne is in no way affiliated with any brands, songs, musicians or artists mentioned in this book.

This book is written in New Zealand English, and as such contains phrasing and kiwi colloquialisms.

*Content Warning - contains attempted sexual assault, and character with PTSD

❀ Created with Vellum

BLURB

After an explosive end to his relationship, Drew Campbell heads home. Sparks fly when he meets local midwife, Hayley, and she and the young doctor end their argument in a way he never saw coming.

As their relationship grows, Hayley's torn between staying in the small town she's made her home, and moving to the big city with Drew. An emergency situation sees her on his doorstep, and Drew's reluctant to let go.

Especially with the attention she's attracted from an unwanted source. One who's used to getting his own way.

The second book in the Copper Creek story also features the continuing story of Adam and Lily. Adam's demons are never far way, and his past still has the ability to hurt them both.

1

DREW

TODAY HAS DISASTER WRITTEN ALL OVER IT. I SHOULD HAVE seen it coming.

"Drew, hurry up in the shower."

"Nearly done." I don't even know why she's yelling. It's not like she'll be out of bed anytime soon. I shut off the mixer and dry off before wrapping a towel around my waist, heading back to the bedroom.

She glares at me as I step out of the bathroom and into the bedroom. Still sitting in bed, her arms are crossed, and I continue to get the evil look as I cross the room. "Do you have to use all the hot water?"

"Yep." I haven't, but I enjoy teasing her. It's too easy.

"Maybe I'll call Ray today. We pay enough in rent and surely he can install a larger hot water cylinder."

We.

Rolling my eyes, I open the wardrobe, pulling out a clean shirt and slipping my arms into it before retrieving a tie.

Chances are by the end of the day, it'll be a mess, but it's the look that matters. I have outpatient appointments this morning, and I like to come across as professional.

Things aren't good with Lucy. After going out a few times, she moved herself in. I didn't mind. I hadn't lived with a girlfriend before, and we were getting on great.

It was when she quit her job without talking to me that I had a problem.

I always thought I'd have a family one day to support. That my wife could choose whether to work or not. But when your girlfriend quits her job a month into living with you, and you suddenly realise you don't actually know her that well? Yeah, not so great.

Especially when she's so good at spending my money.

I get out the door with her still ranting from the bed about the hot water, even though I guarantee the minute I'm gone she'll go back to sleep for another couple of hours. A real lady of leisure.

Reaching for the door handle of the car, my iPhone slips from my grip and lands with a crack on the concrete driveway.

I sigh, bending to pick it up. The screen's splintered, but not shattered, held in place by a protective cover. I can read the screen at least.

Kind of.

If this is the start of the day, I'm not looking forward to the rest.

The drive to work isn't long, but it's slow in the traffic, and it's hard not to be annoyed with myself for how my day's started.

There have been too many of those lately.

As I stride into work twenty-five minutes later, I smile at everyone I pass in the corridors. I love my job. Every day brings me into contact with parents and children, and I can't help but smile.

I'm just about to grab some lunch when I get a page to go to one of the delivery suites.

"Doctor Campbell." I'm met at the door by Caitlyn, one of the hospital midwives. Her eyebrows knit in concern.

"What's going on?"

"Clare Peters. The baby's starting to show signs of distress. It's been a long labour, and I'd like your opinion."

"Sure. I met Clare a couple of weeks ago. She has high blood pressure, right? Let's get her through this."

She gives me a thin smile. Of all the doctors here, I think I have a better relationship with other staff than most. Midwives often call me in preference to the others.

I beam at the patient as I walk into the suite. She's clearly exhausted, sweat dripping from her brow, and I note she has no support person with her. That always bugs me. Everyone needs someone.

"Hi Clare, I'm here to check on you and your baby. How's it going?"

She glares at me. "How do you think it's going?"

"I know you just want this over with, so I'm here to help." I flash her a reassuring smile.

Even in her angry state, Clare gives me a faint smile. "Please."

I check her chart. She's not long been given a dose of pethidine.

"Right. I think I need to take a look, if that's okay with you."

She nods. With a loud retching noise, she projectile vomits. Over the floor, and all over me.

I grimace as I reach for a towel to wipe down. It's not her fault. Pethidine's given with an anti-nausea med. One that's clearly failed to work.

"I'm so sorry." She sniffs, gripping the edge of the bed as another contraction hits her.

"It's no problem. Let's get that baby out and you can have a rest." I grab another towel and wipe down the side of the bed.

As I turn, the midwife shoves the latest readings of the baby's heartbeat in front of me. It's enough to concern me, and I finish cleaning myself as best I can with the towel. I smile as a set of clean scrubs are brought in.

Sliding off my shirt and the T-shirt underneath that's got vomit on it, I decide I can live with the pants. I need to get that baby out, and smelly pants are the least of my problems right now.

I look up, and Caitlyn's eyes are fixed on my chest. I'm pretty proud of my physique—lord knows I've paid enough to maintain it. Smirking, I pull the clean shirt over my head and raise my eyebrows, knowing her gaze will shift. As she meets my eyes, her mouth drops open, and bemused, I turn back to my patient.

"Okay, Clare. Next contraction I need you to push hard."

"Yes, Doctor," she huffs.

I meet Caitlyn's gaze again, and she nods. If this baby isn't born soon, Clare will be in the theatre having a caesarean. They're not my favourite way to deliver a baby, but in cases like this it sometimes becomes impossible to avoid.

The last thing I want is to freak Clare out. So, right now,

my focus is on trying to get this baby out before I make that final decision.

Clare tenses, and the pain is on her face before she groans.

"Here we go," I say softly.

She nods.

"Push. Let's see that baby." *Come on Clare, you can do it. We're in this together.*

She's so close, and from the pained look on her face, she knows what's coming out of my mouth next.

"The baby's crowning. You got this, Clare. Just a few more." I position my hands and nod. She cries out, and I see a little more of the baby's head. "That's it. Keep going."

"I can't," she whimpers.

"Make this next one a big one."

Clare grits her teeth, and closes her eyes. And then it's done, the baby slides out and Clare cries again, but her tone is relief.

The baby's in my hands, and I grin as I take a quick look. Good colour—good movement. He might have been reluctant to come out, but this little boy looks perfect.

"Your son is beautiful." I say.

She lets out a sob. "We didn't know what we were having. He kept closing his legs."

"I'll finish his APGAR check and then you can have a cuddle."

Her chest rises and falls quickly as she succumbs to the emotion. It's common enough, but it hits me square in the heart every time. One day I'll go through this with someone special, hold my own child in my arms. I can't wait for that day, but something tells me it won't be with Lucy.

The baby looks at me with big, dark eyes, and I grin before laying him on his mother's waiting chest. Caitlyn covers him with warm towels, and I pause for a moment to watch the beauty that is mother and baby bonding.

"Typical. You turn up and the baby comes out. Maybe I should just page you at the start."

I grin. It's not the first time it's happened.

"Her blood pressure's down a little," Caitlyn says, handing me the chart.

I nod. "That needs to be monitored, and if it doesn't come back down further by tomorrow morning, we'll look at our options."

"Thanks, Drew," she says quietly.

"You're welcome."

The door flies open, and a dark-haired, stressed-looking man comes running in, his face red and sweaty as if he's just run a marathon. Clare lights up the room with her smile.

"Did I miss it?" He puffs.

"Only just." She laughs, all the stress she suffered minutes ago completely gone with the arrival of her baby boy. Shifting her gaze to me, she still has that hazy, just-having-given-birth blissful look in her eyes. "We thought we had time for Dennis to make one last business trip before the baby arrived. This little one was just too impatient."

"I'm sorry. I'm so sorry." He covers her in kisses, and it makes me smile. His eyelids droop as he looks at me, he's tired too. "I had to fly back from Sydney, and it took forever."

"You're here now, and that's all that matters," Clare said.

"I'm so pleased for the two of you. Congratulations." My phone buzzes, and before I leave, I pluck my phone out of my pocket. I can't help the grin spreading across my face. "My sister-in-law is in labour."

Caitlyn's eyes widen. "Here?"

"No, back home. She's got a midwife, and I'm sure she's good, but Adam wants me to be there. Although, by the time I drive there, there's a good chance she'll have had the baby."

I shift my gaze to the patient. "I've got to go, but congratulations again, Clare, Dennis."

Clare beams at me. "Thank you, Doctor."

"You did all the hard work. He's a beautiful baby."

Caitlyn nudges my arm. "Get going. I'll finish up in here."

"Thanks."

I head out the door and toward the locker room to get in the shower. I need to get clean again before finishing up and getting in the car to see Adam and Lily.

It's not often I shower here. The water pressure is awful, but the heat is relaxing. I lather up the hospital anti-bacterial body wash, and rub it over my chest. My mind wanders to Lucy again. I need to do something about us. We haven't had sex in weeks, and I've become accustomed to spending more time with my right hand than touching her, despite us sleeping in the same bed.

I close my eyes. When we met, she was everything. She had a blossoming career as a buyer for an upmarket women's clothing store. She was so much fun, and whenever I wasn't at work, we fucked like bunnies.

But once we moved in together, she discovered life with a doctor wasn't that much fun for her. I'd given her all my free time, but it was all I had to give.

My eyes spring open as the water runs cold. After five

minutes, the staff showers stop giving you hot water. I frown, but I'm rinsed off, and it'll do until I get home.

Towelling off, I pull on my spare shirt from my locker. Despite the water, I still have the scent of vomit in my nostrils. After all that, it might just be easier to shower again at home.

Knowing she was due to give birth any day now, I've already asked a couple of friends to be on standby, ready to cover my shifts, and I text them to call in the favour. In a year, I'll be going into private practice, and my boss doesn't want to lose me so he's being as accommodating as he can. I dial his number.

"Hey, John. My sister-in-law's in labour, so I'm heading off."

"Let me know how it goes." During the years I've been working with him, I've established a friendship with John that continues beyond my work at the hospital. It'll help when I leave and have patients who deliver here.

"Will do. Thanks."

I head out to my car, and look at my phone again. A replacement will have to wait. Lily's more important.

It's a short drive to my apartment. I'll shower again, throw some things in a bag and get out of here. I already know Lucy will have zero interest in going with me. She's never come home to meet my family as she loves the city. The thought of being somewhere remote for even a couple of days doesn't do anything for her.

I open the door.

They don't hear me, so busy focusing on themselves, and I have to admit, the thing that bothers me the most is Ray Steele's bare white arse on my leather sofa. The leather sofa

I've sat on so many times watching sport, beer in hand, my feet on the coffee table, tainted by him sitting naked on it.

Lucy's blonde head bobs up and down so fast, she could take off at any moment. Ray's feeling it, his hips thrusting toward her.

I'm still pissed his naked flesh is all over my damn couch.

I push the door, and it closes with a resounding slam. Lucy, her eyes as wide as saucers, looks up and sees me. The fear in her face has to be caused by the gravy train derailing. I'm the engineer, calmly waiting for the crash, and it's too late to stop as Ray cries out again.

All I can do is laugh as cum spurts from his erect cock, landing in Lucy's hair, covering the side of her head as she squeals in horror. I did love her once, or I thought I did, but finding her like this is the final straw.

She hits rock bottom as he blows his load all over her.

Gaping at him, she turns, rising her hand to her face as one last blob hits her in the eye. He reaches for the closest piece of fabric to him—God only knows where his clothes are—and it's her dress. That very expensive designer dress she raved about for ages before she finally convinced me to buy it.

"You know, people usually have to pay to watch the money shot." I laugh as she glares at me.

"It's not what it looks like." She stands, her hair sadly not resembling Cameron Diaz's in *There's Something About Mary*. It's disappointing. Does cum not work the same way as hair gel? Can't say I've ever tried it.

"What's it supposed to be? It's not every day I come home to find my girlfriend blowing the landlord." I turn to Ray, who's desperately trying to cover his cock and reaching blindly for his clothing. "Are we at least getting a rent reduction for this?"

"You're a pig," Lucy screams.

"You're covered in someone else's cum."

Her chest rises and falls rapidly. It might be distracting if I was the least bit interested in her, but after that performance, I no longer care what or who she does.

"Anyway, I'm going to go and take a shower because I just had a woman vomit all over me, and the showers at work suck."

"Don't use all the hot water."

It's the line she uses every time I say I'm having a shower, but under current circumstances, it's comical. "Are you serious? You're worried about the hot water?"

I laugh all the way to the bathroom.

When I'm finally feeling clean, I go through my drawers and throw some things in a bag. Enough to keep me going a couple of days before I come back and sort out this clusterfuck.

"You can't go." She tries the puppy eyes, the ones I fell for way too many times. My brother, Owen, says I'm gullible, but I think I'm just soft-hearted. It's not working this time.

"Yeah, I can, and so are you. Pack your shit and leave."

Her lower lip wobbles. "You can't be serious, Drew. How will I survive?"

"Maybe you can go and live with Ray."

I slam the door, and a feeling of peace comes over me. I'm angry that she's treated me this way, but not heartbroken.

It's over.

2

ADAM

"DREW," LILY EXCLAIMS AS MY BROTHER POPS HIS HEAD IN THE door.

"Hey, Lily-bell. I hear there's a baby ready to come out of the oven," Drew says.

He shakes my hand and sits on the bed beside Lily, embracing her. "Whoa. You got fat."

She laughs, pain still etched on her face. "It's been forever. You can't tell me you just happened to arrive just as this baby decided to come out."

Her face distorts, and she grabs hold of Drew's arm to brace herself as she breathes through another contraction.

"Hey, you're cutting off the wrong brother's circulation." He laughs. "Adam invited me, and he's been giving me updates. I thought it was about time I came to see the lovely Lily."

I slap him on the shoulder. "Can you go flirt with someone else's girl?"

"I would, but there aren't any others around here that I can see."

Hayley appears in the door, a smile on her face and her arms full of towels warmed in the dryer. I take one from her and roll it loosely, helping Lily up a little to replace the one under her lower back.

"Here's one. This is Hayley McCarthy. Hayley's Lily's midwife. Hayley, this is my brother Drew."

I smile to myself as Drew sizes up Hayley.

Hayley nods as she places the towels on the blanket box at the end of the bed. "Drew the obstetrician?"

Drew stands, holding his palms up as if in surrender. "It's okay. I know this is your show. I'm here if you need an extra pair of hands."

She moves closer, standing almost face to face with him. "That'll depend on what my client wants." The tiniest of smirks crosses her face, and I laugh at my brother's cocked eyebrow.

"She's got you there, bro."

Lily moans, and I grab the cup of ice chips from beside the bed. "Want one?"

She shakes her head and reaches for my hand, linking my fingers in hers.

"I'm ready for the death grip." I grin.

Lily laughs and grimaces. "Don't. You're not supposed to make me laugh."

"I'm supposed to take your mind off the pain, and that's what I'm doing."

She nods, breathing deeply before giving me a small smile.

"They're coming fast now, Lily. We need to see how you're going. Did you want an audience or not?" Hayley asks.

Lily shrugs. "Why not? My vagina was on display when I gave birth to Max."

It's so unlike her, and I can't help but laugh as I kiss her hand encased in my own. She rolls her eyes and lifts her legs for Hayley to check. Out of the corner of my eye, Drew's watching Hayley rather than Lily as she feels to see how far Lily's dilated.

"You're so close, Lily. Just a little while longer and you can push."

I reach for a damp cloth, wiping Lily's forehead. "Nearly there, baby."

"Where's Max? Is he okay?"

"You don't need to worry about him. He's downstairs with James."

"I still worry."

Max has been so up and down with the pending arrival of his baby sister. I don't know if he fully understands the impact a baby will have on our household, but his mood swings with his mother's, and as we have grown closer to this day, he's only got moodier.

I kiss her forehead where the cloth has left a sheen of water. "As soon as the baby's here I'll go and get him. He'll fall in love with our little girl, Lily. I swear he will."

She nods, but her eyes tell me she doesn't believe it. Even after all these months together, I'll never understand the way Lily and Max are bonded. It hurts, but at the same time, it's a magical thing to see.

Her chest rises and falls faster, and I know the pain is coming again. I'd do anything to take this hit for her, to stop her feeling the agony of childbirth. The best I can do is hold her hand and be there for anything else she needs.

"I want to push."

Hayley smiles. "Let's check." Her smile widens. "The baby's right there. Next contraction, start pushing."

"Oh, I will," Lily says.

"Are you sure she's ready?" As Drew speaks, Hayley shoots him a look that could kill.

"I'm sure."

"Want me to double check?"

I extend my leg and tap Drew's ankle. He shifts his gaze to me. "Want to back off and let her do her job?"

"You invited me here."

"Not to be a pain in the arse."

He holds his hands up again. "I was just trying to help."

"Adam," Lily says, an edgy tone in her voice.

"Ready, babe?"

She nods. "It's … Ohh."

"Push." All three of us speak in unison, and the strain appears on Lily's face as she bears down.

"You three aren't supposed to gang up on me." She lets out a laugh, only to grit her teeth.

"We're helping," Drew says. Hayley's entire focus is on watching Lily, and she seems to ignore Drew.

Each push brings us closer to our baby, and when she finally slides out, Lily closes her eyes.

"We did it," I whisper

"No, I did it," Lily replies.

I laugh. "You know what I mean. Now we have two perfect babies."

Hayley's checking the baby, Drew hanging over her shoulder. I should have known he couldn't keep his distance.

"She's got great colour and tone," he says.

Hayley turns, and the look on her face tells me she wasn't aware Drew was behind her. "She does. I'll just finish her checks and give her back to her mother."

He nods. "Of course."

It doesn't stop him from hovering as she places the baby on Lily's chest. Lily gives me a bemused look as Hayley covers her.

"You just had to invite your brother," she whispers.

"I'm not going to apologise for worrying. Not after everything you went through with Max."

Her expression softens, and with one hand on the baby, she cups my chin with her other. "We made it through in one piece."

"Two pieces."

She grins, and shifts her focus to our daughter.

"Did you want to cut the cord, Adam?" Drew asks.

"Yes," I reply before I realise Hayley's staring at him.

"I clamped it." He shrugs. "The gear and the hand sanitiser was right there."

She shoots a glare at him, and he shrinks back. "Just trying to help."

I shake my head. "Dude. Maybe you should go and help in another room."

Hayley hands me the scissors to cut, giving me a forced smile as she does.

With trembling hands, I cut it, pushing thoughts that I never got to do this with Max out of my head. I still wish I could turn back the clock and either not leave, or come back to get answers. My hurt pride has a lot to answer for.

I know one thing for sure. I'll be here for Lily, Max, and this new baby now. And any other children we have. If I have my way, we're far from finished.

Lily moans, and I look back at her.

"Are you okay?"

"Just delivering the placenta," Hayley says.

"It looks good." Drew's still hovering, and I roll my eyes.

"I hope you take Hayley out for a drink after this to apologise for being a pain in the arse." I laugh. Drew opens his mouth. "I know, you're just trying to help."

Raising my hand, I stroke my daughter's fuzzy little head. She's so beautiful. Her hair is dark, but I hope she ends up with Lily's colouring.

"What are we going to call you?" I ask.

"Don't you have names picked?" Drew walks around the bed to stand behind me.

"We have a huge list, but we decided to wait until she was born to see what suited her," Lily says. "Go and get Max. I want him to meet his little sister."

Standing, I lean over and kiss her tenderly. "Back in a second." I reach a little farther to kiss the baby on the head. "My girls."

Max sits in the middle of the living room floor, playing with his Xbox, James beside him. He's home from university, and I'm overjoyed to have my little brother here for such a big event.

"Hey Max. Wanna go and meet your sister?"

His eyes stay glued to the screen, but when I look, the game's not even loaded.

"We're between games. Now is a great time," James says. "Max. Come on. Let's go and see Mum."

My son stands, his face long, as if it's been slapped. I frown; something's not right with him. Hopefully seeing his mother will shake him out of it.

I hold out my hand, and Max takes it. His lips curl into the tiniest of smiles as I grab hold of him and pull him into a hug. "Let's go."

Hand in hand, we walk to the bedroom, and Max cracks a grin when he sees his Uncle Drew.

"Hey Maxxy. How's it hanging?" Drew grins, leaning over to bump fists with Max.

We're back in time to see Hayley helping Lily put the baby to her breast for the first time. It's a sweet thing to watch as our daughter latches on and suckles enthusiastically.

"She's very alert," Hayley says.

Lily has tears in her eyes, and I grab her hand again. She doesn't need to tell me what she's thinking. This is far from the experience she had the first time around.

"Max. Come around here and see your sister." Her eyes are so full of love, and he walks around the bed. I follow so he's got me, too. The last thing we want is for him to think we favour his sister over him.

"You were that little once," I say to him as we reach the other side.

"I hate her," Max screams, slapping Lily's arm that supports his sister. He turns and runs from the room before I can stop him. I look back at Lily. Tears well in her eyes, and it stings my heart to see them.

I lean to kiss her forehead. "I'll sort him out. We knew he was going to be jealous, at least for a while."

"I didn't think it would be that bad." She sniffs.

I stroke our daughter's head. "He'll come around. I'll go and hang with him for a bit while Hayley and Drew clean up."

Drew's eyebrows leap up. "Huh?"

"You were a dick. The least you can do is help Hayley."

Hayley laughs. "It's okay. It's my job."

"Your job was interrupted by Drew. He can do his share."

Drew nods. "That's fair enough."

"You don't mind getting your hands dirty, then?" Hayley asks.

I bite down, stopping myself from commenting further as Drew shoots her a look I understand well enough. When Hayley's gone, I'll be teasing him about his reaction to the midwife. It's even more intriguing considering he has a girlfriend. Drew's never been the kind of guy to play around.

"Go and check on Max now?" Lily asks.

Nodding, I peck her on the lips and go searching for my son. I find him sitting cross-legged on his bed, the dog next to him. Those two are so close. Lucky picks up on Max's moods, and today is no exception. His head rests on Max's leg, and he looks as sad as Max does.

"Hey," I say, sitting on the bed.

Max doesn't even look at me.

"I know that having a sister is going to be difficult. You've got to share Mum and me now." Tears roll down his cheeks. Sometimes Max seems so grown up, and it's easy to forget he has learning difficulties that sometimes spread into his behaviour.

"I have four brothers, Max, and I found that annoying sometimes too. Especially when James came along. I was about your age when he was born, and all of a sudden, we had this squawking, pooing baby in our house."

He snorts, breaking down and giggling. I have no doubt it's my use of the word poo. Like a lot of other kids, Max finds fart jokes funny.

"But you know what? We were his heroes. James followed his big brothers around because he wanted to be just like them. That's you, Max. You're the big brother. You'll be your little sister's hero, and she'll adore you."

His eyebrows raise. "Really?"

I nod. "The minute she can crawl, she'll be crawling after you. She might drive you crazy sometimes because she just wants to be with you and she's your annoying little sister, but you're the only big brother she'll ever have."

He straightens his back and puffs out his chest a little. "She's so small. We can't play together."

"Not yet, but she needs you no matter how small she is. Your mum's going to be tired and will need us both to help her as much as we can, too. There'll be nights when none of us get any sleep. But you know what?"

"What?"

"We'll all be together. And Mum and I love both of you so much."

His bottom lip wobbles, and he throws himself into my arms. "I thought Mum might love the baby more."

"No chance, mate. When the baby's as small as she is now, she needs more help because she can't do things like you. But you and Mum have a very special bond, and nothing will ever break that. She loves you so much. So do I."

"Love you too, Dad."

My heart's so full in this moment. It always is when Max expresses his feelings. It's a love I sometimes think I don't deserve given he didn't know me for the first eleven years of his life, but he feels so much more than he ever lets on. Seeing Max's heart is rare.

"So, do you want to go and see your sister again?"

He nods. "Dad?"

"Yep?"

"What was she doing?"

I chuckle. "She was having her first feed. Instead of a bottle, she drinks Mum's milk."

"Mum has milk?"

Oh God. What have I done?

"It happens when mums have babies." I pause as I don't know if Lily breastfed Max. I'm not sure whether she got the chance; he was so premature. "Mum knows more about it than I do."

"Did she feed me like that?" His voice is full of wonder, and it's a bit of a kick to the gut to not be able to answer.

"I'm not sure. Why don't you ask her about it?"

He nods.

"Shall we go and see her?"

Drew's rocking the baby in his arms when we return, and Lily's nowhere to be seen.

"Lily's just in the shower. I get to hold this one." He grins.

"You'd make a great nanny."

I don't miss the snort that comes from Hayley as she makes the bed.

"Do you want to see your sister, Max?" Drew asks.

I hold my breath as Max hesitates, then nods.

Drew holds my daughter down at Max's level. She fixes her sights on him, and he grins. "Dad. She's looking at me."

"She is, Max. Give her a few weeks and she'll have a special smile just for her big brother."

"She will?" His eyes are as big as saucers.

Drew chuckles. "She's going to think you're the bee's knees, my friend. How lucky is she having a big brother like you? I bet you'll take really good care of her."

Max nods, and it's heart-warming.

He leans over and kisses his little sister on the head. "Sorry for earlier." His head shoots up, and he stares at me. "What's her name?"

I shrug. "We've all got to work that one out."

"What about Rose? It's kind of like Mum's name."

"Kind of." I hold out my arms, and Drew hands the baby over. "What do you reckon, little one?"

Those dark eyes fix on me. I'd love it if she takes after Lily.

"What does she reckon about what?" Lily comes out of the en suite. Her eyes are heavy; she must be tired after giving birth. She's still easily the most beautiful woman I've ever seen, with the possible exception of our daughter.

"Max thinks we should name her Rose."

Lily lights up. "That's a beautiful name. I'll have to think about it."

"Mum, the baby looked at me."

Lily reaches the bed and sits, patting the duvet beside her. Max sits as I hand her the baby. "She's so pretty, Max. Did you know she looks a lot like you when you were born?"

He shakes his head.

"I've got photos. We haven't looked at them in ages, but

maybe we should pull them out and you can see for yourself?"

His mouth twists as he keeps his gaze focused on his sister. "Mum?"

Lily smiles. "Yes?"

"Did you feed me like you feed the baby?"

Lily's clearly taken aback from the surprised expression on her face. "I did. Not at first, but I did."

"What do you mean?"

"You were born earlier than we expected, and you didn't know how to feed like your sister does. But that came in time, and at first you had a tube that went through your nose and down your throat. I could put milk in the tube and it went into your stomach."

His eyes widen. "Really?"

"Yes. You were in an incubator for a while to help keep you warm and healthy. The nurses used to fuss over you because you were so perfect."

A smile crosses his face.

"Max, I love you so much. And I love your sister just as much. You two and your dad are my whole heart."

He nods. "Dad says she's gonna follow me everywhere."

Lily laughs. "She probably will. I would have loved to have had a big brother or sister, or a little one."

Max's face falls. "You were by yourself."

She shakes her head. "No. Once I had your dad and then you, I was never alone."

My throat constricts at her words. That she can say that after everything she went through means more than anything.

"Lily, everything's clean, so if you want to lie down again, you can. The placenta's in a bag in the chilly bin and ready to be frozen if you want to." Hayley picks up her bag.

I nod. Lily wants to bury the placenta in the backyard and plant a tree over it. It's a Māori tradition, but with this being our home, she wants to put down roots, and neither of us could think of a better way to cement our family being here.

With Max, it all happened so fast for her, and at eighteen she didn't get much of a chance to do things the way she wanted to. This isn't just about doing something for this baby—it's about righting a wrong from so long ago.

"Thanks, Hayley."

"If you're all comfortable, I'll get out of here and give you some space. Give me a call if you need anything. Doesn't matter how big or small it is, if you have any concerns, call me. Even if it's in the middle of the night." She strokes the baby's head. "She's so beautiful. You're welcome to name her Hayley if you want."

Lily laughs. "Thanks for the offer. Now we can get to know her, we'll work out what she needs to be named."

Hayley nods. "I'll see you tomorrow. Try and get some sleep."

I get up on the bed beside Lily and lean my head on her shoulder. Life is so much better than I ever thought possible.

3

DREW

I CAME HERE TO KEEP AN EYE ON THE BIRTH OF ADAM AND Lily's baby.

The truth is both my eyes are focused on Hayley McCarthy.

I can't fault her work—not that I want to. She has the confidence of a woman who's been practicing a while, and she seems to have developed a close relationship with Lily, given the way they laugh together.

She has a beautiful laugh.

And she's completely and utterly pissed with me.

Leaving Adam and Lily with their new baby, I trail behind her out the door as she takes her things back to her car.

"Want a hand?"

She shakes her head. "I'm fine."

"You did a great job in there."

Opening the boot of the car, she dumps her bag and spins around.

"Really? You think so?"

I nod.

"Didn't seem like it, from the way you were trying to help." She's pissed, and I've never seen anything so glorious. Her dark ponytail swings as she flicks it over her shoulder, and her eyes flash with anger.

"It's a hard habit to get out of. I'm used to being in charge in these situations."

"It was rude."

I step forward, and she follows suit until we're nearly nose to nose.

"I don't know if I want to apologise. I didn't get in the way."

"None of it was needed."

I take a deep breath. I don't want to push her too far. "Look, I'm sorry. Can I make it up to you?"

Her eyebrows raise. "What do you suggest?"

Shrugging, I smirk. "Help you with your next delivery?"

Her mouth drops open. I know I'm being cheeky, but is it really going that far? "That might take a while. I'm on my way home and not on-call."

"Shame."

"I've had a long day and I'm all out of patience for interfering doctors." Despite her words, she's all smiles and it's driving me crazy.

I move a tiny bit closer, and her breath hitches. "You should go home and rest. Doctor's Orders."

Her blue eyes shine, and all I see is her amusement. If there's no mutual attraction here, I'm a monkey's uncle.

And then I do either the dumbest thing I ever have, or the best thing. I cup her face and kiss her, pressing my lips to hers. She doesn't fight it and kisses me back, parting her lips so I slip in my tongue. She responds by touching it with her own. Could she be any more perfect?

When the kiss ends, I pull back a little and look into her eyes.

"Drew," she whispers.

We don't know a single thing about each other, but I'm so drawn to her and I can see in her eyes that she's feeling the same way. "I'm sorry."

"Don't be."

I take a step back. "I guess I should let you go."

She's breathless. "We could always continue this conversation somewhere other than your brother's backyard."

"I like that idea better."

"Adam did tell you to buy me a drink or something."

I can't let the chance of a line bypass me. "How about or something?"

Hayley rolls her eyes. "Are you always this much of a tease?"

"Try me." I hold up my palms. "How about I grab some beers from the supermarket and we go back to your place? If we go to the pub, there'll be gossip."

She grimaces. "You've got a good point."

"All my points are good."

Hayley's lips spread into a grin, and she shakes her head. "You're a shocker."

"At least you're smiling, which is a hell of a lot better than me making you cranky. I don't really want to do that again."

She nods. "If you want to have that beer, I'm in."

The rest of the horrible day falls away at her words. I like this woman.

She's gorgeous, I know she'll understand my world, and she seems to have a good sense of humour. Definitely an upgrade.

Shit. I shouldn't be thinking like that.

But why not? I bet I wouldn't find Hayley McCarthy sucking some guy's cock on my couch.

My phone buzzes, and I roll my eyes. I don't have to look to know who that is, but in case it's work, I need to check.

Where are you?

Lucy.

"Drew?" Hayley's eyebrows draw together as she takes in the sight of me looking at my phone.

"I'll grab the beer. You tell me where you live."

Her smile leaves my heart in my throat. "Sounds good."

HAYLEY MCCARTHY LIVES in a colonial-style cottage not far from Adam and Lily. It's painted eggshell blue, and has a white fence. It's cute and homely with a garden that's alive with colour.

I check myself over and make sure I'm tidy before raising my hand to knock on the door. All I can think about is the kiss we shared.

She opens the door. In the time it's taken me to go to the supermarket and buy a half dozen beers, she's changed out of the trackpants she wore while working into figure-hugging blue jeans. I run my eyes from bottom to top, taking note of the low-cut loose shirt she's wearing that shows a little cleavage. Her dark hair hangs loose around her shoulders, and her blue eyes take me in.

"That was quick. I just got out of the shower. You found the place alright?"

"There aren't a lot of houses on this street."

Hayley smiles. "Come in, then."

I can't take my eyes off her arse as she turns and walks away, and I follow her through to the kitchen where she comes to a stop. When I meet her gaze, the smirk on her face tells me she caught me.

"Nice and cold." I lift the beer and place it on the bench.

She smiles, peeling back the cardboard and loading four of them in her fridge. From my pocket, I fish out my keys. I always keep a bottle opener on hand.

"Thank you," she says as I pass her one.

"Thanks for letting me come over."

She runs her finger around the rim of the bottle. "I don't usually invite men I barely know to my house. But then again ..." Her gaze fixes on me. "I don't usually get kissed like that by someone I barely know either."

"Today's a day for firsts, then. I don't usually kiss women I've just met. Not like that anyway."

Her smile spreads into a grin. She's gorgeous. All dainty features, but there's strength behind it. I just watched her help Lily deliver her baby and not worry about any mess.

"I knew Adam had a doctor brother, and I even knew you were an obstetrician. Didn't expect to have a helper today." She leaves the kitchen and I follow, sitting with her on the couch.

"Adam just worries to the nth degree over anything to do with Lily."

Hayley nods, running her fingers through her hair. "They seem very devoted to each other."

I nod. "They really are."

She licks her lips. "You know, this is kinda awkward."

"It really is. I don't know why. I mean, I only kissed you the once."

Hayley's smile lights up everything.

"What I do know is that I'd really like to kiss you again."

She nods, and my heart explodes.

Taking the bottle from her hand, I place it with mine on the coffee table before turning back to her.

I start slow, savouring the softness of her lips. Her tongue tastes of beer, and I reach up and run my fingers through her hair as I deepen the kiss.

When we break apart, the cutest little gasp catches in her throat.

"You'll be the death of me, princess," I murmur.

"Trust me, the feeling's mutual." Her soft voice drives me to distraction. It's sexy and comforting, and I want her calling my name.

"Best of three?"

She snickers, and leans a little closer.

I claim her mouth with mine, and she grips my biceps, pulling me in tight. Our tongues battle for a moment before she lets out the softest moan, and I run my hands down her back just to touch her.

"Hayley," I murmur as I pull back.

"Drew, we can't. This can't …" She leans back. "You're my client's brother-in-law. This wasn't a good idea."

"We're not crossing any line." I reach out and tangle a lock of her hair in my fingers.

"I know, it's just weird. We literally met today."

She has no idea the effect she's having on me. I haven't had sex with anyone but my own hand for weeks, and that combined with how good she smells leaves me harder than a teenage boy at a beauty contest.

But I'll respect what she wants.

"It's okay. I didn't come over with any expectations. I had an awful day, and then I met you and it made up for everything that went wrong. But I've been part of two births today. So, it's a good day."

She smiles. "You delivered a baby today too?"

"Yeah. Turned out that the midwife had it under control and the mother was really close, but I got called in because the baby was starting to stress and it could have easily gone pear-shaped."

Hayley takes my hand from her hair and squeezes. "So you're not one of those doctors who disses midwives?"

"No. That would be stupid. We all work together to take care of the mothers. You did an amazing job with Lily. I just got a bit carried away. I'm sorry."

She nods. "I appreciate your apology."

I reach up and curl a lock of her hair around my index finger. "I kissed you because you were angry, and that was crazy hot."

Hayley laughs. Her cheeks flush with colour. "You were annoying. I kind of liked kissing you."

"Only kind of?"

"Okay. Really liked."

"I really liked kissing you too."

Any other words I might have been thinking fall out of my head as her gaze fixes on me again. I want her.

She licks her lips slowly, and I'm done for.

With a growl, I kiss her again, trying my hardest to convey my want and need for her.

"Yes," she whispers, reaching for my shirt.

One by one, the buttons come undone, and I still as she finishes her task. I love watching her look of utter concentration. Her gentle hands push my shirt off, palming my chest, and my heart surrenders. I don't even know her, but there's just something about her that's driving me crazy.

I reach for her T-shirt and tug it over her head, kissing her while I unhook her bra.

I've never been so spontaneous, not when it came to women. My brothers would tease me about being a hopeless romantic, saying I was the one who took my time.

Not with Hayley. Being with her just feels right. And today, I want to be reckless and give her everything I have. Even if it's just for one night.

Cupping her breasts, I run my thumbs across her nipples. She shivers, her cheeks turning a light shade of pink. "You're gorgeous."

"Me, or my breasts?"

"Both."

She gasps as I drop my head to one, sucking a nipple into my mouth. Her skin's so sweet, and the whimpering sounds she's making give me a raging hard on. I want this woman more than anything I've ever wanted.

"Drew." She hasn't cried it out yet, but she whispers it. It's a start. It's the only word I want from her lips as I keep my attention on her breasts.

Her hand drops to my lap, and I nearly lose it as she strokes my cock through my pants.

Hayley wants this as much as I do. "Maybe we should go to the bedroom."

I chuckle. "I'm enjoying myself here."

"I'm on the pill, but there are condoms in my bedside cabinet."

That was the inevitable conclusion to this encounter, but the words send me into a spin. The thought of being inside her nearly makes me lose all self-control.

When I nod, she rises from the couch. She's a sight to behold, and I'm entranced by the woman who I only met mere hours ago.

Taking her hand, I follow her to the bedroom, and when she bends to take out a box of condoms from the bedside cabinet, I run my hands from her thighs to her shoulders before rounding her waist and tugging at the button on her jeans.

"You're so impatient." She laughs.

"Can you blame me? You're the one with your hands on the condom box."

She turns, rolling her eyes as she takes over unbuttoning her jeans. Pushing them down, she falls backward onto the bed.

Hayley's beautiful, all dark hair and blue eyes, and I follow her lead, dropping my pants to the floor before leaning over to hook my fingers into the waistband of her panties.

"Drew," she whispers.

The sound of my name on her tongue nearly undoes me on the spot. Her breath quickens as I slide her panties down her legs, and I raise my eyebrows at the sight of an obvious Brazilian wax. "You can get those in Copper Creek?"

Hayley's brows knit. "Get what?"

I nod, and her eyes trace the line of what I'm looking at.

She laughs. "No. I have to travel, but it's so worth it. Not that I've had sex for a while, but it makes it so much ..."

I lean over and kiss her, not letting her finish her sentence. "I love it," I murmur.

She blushes, and that excites me even more.

Bending, I grip her thighs and go straight for her pussy. Flicking my tongue over her clit leaves her grinding against me, and the scent and taste of her is divine.

"God, princess, you taste so good." I take my time, bringing her to the brink and pausing to let her catch a breath. She moans as I tease her, each time getting her closer to coming.

When she does come, it's a sight to behold. "Drew," she cries, and her nails dig into my biceps. I can't wait any longer, and I reach for a condom.

I peel the packaging open and roll it down my cock. Her breathing quickens, and I push her legs farther apart, sliding into her heat and closing my eyes as I do it.

I move hard and fast, needing release but wanting this to last for as long as possible. This isn't how I saw my day going, but I have no desire to be anywhere else but inside this beautiful woman. With real life bullshit facing me when I return home, I want to lose myself in her for as long as possible.

But it's not all about me.

I open my eyes to see her face, so open and full of emotion. Hayley's a woman who wears her heart on her sleeve.

She shifts her hips, thrusting to match me and driving me

in farther. We're a frantic mess, and nothing could be sweeter.

I trace a line with my right index fingers from her chin to her breast, circling the nipple. That this could happen today of all days, when I've decided to move on, must be fate. She's my fate.

Closing my eyes, I give up any pretence of this lasting any longer. She's so tight and hot around me, it's ecstasy to let go, soaring as I come.

For a moment, our gazes lock, and her satisfied expression tells me everything.

I collapse exhausted beside her, and she rolls over, laughing into my chest.

"What was that?" she asks.

"Pretty fucking good. That's what that was. I think I need a cigarette." Her eyes widen, and I grin. "I don't smoke."

She laughs again and plants kisses on my shoulders. "I didn't think this would be the outcome of inviting you over."

I raise my eyebrows. "What did you think would happen once you lured me into your lair?"

She shrugs. "I thought we might talk. Maybe get to know each other a little. As annoying as you are, it's always good to find someone I have something in common with." Her lips curl. "Although, you were a gigantic pain in the arse today."

"Oh, you have no idea how much of a pain in the arse I can be."

"I really don't want to know."

My phone starts vibrating, jiggling out of my pants pocket and onto the carpet. I groan. "I should check that just in case."

She nods. "On-call life. I know *all* about that."

I slip out of bed and retrieve the phone, rolling my eyes at the messages, and get back into bed. It's a shame my screen didn't crack farther down.

"Do you have to go to work?" she asks.

"No."

"All those text messages. You look like you're concentrating on something."

Get back here. We need to sort this out. The messages are coming thick and fast. If there's one thing Lucy's good at, it's texting. That and screwing our landlord, apparently.

I shake my head, distracted by the bleeps coming from my phone. "It's nothing. Just my girlfriend harassing me."

The words are out before I can stop them, and my mouth falls open. "Shit. No. Hayley—"

It's too late. Her eyes well with tears. "Get the hell out of my bed. What were you thinking?"

I drop the phone on the duvet. "It's not like that, it's—"

"Get dressed and leave. What was *I* thinking? I don't even know you. But for some stupid reason I thought we had a real connection. I'm such an idiot."

"No, you're not."

Her face is buried in her hands now, and I feel like shit, even if I've done nothing wrong. "Hayley ..."

"Just go, Drew."

"She's not my girlfriend."

"You literally just told me she was. Go away."

She lies down on the bed and pulls a pillow over her head to cover her ears. It's infuriating, and I lean over to tug on the pillow, only to receive a glare in response.

"Fine. I'll go, but I am seeing you tomorrow, and maybe

you'll give me a chance to tell you the whole story. Tonight meant a whole lot more to me than just sex."

I still hear her sobs as I dress and walk out. We don't even know each other. I screwed up, and I'll own that, but I hate that she won't give me a fair hearing. Although I guess at this point, it'll all sound like bullshit.

I'm sorry.

4

HAYLEY

I'VE NEVER HAD A ONE-NIGHT STAND. NOR HAVE I EVER BEEN the other woman.

Tonight, I did both.

The idea nauseates me. Not so much the one-night stand as the fact that the connection between Drew and me was so strong, I was sure it would turn out to be more than that. But if he has a girlfriend, that's all it can ever be. My heart hurts that he omitted to tell me about her before we had sex.

He leaves before he sees me sob. I could say I'm heartbroken, but that would be a lie. We weren't in love. All it had been was uncontrollable lust between us.

That's a lie too.

I cry myself to sleep with my head wrapped in the pillow. I've spent my whole life running from the men my mother's tried to set me up with. 'Nice boys,' she always says. They probably are, but I don't want to be with someone just because she's chosen them. The reality is that they may be nice, but she chose them because they're rich. Tonight, I thought I'd found a nice boy of my own.

In the morning, I drag myself out of bed. My eyes are sore from crying, but I look semi-decent, and I give my hair a good brush before tying it in a ponytail and heading out the door.

My heart sinks when I see the silver Holden parked outside Lily and Adam's. The same one that stopped outside my gate last night.

If I didn't take my work so seriously, I'd bypass their place and come back later. But I made a time with Lily, and I intend to stick with it. It's my job.

I park outside. The gate's shut, but that's just to keep the dog in. He's a young Border Collie who's so affectionate he'd probably lick a burglar to death. I love visiting here. I only knew Lily in passing before her pregnancy, but she and I have become friends. Adam clearly adores her, and Max is the sweetest kid. I'll miss it when I don't come by so much.

Lucky, the dog, runs toward me as I come through the gate. Max will be in school, and Lucky's hanging out for him to come home. He nudges my hand as I walk, and I scratch his head, walking around the corner to the house.

"What the hell is wrong with you?"

I freeze when I hear Drew's voice. We didn't part on good terms, but thought he might at least be civil.

He's sitting on the swing-seat on the deck, swaying gently in the breeze.

"Drew, I ..." As I draw closer, I realise it's not me he's talking to. He doesn't hear me, or at least he doesn't seem to, and he rubs his forehead with his fingers, his phone in the other hand.

"It's really simple, Lucy. Pack your shit and get out of my flat." He sighs loudly. "No, there's no point. Even if you don't want to be with him, you were cheating on me in my own home. I repeat. What the hell is wrong with you?"

My heart sinks. I might have made a snap judgment after all.

Mounting the steps, I watch for a moment, my heart aching for him. He's in obvious pain, but I get the feeling it's not because his relationship is broken. With his hand pinching his forehead, he doesn't seem to have seen me.

The seat sinks as I sit, and he turns his head, his eyes widening when he sees me. I give him what I hope is a reassuring smile and place my hand on his shoulder, gripping it gently.

"Fine. I'll tell you what. I'll leave, and you can stay in the flat. Maybe Ray will rent it to you cheap, or even free." He rolls his eyes. "You can even keep the couch. As if I'd want that."

He hangs up the phone and drops it to the seat beside him. "I'm sorry you had to hear that."

"I'm sorry I told you to leave. I should have listened to you."

Drew shrugs. "You weren't to know." He turns his head to catch my gaze. "My relationship with Lucy wasn't that great to start with. Yesterday morning, I came home from work early and found her blowing the landlord. On my favourite couch."

My jaw drops. "What a bitch."

He gives me a lopsided smile. "Yeah. I mean, I kinda knew that things were screwed for a while, but when you're working, life has a habit of creeping by without you realising. And all of a sudden, you've been cheated on, you've broken up, and then you've ended up in bed with someone much better."

I laugh, my cheeks heating with embarrassment.

"You're something special, Hayley McCarthy. I hope you know that."

Shrugging I turn away, and he places his hand on my knee.

"I don't know what that was last night, but I've never experienced anything quite like it."

I nod. "Me too."

"I'd really like another chance."

Turning back, I see his eyes are full of emotion. There are moments when this thing between us feels like pure, unadulterated lust, but there's something behind that. A man who wants more.

I want more. Or at least a repeat of last night.

"I'm not going home until tomorrow. Have dinner with me."

There's no way I can stop the smile now gracing my face, and I nod.

"We can either go somewhere fancy, or grab fish and chips and sit down at the cove."

My grin widens. "I like the second idea. The cove is one of my favourite places."

"Mine too."

"I need to go and see Lily."

He nods. "Give me your number, and I'll text you later. I'll come by and pick you up around six if that suits."

"Sounds great." I bite down on my bottom lip. "I'm sorry for last night. I should have given you a chance."

Drew shrugs. "I shouldn't have let her distract me. What

was happening with us was far more important than her crazy texting. Next time, I'll just turn my phone off."

"Next time."

He squeezes my knee. "If you want to."

"I want to."

LILY'S in bed when I get inside, all snuggled up and feeding the baby.

"How are you feeling today?"

She gives me a blissful smile. "Better than I thought I'd be. I guess having a healthy full-term baby is a really different experience to what I had before."

"I bet. How's she doing? Is she feeding well?"

Lily nods. "She's so hungry. But I managed to get a little sleep last night too. Adam took her between feeds."

"That's awesome. How's Max doing?"

She laughs. "He popped his head in the door at about two this morning and told her off for making noise. We gave him the option to stay home from school today because things are so crazy, but he wanted to go and tell everyone about his little sister."

I grin. "I'm so glad he came around."

"So am I. I knew he'd have a problem with it. It was just me and him for so long. But we'll get there." She shoots me a sly smile. "So, you and Drew ..."

"That obvious?"

"The way he was looking at you, and then how he disappeared when you left? It was just a guess, but given how red your face is, I'd say I guessed right." She grins.

I let out a loud breath. "Yes, you guessed right."

Lily chews her lower lip, and places her hand on mine. "Did he tell you he has a girlfriend? Maybe I shouldn't be so blunt, but it's not like Drew to lead someone on, and I think you should know if he hasn't told you."

"They broke up."

Her eyes widen. "Really? When?"

"Yesterday, before he came here." I pause. "What was she like?"

Lily shrugs. "I don't know. They were together for a while, but I never met her. He'd say she was a city girl, but she just sounded like a snob."

I laugh, despite myself.

"But I do know you, and I know Drew. He needs someone good in his life, and you're amazing."

"Thank you."

She squeezes my hand. "I mean it. There was no way I could tell Adam how nervous I was about giving birth again after everything that happened with Max. You were a godsend helping me through that."

"It's been a pleasure. Drew seems really nice."

"He is. If you do start seeing him and he doesn't treat you well, I'll kick his arse."

I laugh, but I can picture her doing it. One thing I have picked up on in the time I've spent with Lily and Adam, is that his brothers are very protective of her. I wish I'd had a reason to get to know her earlier. While I've made friends in this town, it's a place full of gossip, and I've been reserved. Lily's one of the few people I trust.

"Have you got a name for that baby yet?"

She shakes her head. "That's still up for debate."

I smile. "You've got a little while."

The baby screws up her face, and lets out an almighty wail.

"How about I leave you to it and I'll see you again tomorrow?"

"Maybe I'll be organised enough to make you coffee."

I shake my head. "You take care of that baby, and yourself. That's all I need you to do."

I SPEND AN HOUR GETTING READY, only to end up wearing a similar outfit to the one I wore the night before.

Drew knocks on the door, right on time at six p.m, and lets out a low whistle when I open it.

"You know how to drive a guy crazy."

I laugh. "I'm comfortable. Might as well be if we're sitting on the sand."

He rolls his eyes. "I'm a bit more civilised than that. I've got a blanket."

Stepping past him, I pull the door shut and lock it behind me. He speeds past me on the path to the gate, and opens the passenger door of the car for me.

I pat his chest as I step into the car. "Such great service."

"I aim to please."

There's the familiar scent of paper-wrapped fish and chips coming from the back seat, and I grin as Drew gets in the driver's side. "You came prepared?"

He nods. "To feed an army actually. I didn't know what you wanted, but leftovers are good for a midnight snack."

I lean over and peck him on the lips. "I'm glad I found out the truth."

Drew has these tiny dimples in his cheeks when he smiles, and they make my heart flutter. "So am I. I was thinking of turning up on your doorstep to explain tonight. If you listened."

"Well, I'm here now, and we have food to eat before it gets cold."

"Is that you bossing me around?"

I lick my lips. "Better get used to it."

"Yes, boss."

I lean back in the seat of his late-model Holden as we take a drive to the cove. The weather's warm, and we're far from alone on the beach, but there aren't that many people there.

I carry the bundle of food and Drew carries the blanket. He lays it down on the sand, and I unwrap the parcel. The Copper Creek Fish Shop makes the best fish and chips I've ever tasted. I inhale the amazing smell.

Drew sits next to me, and for a few minutes we eat in silence, sharing smiles and glances.

My cheeks heat at the memory of last night, how Drew's hands on me felt, how he put me first the entire time. It was frantic and hot and everything I never knew my body was capable of.

I want it again.

"I hated leaving last night when you were so upset," Drew says.

"It really hurt. I didn't get a lot of sleep after that."

"Neither did I. I spent most of the night trying to work out how to put things right."

"Where did you go last night?"

He picks up another chip. "I went to Mum and Dad's. We've all still got rooms there if we want them. Except Adam. They changed his into a spare room."

"Why?"

"I think they thought he'd never come back. Then he did, and moved in with Lily, so I guess changing it wasn't a waste of time."

I rest my head on his shoulder. "I'm sorry again for kicking you out. I could have done with a giant hot-water bottle."

Drew laughs. "If you're interested, the offer's good for tonight."

He plants a kiss on the top of my head, and I sigh. "Might just have to take you up on that."

"Promise?"

"We'll see."

I lean back on my arms and close my eyes.

"I always loved coming down here. When we were kids, we'd spend a huge chunk of the summer holidays at the cove," Drew says.

Grinning, I roll onto my side, propping myself up on one elbow and look at him. "That must have been nice."

"Four horny teenage boys with a bunch of girls in skimpy bathing suits? It was awesome." He laughs, and reaches to run a finger down my cheek. "I like being here with you now, though."

"Even if I'm not wearing a skimpy bathing suit?"

He smiles, the dimples in his cheeks setting my heart alight. "Even then."

I swallow and lick my lips. "I'm glad you're giving me another chance."

Drew shakes his head. "Don't worry about it. All those texts made me a little nuts." He leans over and brushes my lips with his. "We did have a real connection. Do have a real connection. I spent all of today thinking about you."

"I did the same."

"What am I going to do about it, Hayley McCarthy?"

"I don't know, Drew Campbell. What *are* you going to do about it?"

He gives me this wistful look, one that says he's feeling the same as I am. "Drop you off home and go back to Mum and Dad's for the night. That's probably what I should do."

"I don't know if that answers my question." I poke my tongue out, and his mouth is on mine with soft, romantic kisses as he rolls me onto my back.

Parting my lips, I sigh as his tongue touches mine. The feeling from last night is lingering, and all I want right now is him. Are we rushing this, or is this going at the pace it needs to?

"I really like you. Does that answer your question?" He's breathless, and it's so hot.

"I like you too."

His blue eyes penetrate my brain with their stare. "Should we go back to your place?"

"I thought you'd never ask."

His mouth covers mine again, and my entire body is on fire, needing his touch. "Maybe I should take you to your place before we end up naked on the beach."

I reach up and run my fingers down his cheek. "There's a great idea. It's a bit too public."

"Don't think I wouldn't do it." He waggles his eyebrows.

I laugh. "You don't have to live here."

He pushes himself up and stands. "Come on, then. I'll save you from the gossip."

"With your car parked outside my place all night?" I tease.

Drew offers me his hand, and I take it, pulling myself up.

"Okay, maybe some of the gossip." He wraps his arms around my waist.

At my place, he makes good on his promises with more gentleness than I'd thought a man was capable of. What we have is special. I guess we just have to work out exactly what it is.

When I close my eyes to sleep, Drew's naked body is curled around mine.

All is right with my world for a change.

How long will this last?

5

DREW

I WENT TO UNIVERSITY IN AUCKLAND, AND THEN STRAIGHT onto Hamilton, so the city has been my world for a long time.

As much as I enjoy going home, I love being in the 'big smoke', as the people back home would say. My apartment isn't far from work, and the life there suits me.

When I left the city two days ago, my mind was full of Adam and Lily, as well as the mess I'd left behind. All the way home, the only person I think about is Hayley. For the first time in a long time, I hate leaving Copper Creek.

I unlock the apartment door, and frown at Lucy sitting on the couch.

"What are you doing here?"

She flutters her eyelashes. "Waiting for you."

"That shit's not going to work on me this time."

I make my way into the bedroom and open the wardrobe.

Pulling out my large suitcase, I fill it with shirts and pants before hitting my drawers.

Hands with long, red painted nails run up my chest.

"Don't," I say.

"But Drew, I don't want us to end this way."

"Should have thought of that before you sucked another guy's cock." I turn around and glare at her.

"It was a mistake. I swear."

"Your lips fell onto it?"

She tries that femme fatale look she does so well that's sucked me in before. Not anymore. Her right hand slips to the front of my pants. I grab her wrist to stop her.

"No. You don't get to do that anymore. I'm packing, and I'm leaving. I'll be back to get the rest of my things next weekend."

Her face falls. "But ..."

"There are no buts. I dealt with you quitting your job without speaking to me. I dealt with you spending my money like there was no tomorrow. It wasn't the first time you cheated, was it?"

Lucy's expression tells me everything.

"Was he the first one? Do I need to get tested?"

"You always wore a condom."

"I'll do it anyway."

Her eyes narrow. "I was never unsafe."

"Never? How many have there been? Fuck, I'm just a sucker, aren't I?"

"Stop twisting my words."

"Really? How would you have felt if you'd walked in on me going down on another woman? I'm sure you wouldn't just shrug it off."

I let go of Lucy's wrist. "I'm going to a motel, and I'll find somewhere else to live. I'll give Ray notice, and you can either stay here alone or go somewhere else. I'm not going to be your doormat." Picking up the suitcase, I wheel it out of the room.

"Drew." She whines, and I realise it's been so long since we've had a proper conversation. It's funny how when you're busy and life is passing by that you don't notice these things. Now, I notice everything.

"Just don't." I don't look behind me, and I walk out the door, pulling my case. There are plenty of motels in town, and I can do with a bit of time taking care of myself.

Besides, I have something so much better to look forward to.

I FIND a motel near the hospital. If it's going to be home for a few nights, I might as well make it convenient.

It's a small room, but it has a bed, and I'm so tired after my trip that it's all I need.

I kick off my shoes and collapse onto the soft mattress. Today's been exhausting, between driving and dealing with Lucy. What I really want to do is curl up around Hayley and sleep.

She seeps into my every thought, and spending last night with her made us way more than just sex.

I pluck my phone from my pocket and grimace. First thing tomorrow, I'll go and buy a new one. A new phone for a fresh start.

Scrolling down to her name, I smile as I press the message button.

I'm back in Hamilton, and I'm alone in a motel thinking about you.

It takes a few minutes, but I soon get a response.

You're in a motel?

She can have the flat. I'll find somewhere new.

Don't forget to replace your couch.

I chuckle and shake my head. This girl has me tied up in all kinds of knots, and I don't even really know her. Guess it means I'll be going home more often.

I'll buy something bigger and better. So when you visit, there'll be plenty of room for us to lie down on it together.

I like that idea.

So do I. I really like that idea.

I like that you like that idea.

I like that you like that I like that idea.

Laughing, I gaze at my phone as if it's about to spill some big secret. It's been a long time since I've felt so alive, so wanted. How had my relationship with Lucy been so bad, and how had I been so blind to it?

Wish you were here. There's room service and a mini bar.

I'm sold. Or I would be if I didn't have work tomorrow.

If you're going to Lily's, give my niece a cuddle.

Of course I will. Goodnight, Drew.

Night, princess.

TWO DAYS, and a lot more text messages later, I stumble across a place to live.

Today there's a farewell at the hospital for one of my co-workers. Daryl Murray has about ten years on me, and is not only leaving the hospital to go into private practice, he's going overseas to do it.

He's been a friend and a mentor, and as excited as I am for him, I'll be sad to see him go.

"You, Drew. You'll go far when you get out of the hospital. I mean, it's not a bad place to work, but you have so much potential." He slurs after a couple of beers, and I smirk. Daryl is a lightweight when it comes to drinking.

"Thanks, mate. I'll miss your help."

"You don't need it."

I nod. "So, you all ready to go?"

He grimaces. "Almost. I thought my house would have sold by now. It's supposed to be a buyer's market, but someone should tell the buyers that."

Laughing, I pat his back. "Well, I'm looking for somewhere to live. I can't buy yet due to the ex's spending habits, but if you end up renting it out, I'd be keen."

He gapes. "That's a really good idea. I know I can trust you."

"Of course you can. Let me know how much you want, and I'm sure we can work it out."

"It'd really help me out of a bind. I'm a bit reluctant to leave it empty."

I've seen his house. It's huge and would be a great place to give myself some space. Hopefully he remembers this conversation in the morning.

When I get back to the motel, I send a quick text to Hayley. It's funny. We still don't know each other well, but having her to talk to gives me something to look forward to.

I might have found a place to live.

The phone rings, and I smile when I see her name appear on the screen.

"Tell me you need to hear my voice."

She laughs. "Of course. I also thought it'd be easier than sending dozens of texts."

"Dozens? That's ambitious."

"Okay, it might be a slight exaggeration, but it seemed like it last time we started a texting conversation."

"I miss you."

There's silence for a moment, and I know I've hit her with something she wasn't expecting.

"I miss you too." She lets out a loud breath. "So, tell me about this place you found."

I smile. "Well, I don't know for sure if I can have it, but it's a house. He's got it for sale at the moment so I'll find the link for it online and send it to you."

"I'd like that."

Lying back on the bed, I close my eyes. "How was your day?"

"I stopped by and saw Lily again. She's doing so well."

"Have they named the baby yet?"

Hayley laughs. "No."

"They should just let Max do it."

"Max is still pushing for Rose, but Lily has final say and isn't quite sure."

I smile at the thought of that little family. Lily will be keeping Adam on his toes. With any luck, she's got him running around after her, just as he should have done all those years ago instead of running from her. He's the luckiest bastard on this planet to get back what he walked away from. Lily's one of my best friends, and I'd do anything for her and for Max.

I chuckle. "Good for her."

"Other than that, today was crazy busy. I can tell you …"

Hayley's voice soothes me as I settle in for sleep.

I do miss her.

THE HOUSE IS AMAZING. By the weekend, I'm standing in the living room in silence.

There are no sounds from the street outside, as there was in the motel. No Lucy. She has no idea where I am, and I intend to keep it that way.

I've taken the furniture I wanted from the flat, and replaced what I need to from the savings I'd managed to squirrel away. Tonight's the first night I sleep in my new bed.

Every night, Hayley and I burn up the phone line with texts and calls. Little by little, we get to know each other, and maybe it's what we should have done before sleeping together, but the distance is helping, in a way. It means our fledgling relationship isn't just about sex. It's becoming so much deeper.

Although, as I lie on my super-king-size bed for the first time, all I want is for her to be here with me.

Memories play through my head. The instant attraction, kissing her for the first time, needing to touch her.

My fingers hover over the onscreen keyboard of the phone. I feel as if there's so much to say, but we've known each other for five minutes, and I don't want her thinking I'm some kind of crazy stalker.

I don't need to start the conversation.

Are you settled in your new house yet?

I smile at the text as it pops up on my screen.

Getting there. I was just about to get some sleep.

Sorry. I just wanted to make contact.

My phone was in my hand to do the same.

Great minds and all that.

She makes me happy even when she's not with me.

Something like that. I wish you were here. You'll love this place.

There's so much more I want to say, but it's too early. Way too early.

I looked at the link you sent me. It looks lovely. Is that you inviting me to visit?

I grin at my phone and let out a loud breath.

You're welcome any time, princess. The sooner, the better.

My first night in my new place, I sleep better than I have in ages. It's not just because of this house—it's because of Hayley.

I think I'm falling for her.

THE MORNING SUN floods through the huge bedroom windows. I could be pissed with myself that I forgot to pull the blinds before going to bed, but the privacy screens leave me hidden behind the glass and I can enjoy the rays.

I'm going to love living here.

Slipping out of bed, I pull a pair of dress pants on before opening the wardrobe for a shirt and tie. The plush carpet is soft, and the warmth continues as I step onto the heated tiles of the kitchen. Darryl pulled out all the stops for this place.

I flick on the electric jug, and while the water's boiling, I pull my shirt on. Standing by the bay windows that face out to the backyard, I look over the pool. This is a home for a family—not that it's ever been one.

It was a no-brainer moving in. When we got to talking rent, it wasn't much more than what I'd been paying for my flat. It's farther to drive to work, but it's a nice house in in a nice neighbourhood.

The jug flicks off, and I finish buttoning my shirt as I cross the room. Am I crazy for wanting this much space?

When I was a kid, I shared a room with Owen until we moved to Copper Creek. Even in a bigger house, I was always surrounded by people, and in uni and when I started at the hospital, I flatted with others. I'd finally got a flat for myself just before I met Lucy.

Now all I can think about is getting Hayley here to spend some time together. Being with her isn't like being with anyone else—it's just so easy.

I mix my coffee, and pick up my phone, smiling as I see the message on it.

Have a good day.

But there's another message.

We need to talk. Come home.

I need to go back and get the rest of my things, but as far as I'm concerned, I *am* home.

6

HAYLEY

"HAYLEY MCCARTHY?"

A phone number I don't recognise rang my mobile seconds ago, and while I'd love to ignore it because I've been up since 1.30 a.m, I have to answer it just in case it's important.

"This is she."

"My name is Ash Harris. I need your help."

I don't need any further introduction. Partway up McKenzie's Mountain is a massive compound, hectares and hectares blocked off by a massive wall that I assume goes all around the property. Ash Harris is the leader of the people who live there.

From what I've heard, his father used to run the commune, and while they tended to keep to themselves, the people who lived there were a lot more open. There are stories of the women coming into town to shop. I have to admit, that place scares the shit out of me.

"What can I do for you, Mr Harris?"

"One of the ladies here. She's in labour, and the woman looking after her thinks she's in some kind of trouble."

My stomach drops. If they're having babies in there, who's looking after them? "How long's she been in labour?"

"Uhh, it started a day ago, maybe? I don't know a lot about it, but she's in a lot of pain, and I think she needs help."

I've been up for fifteen hours so far. What I really need is some sleep. "Either myself or Margaret Joyce can be there in the next fifteen minutes."

"The sooner the better."

I get Margaret's voicemail. She was up most of the night too, so it looks like it's me.

It's funny. There are times when it's quiet, but like so many other things in a rural community, babies seem to be seasonal. And it's the season. Margaret and I cover a massive area between the two of us, and we intersect with two midwives in the next town over to fill any gaps. The population of Copper Creek isn't huge, there's maybe three thousand people, but there are a lot who live on farms and not in the town centre. My fuel bill can be insane.

McKenzie's Mountain is at the back of Copper Creek. It and the mountain range it belongs to wraps the town. There's one road into town and one road out. It's off the beaten track and wonderfully peaceful.

I drive up to the large gate. There are no signs of guards or anyone else around, but the gates slowly open, and my stomach flips with nerves as I drive inside. In the four years I've lived in Copper Creek, I've never been inside this community. They're so secretive.

A large compound is at the end of a very long driveway.

Behind it, there are rows of greenhouses. I never thought about how these people must feed themselves, but I guess they've been here long enough to be self-sufficient. For all intents and purposes this just looks like a big farm.

The concept has always seemed sinister to me. People locked behind a large gate, not seeming to venture out into the world. One of the things I love about Copper Creek is that it's rural and there are a lot of wide, open spaces. Coming from the sometimes cramped city, it's heaven on earth.

Unsure of where I'm supposed to go, I drive closer to the largest of the buildings. At the entrance is a tall, dark-haired man who waves at me. I guess that's who I'm supposed to see.

I retrieve my bag from the back seat and climb out of the car.

The man extends a hand for me to shake. "Hi, I'm Ash Harris." This is the leader of this group.

Ash Harris is beautiful.

There's no other way to describe him. With short, jet black hair, and piercing blue eyes, it's enough to make a girl's heart flutter. But I'm not any girl, and men like him are a dime a dozen in the world my mother wants me to live in.

That doesn't make him any less intimidating.

He smiles at me like a cat who got the cream. "And you are?"

"The midwife. Where's my patient?"

His smile disappears, and I immediately regret how short I am. Not because I'm worried about offending him, but it does concern me that he might not let me see her.

He nods. "Come this way."

If there was a bridge, I think I've burned it, but the important thing is that he's leading me into the building and through a maze of corridors before we stop walking.

A tall, bearded man stands like a guard at the door of the room. I hear the exhausted groans of a woman who's been in labour too long. Gritting my teeth, I summon my courage and push the door open. No one stops me. Ash follows behind.

In the centre of the room is a bed with the labouring woman in it. Her dirty blonde hair hangs loose, and she's dripping in sweat. There are women either side of the bed, dressed in the plain grey dresses I've heard women from this group all wear.

Ignoring them, I walk to the side of the bed. "Hi. I'm Hayley, and I'm a midwife. You are?"

"Julia."

"What's going on, Julia?"

One of the women speaks. "She's been in labour for hours, and nothing's happening."

I wait for any more information. "Is that it?"

"That's all we know."

Holy shit.

"I just need to examine you."

She nods, pain written all over her face. How they let it get to this stage, I'll never know.

I open my bag and pull out my stethoscope and Doppler. I've never been in a room so quiet when someone's giving birth. It's like she has an audience instead of anyone helping her.

Her blood pressure's high, and at first I can't find the heartbeat of the baby. I swallow hard. I can take her to the clinic for an ultrasound, but that's something I suspect she won't let me do, despite needing it a long time ago.

There's a faint echo of a heartbeat, and it's too fast to be Julia's. I place my hands on her to feel how the baby's body's lying.

My heart sinks. The baby's transverse.

This is one of the worst things that can happen.

Lying sideways, this baby won't come out. At least not here.

"You need a caesarean. The baby's lying the wrong way," I say.

"Can't you turn it?" one of the women asks, and it takes everything in me not to roll my eyes. If they're going to look after a woman in labour, they should at least know that it's too late for that.

"No, I can't. The baby's transverse. There's an elbow where the head should be."

She blanches, and I look toward the door where Ash stands.

"We need to get an emergency evacuation for her."

"Really?"

"If you want her and the baby to live, yes." I regret the words, and I would never say anything like that in front of a patient normally, but time is of the essence, and this could easily turn into a tragedy.

Without his reply, I pick up my phone and dial a number Margaret gave me four years ago, which I've never had cause to use. I've sent patients out of town before to get specialist care, but never an emergency evacuation.

Ash moves beside me. "Whatever you need."

"The helicopter will land beside the clinic in town. We'll

have to get her there."

Ash nods. "There's nothing else you can do?"

He might have a gaze that penetrates to my soul, but Julia's life is at risk, and I can't back down.

"The baby can't come out this way. She needs a doctor."

"Doctor Paton is in town."

"She needs an obstetrician."

He nods again, but his blank reaction irritates me. It makes me want to scream at him, but I need to keep my cool for Julia's sake. He's standing over me, and I'm unsure if it's because I'm putting my foot down and he doesn't like it, or if he's hovering because he cares about Julia. Chances are it's the latter, but it's unnerving. I doubt anyone has ever told this man what to do.

"We've got a van we can use."

"That's a good idea. I'll go with her."

He gives me a thin smile. "Thank you."

The man from the corridor steps in and scoops Julia into his arms as if she weighs nothing. She grimaces, and the pain of another contraction is clear on her face. She moans as he carries her out the door.

Following my new patient back out, I watch as a mattress is carried out of the building and placed in the van, and she's gently laid on it. Without any hesitation, I hop in the back with her and sit on the floor. Ash gets in the front.

"How are we doing, Julia?"

She nods, fear in her face, tears in her eyes.

"It'll take a while for the helicopter to get here, but I don't want you to worry. You're with me, and I'll take care of you."

I'm shaking, but I can't let her know how scared I am. My career's been on the line once before, but this time I'm in charge and I have full confidence in getting her to help in time.

It's a fifteen-minute ride to the helicopter pad, and it's at that point I think about my car. It's still parked outside their main building, and I'll have to face these people again to get it back.

We have to wait until help arrives, and I hold Julia's hand tightly through her contractions. I'm timing them, but I don't need a watch to know they're speeding up. The sooner we're out of here, the better.

When the helicopter arrives, the paramedics move her to a stretcher and into the helicopter.

"Hayley."

I turn back to see Ash walking toward me.

"I'll give you my number. Text me any updates on Julia, and let me know when you want to pick up your car. I'd follow but I think she's in safe hands and I have others to look after."

Bile's in my throat because this man makes me uneasy, and yet if he's the leader of these people I don't have a choice but to be in contact with him.

I nod, and open my contacts. His much larger hand is on mine to grab it and enter the numbers.

He hands it back to me, and I turn toward the helicopter, the paramedic motioning me to get to it. There's no time for anything else, and I run without looking back, stepping up and smiling at Julia. She's pale, and I sit, buckling in before closing my eyes and giving a silent prayer that I've identified the issue in time.

If I haven't, I don't know if I can live with the consequences.

7

HAYLEY

"We can't get into Tauranga. The hospital wants overflow going to Hamilton." The helicopter pilot's tone is calm, and we all need to be for Julia's sake.

"Do we have a choice?" Julia squeezes my hand as I ask.

My stomach churns. I already know the answer.

"I've already laid a flight plan. It'll take a little longer, but we'll get right in."

I raise my eyes to the roof. Delays could be dangerous, but if we land at a hospital that's at capacity, there'll most likely be delays anyway.

"Hayley?" Julia says quietly.

"We'll get you there as fast as we can," the pilot says.

Julia grimaces in pain and grips my hand tighter. How did things ever get this far?

"Can you take her hand for a second?" I ask the paramedic. He nods and I transfer Julia's hand to his. Smiling at Julia, I cock my head. "He can handle the hard squeeze better. I just need to check in with someone in Hamilton to see if they're working."

She nods and takes a deep breath. I've managed to keep her calm, which is half the battle, but the pain seems to be intensifying.

I pull my phone out of my bag and text Drew.

Are you working? I'm incoming on a rescue helicopter with a transverse.

Taking a deep breath, I look back at my patient. She's in conversation with the paramedic. He's keeping her talking, and the distraction hopefully helps.

I'm here, princess. See you soon.

Drew's waiting as the helicopter lands, and a feeling of relief washes over me that it's him working tonight. Not that I think he's necessarily a better doctor than the others here, but I know how he works, and I know my patient's in good hands.

"Hayley," he says as I draw close. "How is she going?"

"The baby's transverse, as I said. I've got my notes, and—"

"I'll take those." A hospital midwife steps forward, and I hand her what I've got. "This doesn't seem like a lot."

"I don't think she's had any pre-natal care. She lives in a very sheltered community."

The midwife grimaces.

"Let's get her inside and I'll assess her," Drew says as Julia's carried past. "I'll decide where to go from there."

I nod, and we all follow my patient as she's taken inside. Drew reaches for my hand as we walk, and he squeezes. It doesn't help my shaking. He runs his thumb across my knuckles, and as we step into the elevator, he pulls me into him. It's subtle enough that not everyone notices, but the midwife who took my notes does and raises an eyebrow.

"Hayley?" Julia speaks, and I shuffle toward her. She reaches for my other hand. "Is my baby going to be okay?"

I give her what I hope is a reassuring smile. "I've got the best of the best on the case. Doctor Campbell will do whatever it takes."

She nods. "I'm scared."

"Of course you are. But we're in the right place now."

"Do you think Ash is mad I left? He doesn't like us leaving."

All of the eyes in the elevator are on me, and Drew lets go of my hand and places his on my back.

"I think if you're pregnant, you need proper maternity care, so Ash has to take some responsibility for that. I'm not saying that the ladies in your community aren't competent, but they're not medical professionals."

"I'm glad you came."

"So am I."

"I'm glad you told him what could happen. Even if it was scary."

That's what's still leaving me trembling. I doubt it's often that anyone stands up to Ash Harris. At least in his community.

"What was that?" Drew murmurs.

"Later."

I turn back to Julia. "That's what a midwife's for, Julia. Not just caring for you and your child, but to be your advocate when you need one. Maybe you weren't my patient, but I'll fight for you to get the help you need."

The elevator arrives, and she's wheeled out to the exam

room. Drew checks her and the baby over quickly and gently. It's hard not to watch as he does it; he's the consummate professional and it makes my heart flutter more than ever. It would be so easy to fall in love with him.

"We need to get this baby out, so let's get you in for an emergency C-section."

Julia's eyes widen. "Is that really necessary? I thought maybe when we got here ..."

"This baby's not going to turn now, and you're both at risk if we wait any longer."

She nods and looks at me. "What do you think?"

"I think you should do what Doctor Campbell says. Told you, best of the best."

She shifts her gaze to him. "Whatever it takes."

AT THIS POINT, I'm here to hold Julia's hand.

Drew and his team work quickly. As much as you want to avoid a client having a caesarean, the doctors have it down to a fine art.

It's clear the nurses like working with Drew. He never skips a beat, being cheerful and making all of us smile.

He's so good at what he does.

Julia cries as Drew shows her the baby, and I squeeze her hand as he's laid on her chest. Tears run down her cheeks, and I realise that I'm her support. I've been so preoccupied in getting her here, I never stopped to think. Is Ash the father? Who in that community will be her support?

"He's beautiful. What are you going to call him?"

She looks at the curtain between us and Drew. "What's that doctor's name?"

"Doctor Campbell?"

"His first name."

I smile. "Drew."

"I'll name him Andrew."

I bite down on my lower lip and nod.

"Do you think Ash will like the name?"

With anyone else I'd think that would be an indicator that he's the father, but then again, he seems to have that weird hold on his group. I shrug. "It's a beautiful name."

Drew's stitching her up, and the baby distracts her. It's a beautiful sight to see a new mother and her baby, and relief floods through me that I got her here, and that they're both safe and sound.

That's all that matters.

Julia's taken to a ward, and I take a big breath for the first time in what feels like forever. My nerves have been raw for hours, and finally it's over.

After we get cleaned up, Drew wraps his arms around me from behind, and I close my eyes, bathing in that feeling of security.

"You did good tonight," he whispers. "That mother and baby are still alive because you acted so quickly."

I'm still shaking, and I know it. I've been on a knife's edge ever since I drove in the gates of that compound.

"Are they both going to be okay?"

"Better than okay. Do you want to see them tucked up in the ward?"

I nod.

"Are you coming home to stay with me for the night? It's a bit late to think about heading back."

"I'd like that," I murmur.

"Good. There's nothing more I want than to hold you. At least until the shaking stops."

"You noticed."

"There's very little I don't notice about you."

I open my eyes and spot one of the hospital midwives over his shoulder, her eyebrows arched as she watches us. If I wasn't so exhausted, I might act a bit more possessively, but I'm the one Drew has his arms around. I have faith that I'm the only woman in his life.

He kisses my ear and loosens his grip. "How about we go and get this visit over with so I can take you home to bed?"

I turn and look into his eyes. This man just got my patient through a situation that could have killed her, and I'm so glad he's mine. "Thank you."

"For what?"

"Everything. For being the one who was here for me and my patient. For knowing exactly what I need."

His blue eyes sparkle, a small smile on his face. "It's what I'm here for. All of it. I'm glad I was here for you and your patient, and I'm also glad I get to be a little selfish and get you to myself, for tonight at least."

I lick my lips. "I'm looking forward to seeing your place."

His smile spreads. "I can't wait to show you. Especially my nice, new, big bed."

"How big?"

Drew plants a gentle kiss on my lips. "Huge. The bathtub is also massive."

"I think I might need a soak."

His eyebrows twitch. “Sounds like a great idea to me. Let’s go see your lady and get out of here. The sooner you’re in the bath, the better.”

I waggle my eyebrows. “That’s what I think too.”

“Come on.”

Julia gives me a tired smile as I enter the room.

“I won’t stay long. I just wanted to check in and see how you’re doing.”

She shoots a glance at the plastic crib next to the bed. “We’ll both be fine. I think I need a good sleep.”

“Good luck with that.” I grin. I lean over the crib to see the chubby-cheeked, dark-haired boy with his eyes closed, at least for the moment.

“He’ll be good. I know it.”

“So, you’re stuck in here for a few days at least before you’ll be allowed home. Do you want me to bring you up anything in the morning? Magazines? Food?”

Her smile widens. “Something to read would be good. Have you let Ash know we’re okay?”

“Not yet, but I’ll text him when I leave here.”

She winces as she pushes herself into a seated position “He needs to know.”

“It’s okay. I’ll let him know. Catch a breath. You need to take care of yourself and this one now.”

Her shoulders slump, and she nods.

“You’ll be in hospital for a few days, and then we’ll need to work out how to get you home again. No more emergency helicopter rides.”

She laughs, and then grimaces. “I might have enjoyed it if I wasn’t in so much pain.”

I pat her hand. "I'll leave you to it. See you in the morning."

Before we leave the hospital, I shoot a text to Ash.

Julia and her baby are safe. She had a boy.

After sending another to Margaret to let her know what happened, I drop my phone in my bag.

What a night.

"What's with this Ash guy?" Drew asks in the car.

"You know he's the one who runs that group on the mountain?"

He nods.

"That place is creepy, but I'm glad I went. They just had her labouring away, and there would never have been a happy ending to that."

Drew frowns. "When we were kids, the people up there seemed friendly enough when you saw them in the street. Whole thing seems really cultish."

"Yeah, which is what's making me nervous about going back. But this can't happen again, Drew. Something needs to happen in that place to let women like Julia get the help they need without the dash to the hospital for an emergency C-section."

He turns the corner and nods toward a large, cream-coloured house. "That's where we're going. And for what it's worth, I agree. Maternity care is probably just one thing they're lacking in there. Makes you wonder what else is going on. As much as they might need help, I don't know if I want you going back."

I shiver. "I don't really want to. What I want to do now is to have a night with you and forget about going back just for a little while."

Drew grins as he pulls into the driveway and stops the car. "That can be arranged."

DREW'S HOUSE IS IMPRESSIVE. He's got a ton of space for someone who lives alone, and I swear his living room is the same size as my little cottage. I take a step and my feet sink into some of the softest carpet I've ever felt.

"This is your place? It's even bigger than I imagined from the photos."

He laughs. "It's perfect." I close my eyes as he wraps his arms around my waist. "There's way too much space for me, but it's comfortable, and now I get to bring you home. For the night, at least. Although, if you stay for two, I can take you home."

"I'll stay for a couple of nights, then. I've at least got my bag if I need anything. I sent her a text, but I need to call Margaret to update her."

"Stay as long as you want. I'm famished. How about I cook something and then we'll take a bath together?" Drew plants a kiss on my neck.

As if on cue, my stomach grumbles, and I look at him and shrug helplessly. "I guess I didn't realise how hungry I was."

"Bacon and eggs? That's what I feel like."

I nod.

"I'll go rustle up some dinner. You go and lie on the couch. I'll wake you to eat if you fall asleep."

"I think after all that I'm too wired to sleep. What I need is food."

"Then food you shall have."

I flop on the couch and watch as he heads into the kitchen. This place is all open-plan, so I can watch him cook while I relax. I'm tired, and I close my eyes for just a moment.

"Am I that boring?"

Drew stands over me, a dinner plate and cutlery in each hand. I smile and sit up.

"I was just resting my eyes."

"I'd let you sleep, but for the fact that I think you need food and the bed's much more comfortable." He sits beside me and hands me a plate. My stomach grumbles at the sight of bacon and scrambled eggs on toast.

"I think I could inhale this. It looks so good."

He grins. "I like cooking. I've always done it for myself."

I take a bite of scrambled egg. It's so soft, it melts in my mouth. "You can cook for me any time."

We eat quickly, and my hungry stomach is soothed by the food. It just leaves me wanting sleep.

Drew takes my plate from me and places it with his on the coffee table.

"Come here," he says.

I let him envelope me in his embrace. Being with him after the endless nights of texting and calling is wonderful. Maybe I found my way to Drew tonight due to someone else's unfortunate circumstance, but being here is a benefit I intend to make the most of.

"Is this weird?" he asks.

"What do you mean?"

"We've been texting up a storm and getting to know each other. This is still so new, but I feel like I know you so well."

"That's how I feel," I whisper. Snuggling into his chest is just so easy.

"I really want to make a go of this, Hayley."

I sit up straight and nod. "So do I, but the long-distance thing scares me."

"Well, I don't much like it either, but I want to try."

"It's just that I've seen how much damage distance can do to a relationship."

"Do you not trust me?" His eyes are pained, and my stomach churns.

"It's not that."

"I'm not Owen."

I don't have to know his brother Owen to know his reputation. "No, you're not. I've seen more than enough of Owen and what a player he is. Thankfully I've only ever had to attend one birth of …" I stop. My tired mouth has run away on me, and I pray to God that Drew hasn't picked up on it.

Of course he has.

"One birth of? What? What's the rest of that sentence?"

I shake my head. "Nothing. I'm just tired and talking too much. Can we go to bed?"

"We're having a bath first, which you get once you tell me what's behind that. Something to do with Owen?"

Running my fingers through my hair, I shake my head again. "I already opened my mouth to probably the worst person I could have."

"I won't tell anyone. Oh, and the worst person you could have told was my mother. She'd probably find some way to use it to screw up Owen's life."

I grimace. "She's that bad?"

"After what she did to Adam and Lily, I wouldn't trust her with any personal information."

This was news. I'd picked up from Lily that there was some kind of rift between her and the boys' mother.

Drew's eyebrows twitch. "What did Owen do?"

"There's such a thing as patient confidentiality."

"You opened this can of worms. Even if it was by accident."

I let out a breath. "You had better promise me that this goes no further."

He nods.

"Do you know Cara Mitchell?"

A smirk spreads across his face as he nods again. "I know Owen screwed around with her."

"She and her husband, Ryan, they tried for a baby for several years. She wanted to do IVF; he didn't want her to go through the pain of having it fail."

Drew's lips curl. "So, my little brother ..."

"Apparently the two of them had a fling, and she became pregnant. Ryan was so happy that it had finally happened that he never questioned where the baby came from. They've got a three-year-old daughter ..."

"Who's biologically Owen's."

I nod. "She was one of the first babies I delivered. Cara was a mess after the birth and told me, but she was my patient, and I couldn't tell anyone."

Drew smiles. "Your secret's safe with me. Personally, I think Owen deserves to know, but if the kid's got a stable family ..."

"She does. You can't tell Owen."

"I know." He places his hands on my shoulders, giving

them a quick rub. "I'm going to run a bath. Are you joining me?"

"Wouldn't miss it for the world."

Drew leans forward and gives me a soft kiss that gives me tingles. "I love you being here. Hope you know that."

"I do."

I close my eyes and take a deep breath of the steam rising from the bathtub.

Drew wraps his arms around me from behind, running his hands up until he cups my breasts. I lean my head back on his shoulder and let out a moan.

"You're wearing too many clothes," he murmurs. He nips at my neck.

My shirt is lifted over my head, and my bra falls to the floor.

"Nearly." He chuckles against the nape of my neck.

I reach to unbutton my jeans, and his hands land on mine. The fly of my pants is peeled away, and he pushes them down along with my panties. "As much as I love your arse in jeans, it's so much better without them. Get in the tub."

Placing one foot in the bath, I moan with delight. After the day I've had, sinking into this will be amazing.

As I sit, I turn my head. Looking at a naked Drew Campbell is a treat. From his thick, muscular thighs, up to that eight-pack, and then onto those broad shoulders ... Not to mention that happy trail from his navel headed south, and that deep *V* that leads places I'm now intimate with.

I sit up to let him climb into the bath behind me.

The water's hot, the steam comforting, and I lie back in Drew's arms as he runs the sponge over my breasts.

"Relaxed?" he murmurs in my ear.

"This is amazing. Just what the doctor ordered. I could go to sleep."

He chuckles, sending tiny ripples of water against my back. "Well, this doctor thinks you can if you want. Today must have been tiring."

"I've been on the go since early this morning. Do you know Aroha Clark?"

Drew plants soft kisses on my shoulders, which don't help my drowsiness. "Her sister was in the same year as I was. I think she was a year younger."

"She gave birth to a baby boy at five-thirty this morning."

He pauses. "You've been up since then?"

"No." I laugh. "I've been up since one-thirty a.m. It's her third baby, so it was all over quickly."

"You must be exhausted."

I nod. "I am, but I think I've been running on adrenalin all day. First time in four years I've had to airlift a patient out. Margaret's had a couple, but not me."

"As stressful as it was, I'm glad it was you. I don't want to have a bath with Margaret."

I'm so tired, but I laugh. "I don't want that either."

His lips are up behind my ear, and I sigh, leaning into him. "I know we've only been together a few times, but being with you is different," he murmurs.

"Different how?"

"It's like you're the missing piece to my puzzle."

My heart beats faster when he says the words. They sum up how I've been feeling about this whole thing. Somehow, Drew makes me feel complete.

"Don't puzzles usually have more than two pieces?"

He shrugs. “I guess that means there are more pieces to come.”

My heart explodes. He sees a future with me, and I see that future, too. If we can work through the one thing that’s a barrier to our happily-ever-after—the distance between us.

“How many more pieces?”

He chuckles, his lips against my skin. “I don’t know. Three or four?”

“That many?”

Drew lets out a contented sigh. “All I know is that I haven’t stopped thinking about you since the day we met.”

“The feeling’s mutual.”

He groans. “Hayley McCarthy, I don’t know what you did to me, but I want this feeling to last forever.”

“Me too.” I turn on my side in the bath and lay my head on his chest as he leans back. Drew is safety and security, and it’s been a long time since I’ve had either. If we’re a puzzle, he’s the corner piece, anchoring me.

He strokes my hair. “How about we get out of this bath and go to bed?”

“I could stay here like this all night, or at least until the water goes cold.”

Drew chuckles. “Me too, but I think we’ll be more comfortable in a nice, warm bed.”

“That sounds equally good.”

I sit back up, and he pulls his legs back and stands, stepping out of the bath. He grabs a towel and wraps it around his waist, picking one up for me.

“Come on, princess. It’s bed time.”

It’s with great reluctance that I push myself up and out of

the warm water. But then, Drew's bed is incentive enough to move.

He stands beside the bath and wraps a big, fluffy white towel around me.

"Feel better?"

"I feel sleepy." I yawn.

"I'll keep you awake just a while longer." He slips his arm around my shoulders as we walk to the bedroom, stopping at the end of the bed.

For a moment, we gaze at each other, and it's enough. This isn't just sex, and it never was, no matter what either of us might have thought. There's something deep, and it's just waiting to unfold for us. I feel it, and I know he does too.

"Drew," I whisper before his mouth closes on mine. This is slow, sensual, and more tender than ever. Tonight is different; it's like we hit a reset button.

He tugs at the towel, and it drops as his hand finds a breast to stroke. My breath catches as my nipple hardens beneath him. My body's alive with the energy between us, and I close my eyes as he caresses my back.

"You're the most beautiful thing I've ever seen," he murmurs as he nuzzles my neck. Tears sting my eyes because I know he's being honest with me. Because I know him.

He scoops me into his arms, and carries me around the side of the bed where he lays me down with all the gentleness I've come to expect from him.

"I wasn't sure when or if I'd get the chance to do this again." He slides over me and to my side, cupping a breast with one of his hands, his body pressed against mine. As he caresses my nipple, his lips brush my neck. It leaves me sighing.

"Why wouldn't you?"

He shrugs. "I thought maybe you might change your mind about this. About us."

"Not a chance. Not when you touch me like this."

Drew grins. "There's plenty more where that came from."

"Show me."

He drops his mouth to my other breast, gently sucking on one nipple as his fingers lace a trail down my chest and stomach before reaching my clit. His hands are soft, surgeon's hands, and with clinical precision he parts my legs and slips two fingers into me.

I gasp as his fingers slide in and out, and he drops his thumb to my clit. I've never come so fast nor as hard as I do with Drew. That's another talent my favourite doctor has and another reason for me to not want this to end.

"I've been thinking about this ever since I last saw you," he murmurs. His lips are on my breast, my shoulder, my neck. Drew is everywhere, and my body's getting the fix it needed. I've missed him.

"I've thought about you a lot." My stomach clenches as I ride the wave, and a moan escapes my lips. I want more, but I don't want him to stop what he's doing. My head's in a spin, and I'm so tired, but this could go on all night and leave me happy. By the time I get to sleep, I'll be so relaxed, but I'm sure that's not why Drew's so persistent.

He takes me over the edge again before dipping his head and spreading my legs. Kissing my thighs, he plunges his tongue into me, his hot breath leaving my insides quaking. It doesn't take much of his teasing for me to come again.

"Drew," I cry out, running my fingers through his hair as his tongue flicks over my clit. It's sensitive from the two climaxes he's already given me, with no sign of coming up for a breath. "I need you inside me."

He grins as he reaches for a box of condoms sitting in his top drawer. "I'm just trying to make the most of this. I don't know when I'll get you here next."

"I'm not complaining."

"You look tired. Don't fall asleep on me."

"I won't. Don't be surprised if I fall asleep under you though." I laugh as he strokes the condom on and positions himself above me.

"Ordinarily I might be offended at that suggestion, but given the circumstances, I think I can handle it." He slides into me, and I let my eyes roll back in my head at how good he feels. Drew's touch sets me on fire, my body rising to the occasion despite my exhaustion.

When I'm with him, I feel like I can climb mountains.

And I know he's there to catch me when I fall.

AFTERWARD, I lie by his side, my head resting on his chest. His arms are around me, and I feel safe and relaxed.

"Why did you become an obstetrician?" I ask, running my fingers down his arm.

"Mostly because of Max. It was a toss-up between obstetrics and paediatrics, but I loved the idea of helping parents bring their children into the world safely."

I plant a kiss on his bicep. "I like that. Lily told me about Max, that he was born early."

"Yeah, complete with umbilical cord around his neck.

Every time I see that kid I think about what a little miracle he is."

Grinning, I bury my face in his chest. "He's got so much character. I love how he always has a smile on his face."

"Even when everything's turning to shit around him. Yeah, that's Max."

"Have things been that bad?"

Drew rolls toward me. "Before Adam got back, Lily struggled. We all did what we could to help her, but Max never cared that he had to go without, or that they didn't have all the gadgets and things other families did. They couldn't even get internet on that farm except for the ridiculously expensive kind." His eyes shine, full of happiness. "He's like a pig in mud now. He's got everything he ever wanted."

"I'm glad. They're such a nice little family. Adam clearly dotes on them all."

"You have no idea." He chuckles. "He spoils Lily and Max rotten, and they deserve all of it."

"They seem very happy."

"They are." He sighs. "I want what they have, but I just never found the right woman." My heart flutters as he fixes his gaze on mine. "Something tells me I'm on the right track now."

I don't know if I want to leave.

8

ADAM

Ben.

My ears ring and everything moves in slow motion. I hold my hands either side of my head, trying to get rid of the sound that plagues my brain, but there's only one thought nagging at me right now.

Ben.

I see him lying on the ground, and I crawl toward him. His eyes are open, as if he's staring into the distance, but I know there's nothing behind that stare.

No.

I make it to him, and ignoring any danger, I sit and pull him onto my lap. One of his legs is gone at the knee, not that it matters anymore. Ben's dead.

Cradling him in my arms, I rock, tears rolling down my cheeks. He and his family welcomed me into their home when I was so lost. He'd become my best friend, my brother.

Things might long be over between his sister and me, but nothing ever changed between Ben and me.

Pain rips through my shoulder, but I don't care. The agony of losing my best friend is so much worse than any physical pain I could endure. He has a wife at home, and a baby on the way. This was our last deployment. We've both had enough.

It's not fair.

Right now, I'd give anything to swap places with him.

I have nothing. No permanent ties to anyone. That all went when I left Copper Creek. I've spent years pretending for the most part that my family doesn't exist, and hiding myself from any updates I might accidentally stumble across. Once I lost Lily, I lost everything.

There are times when I feel utterly empty, like my soul is lost and can't be found. That emptiness is much worse with the loss of Ben.

My heart's raw, and I barely notice gunfire around me as another team swoops in to pick up the pieces. I can't let go of Ben—I won't let go.

I WAKE to Lily's steady breathing, and it calms me. I'd never confess this, but the lights we set up to help her through her fear of the dark also help me when I dream of Ben.

It's the same dream, over and over. I go weeks without having it, and then he haunts me every single night for days on end at a time.

Maybe it's payback for him dying instead of me.

OPENING the garage is the best idea I've ever had, but it's not easy.

I have two mechanics working with me now, one qualified, one under an apprenticeship. Today, I've been down one as my second mechanic has been working out on a farm on the other side of McKenzie's Mountain.

It's late when I walk around the garage and toward the house. Corey's ute sits in the backyard, and I smile as I walk in the door.

Lily greets me with a kiss.

"Corey's here?"

Lily smiles. "He hasn't been here long. He's—"

The sound of a gunshot echoes in the empty night. It's close. Too close.

My head swims, and my vision blurs. Lily squeals as I grab hold of her and push her to the ground, shielding her with my body. Not Lily—anything but Lily. I'll sacrifice myself before anything happens to her.

The taste of sand is in my mouth. The acrid smell of burning flesh fills my nostrils.

"Adam?" She's scared, but so am I. The last time this happened, I lost Ben. I won't lose Lily.

"Keep your head down," I whisper, clutching her tighter. "Close your eyes."

"You're scaring me."

"It's okay, baby. Everything will be okay, I swear." What about Max? Where's he? The baby? My heart burns with the need to protect my children, but there's no way to get to them without leaving Lily.

"That got the bastard." Heavy footsteps land in front of us. I raise my head to see the butt of a rifle. My heart races. "Adam, what the fuck?"

"Don't hurt her. It doesn't matter what happens to me, but please, don't hurt her." My eyes sting with tears as I croak the words.

"Adam." Her voice is soft, but I won't let her sacrifice herself for me. I dig my nails in to keep hold of her.

"Dude." A hand lands on my back, and I shake it off. All around me is death, and I can't handle it. My shoulder aches where I was shot, as if it's a fresh wound.

"Adam. You're scaring Lily. You need to get off her."

"I can't. I can't lose her." I'm a snotty mess, my nose streaming as my eyes do. I let her down once, and I'll never do that again. I need her to be safe.

"I'm right here," she says.

"Are you okay?" The voice is deep and familiar, but whoever fired that gun is a direct threat to my family.

"Not really. I twisted my ankle when Adam pushed me over, and my foot's still stuck under him."

I hear her voice, but my ears still ring. It's as if I'm in a tunnel, and she's outside and so far away from me.

"Adam, I'm going to move you. Lily's hurt."

No. My ears rush with blood.

"You might have to just do it, Corey."

The hand moves to under my arm and is joined by another under my other arm. I'm lifted off her, and I struggle as Lily slips out from under me.

"No. You can't take her. Take me."

"You're not going anywhere."

Lily pulls herself to her feet and takes a couple of steps

toward me. I reach for her, and she cups my face, bringing everything into focus with her. Her blue eyes search mine. "You're safe. Adam, you're safe. You're here with me in our home with our kids. No one's going to hurt me, or them. We're safe."

I let out a sob.

I'm on my feet, and she slips her arms around my waist. The movement grounds me, and I look around to see my older brother holding onto my arms. "Corey?"

Lily rests her head on my chest, and I breathe in the scent of her blueberry shampoo.

Corey retains his hold on my arms. "What happened?"

"I don't know. One minute I walked in the door, and the next ..."

"The shot set him off. He pushed me to the ground, and I think he was trying to save me."

"Save you from what? He hurt you."

Lily reaches to touch Corey's hand. "Not deliberately. From what Adam was saying, I don't think we were even in our kitchen anymore. Were we, Adam?"

I shake my head. "I can taste the sand," I whisper.

"Shit." Corey lets go of me, and I turn toward him.

"I would never hurt Lily."

"I'll make us all a coffee and we can sit down," Lily says softly.

Corey shakes his head. "Not on that ankle. You sit down, and I'll make the coffee."

He eyes me suspiciously, and I can't blame him. I haven't had anything like this happen since I've been back in New Zealand. I thought it was something I'd got over long ago.

Despite her arms having been around me, when I take

Lily by the arm, she flinches, and she grimaces as she takes another step.

"What's wrong?"

"My ankle. When you dived on me, I fell awkwardly."

It tears me apart. My girl, still recovering from childbirth, and I threw her on the floor, injuring her in the process.

"I'm sorry, Lily."

She shrugs. "It is what it is. Help me to the table, and we'll have to work out where we go from here."

I haven't heard her so deflated since we've been back together. All these months our relationship has been happy and full of love and laughter. That's what she needs, not me falling apart. My guard's so far down, I didn't even think to use those stupid breathing exercises that Jenna taught me. Would they have helped? Maybe not, but I could have tried.

Pulling Lily's arm over my shoulder, I help her as she hops to the table. I fall to the floor at her feet. "I'm so sorry."

She sighs, and runs her fingers through my hair. "I have no idea what that was, but we need to get you help."

"I think I need to tell you a story." She's asked so many times, but I've deflected, not wanting to wound her with knowledge of how I tried to move on from her. If I tell her about Ben, I tell her about his sister, the first girl I was with after Lily. "Please?"

Corey stands behind me with the first-aid kit. "Get out of the way. I'll take a look at your ankle, Lily."

I move to the side, and keep scanning her expression. Her face is devoid of colour, and her eyes have dark circles underneath. She's under enough pressure with a new-born baby without me adding to it.

"We need to ice this and rest it before bandaging it."

Before he can say anything else, I retrieve a packet of peas from the freezer and a tea towel while he grabs an ottoman from the living room. We work in silence, placing the frozen food on her ankle with the towel to hold back the ice.

"Thank you." I think she's speaking to Corey, but at the same time, she reaches down to stroke the stubble on my chin.

"I love you, Lil. I'd never hurt you deliberately."

"I know. You were trying to save me."

Corey snorts, and I glare at him.

"Did you get the possum?" Lily asks.

He nods. "He won't be eating Lucky's food again."

"I hate that you have to do that."

He nods. "They're pests. There are so many native animals around here, and if you let the possums get out of hand, they'll destroy that."

Lily sighs. "I know. It just makes me sad. I love the bush behind our house; it'll be great for the kids to learn about nature."

"Then we need to make sure that there are plenty of animals left for them to learn about. It's why I love where I'm living. That group that owns a huge chunk of the mountain have been after my land for ages, but they can bugger off." He stands and goes to the kitchen bench, plucking two mugs from the cupboard.

"I'm pretty sure Adam will want one too."

Corey grunts, and reaches for a third cup, flicking on the kettle. He's pissed, and I don't blame him. He's always been protective of Lily, and even offered to take care of her and Max in my absence. While he's said it's not because he has feelings for her, I have my doubts. Lily said no to his offer of help, but I'll always wonder if she'd said yes if it would have become more than a relationship of convenience.

All I know is that she has a way with him that no one else does.

And right now, she probably prefers him to me.

Lily's still distant at bedtime. I try and make things up to her by making sure Max is in bed on time, and I've changed every nappy since the incident in the kitchen.

When the baby is fed and asleep, she slides into bed with me.

"Everything okay?" I ask, knowing it's not.

"It's fine."

"Come here then." I hold my arms open, and after a brief pause, she lets me wrap them around her. There's nothing better than having her in my embrace, and I close my eyes.

"You scared me," she whispers.

"I scared myself. It was all so real, and I couldn't bear the thought of anyone taking you away."

Opening my eyes, I meet her gaze. Her blue eyes are full of concern, and tears well in them as we look at each other.

"Nothing and no one will ever take me away. Not again," she says softly, raising her hand to brush my cheek.

"I know that. It was just my reaction to that gunshot. Everything's been so good, and I've been so relaxed that I let things go too far."

She swallows. "Tell me what happened. Please."

It's not the first time she's asked, but it's the first time I'll give her an answer. After everything, she deserves to know the full story.

I kiss her, savouring the taste of her lips as if it's the last time I'll enjoy them. It'll be a few more weeks until we can do anything more with her so recently giving birth, but right now I need her to know how much I love her. How much I've always loved her.

"Adam," she whispers. "Let me in."

I take a deep breath. "When I left town and went to the States, I stayed with friends of Mum and Dad. They had a son my age, and we got along so well—it was like finding another brother. We enlisted together. I thought I'd lost you, and it was what he'd always wanted."

She nods.

"To cut a really long story short, we travelled the world together. We saw so many different places, met so many different people. We fought by each other's sides, and we came home together. Ben met someone and fell in love. I was the best man at his wedding." I scan her face in anticipation of her reaction. "I had a relationship with his sister."

It hits her; I can see it. I don't have to ask to know her mind's ticking over, and she knows all this went on after I thought she'd left me. While she was back here, struggling with a young child, I was half a world away trying desperately to fall in love with someone else. Not that it ever worked.

"Anyway, my last deployment, we'd been really lucky to have been through so much. There were mental scars, but not physical. We were both getting out. He and his wife had a baby on the way. I just wanted a new life."

Lily wipes my tears with her fingers.

"He died, Lil. Our Humvee hit an IED, and I was the only survivor. I held him in my arms, but he was already gone. That's when I got shot. It was a miracle it was my shoulder and not a bullet through my head. It was only because there was a team behind us who came in and dealt with the insurgents that nothing worse happened to me."

Warm tears fall on my chest.

"Hey, it's okay. I'm right here." I grasp Lily's chin and pull her gaze to mine. "I got better physically, but mentally, I was a mess."

"And then you ended up with me."

"We both have our scars, and they're pretty deep. I see you struggle sometimes, those nights when you still have nightmares. The bedroom lights help with your fear of the dark, but they don't take it all away."

She nods.

"I stayed in the army to try and make up for something. I don't know what. When I left, I fell apart, and at first, there was no one to help. I'm pretty sure it's the same wherever you go. Being in the army is one thing, and there are groups you can get support from. But there's a reason why there's such a high suicide rate among veterans."

Her grip on my arm tightens.

I swallow. "Then I met someone. She'd worked with people like me, people with PTSD. She spent hours talking it through with me, teaching me ways to cope. I was busy burying myself in alcohol."

"She helped?"

There's no easy way to put this, and I wrap my arms around her and brace myself for her reaction. "We fell in love. At least, that's what it felt like. After a while, she moved in with me."

"That was the woman you told me about," Lily whispers.

"It was. I got so caught up. She and I were so close, and I nearly asked her to marry me. But she wasn't you, Lily. I realised I wasn't prepared to marry some other woman when I didn't feel a fraction for her of what I felt for you. It wouldn't have been fair to her or to me."

Tears roll down Lily's cheeks.

"I chose you, or at least the feelings I had for you. How could I commit to someone without feeling that way about them?"

I break myself out of my thoughts. I hadn't been fair on Jenna at all. Not from the start of our relationship to the end. She hadn't deserved what I'd done to her.

"Adam." She sobs

Now, I not only have the love back I thought I'd lost so long ago, I have the original target of those feelings. My beloved Lily.

"I'm so sorry about today. It's been a long time since …"

"No, it hasn't."

"What?" Her eyes are so hurt, and I'm so confused.

"I'm not the only one who has bad dreams. You hide it better than I do, but I hear you cry out in the night. I see you sit up to get your bearings and I understand because I do the same."

I nod. Despite me trying to hide it, she knows. I should have known she did. "When I came back and found out what had happened to you, all I could think of was how I could make things right."

Lily rolls away and onto her back. "It wasn't you who abused me. It was my mother."

"I know, but I still feel guilty about it. I always will. It might have been her, but I could have done more."

She sighs. "What's done is done. We've moved forward so much, and we need to keep on going." Focusing her blue eyes on me as I nod, she gives me a small smile. "We are going to have to find you some help though. You can't live in the countryside and do that every time a gun's fired."

"I know, and I'm so sorry I hurt you today."

Lily shakes her head. "I'm not blaming you for that, and I'm not saying this because of what happened to me. If this sets you off every time, it's the impact in here I worry about." She taps me on the forehead. "You've done a wonderful job of looking after us, but now we have to look after you."

I let out a relieved breath. If there's one thing I know about Lily, it's that she has a big heart. I should have known she'd do anything to protect me, just as she does our children.

"I'll work something out. You and the kids are everything to me. I couldn't bear it if I lost you."

Her eyes, so full of concern, search mine. "You will never lose us. Got it?"

I nod, but this latest episode fills me with fear for the future. "Tomorrow, I'll do some research on the net. Work out what the next step is," I say.

"Tomorrow, I'm going to need some help getting around with Rose."

"Rose?"

She smiles. "Max was right. It's the perfect name. She is my little rose."

I kiss her. I love her. "You're all so precious to me. We should be back up to full staffing at the garage tomorrow. I'll work something out after I've taken you to the doctor to look at that ankle."

"It's only twisted. I'm sure I just need to take the weight off it for a while."

"Even so, I think we'll get it checked out. The last thing I want is for it to get worse."

Lily runs her hand down my arm, and gives me a tender kiss. "I love you. We'll get through this just like we've got through everything else."

I close my eyes as we snuggle together. There's nothing I love more than Lily and our family.

Nothing will destroy that.

Ever.

9

HAYLEY

DREW'S ALREADY OUT OF BED WHEN I WAKE UP, BUT STILL HE surrounds me, the sheet and pillows smelling of that light cologne he wears. I could wake up like this every morning and be happy. My nose twitches as it picks up the scent of coffee and toast, and I roll over onto my back and smile.

Last night was stressful and exhausting, but Drew had this way of calming me, surrounding me in him until I forgot about my worries. It'd be far too easy to become addicted to that.

There's no sign of my clothes, and I sigh as I remember him placing them in the washing machine. I climb out of bed, and open a drawer, finding a light blue T-shirt that I pull out and tug on over my head. It might be clean and smell of laundry powder, but it's *his* laundry powder and he's the one who cleaned it. He'll be lucky if he gets this shirt back again.

He's hovering around the dining table as I approach,

fussing over the plates and rearranging the cutlery three times as I watch in silence. I sneak up behind him and wrap my arms around his waist, smiling at the way he shivers.

"I didn't know you were awake," he murmurs.

"Only just. I hope you don't mind me stealing one of your shirts."

I let go as he twists and turns to face me. "You can wear my shirts any time. Your clothes are in the dryer." He bends a little to kiss me, his warm, soft lips pressing against mine with so much tenderness.

"Guess I'm wearing this until they're ready."

He runs his hands down the length of my spine until he cups my arse. "Suits me. Are you hungry? I hope so. I'm cooking breakfast."

"I can smell."

"I was wondering whether to bring some in to you or just leave you to sleep. Last night would have been exhausting."

"No thanks to you."

His smirk makes me chuckle. When I'm around Drew, I'm always smiling, laughing, having fun. I like this so much —I just hate that he's so far away.

"It was pretty good. Even if I do say so myself." He pecks me on the lips again and lets me go. "Now, I've got more bacon to cook because I'm starving. There's some toast out on the table, but I wanted something a bit more."

"Bacon is good." I walk around him and sit at the table.

"Coffee? I just made some and I can make one for you."

I smile. "Coffee would be amazing."

"Then I might let you get dressed and we'll go to the hospital. I'm sure you want to check on your patient."

I nod as he walks to the machine, and the sound of the coffee pouring fills the room. "Hopefully she's doing well."

"She is. I've already called to ask." He places the cup in front of me. It's got milk in it, just how I like it, and I bet it's got the required two sugars, too. The man has a good memory.

I look up at him. "Maybe I'll keep you around. This is such great service."

"Give me a chance and this'll be just the beginning."

My breath catches looking at him. His eyes are so earnest, and I know I can believe him. Drew Campbell wants to give me the world, but I'm so scared of taking it.

"Drew, I ..."

"Take your time. We have plenty of it. If you're staying another night, I'll have another opportunity to prove to you how good this can be. How good we can be."

I take a sip of my coffee and close my eyes. "You don't need to prove anything."

He squats in front of me, and I open my eyes again to see him face to face. "I don't want you to be afraid to try."

I shake my head. "I'm not afraid. Being with you is amazing. I'm just worried about when I'm not with you."

"Do you think I'll muck around?"

"No." I shift my gaze away.

"So, what is it?"

I bite my bottom lip to give me courage. "Every time I'm with you, I just get confused. I thought I had my life all mapped out." I raise my eyes to meet his. "When I worked in Auckland, I didn't cope. Copper Creek gave me the peace I needed."

"I won't ask you to give up that peace. Not yet."

"It's the 'yet' I'm scared of."

He places a hand on my left knee. "So, we'll take things slowly. I mean, it's gonna be slow with the distance, but I don't want to give up on this. Whatever it is we have is so special, and I'm really glad that Lucy chose the day Lily gave birth of all days to blow the landlord."

I can't help it. I giggle, and a huge smile spreads across his face. "So am I."

"It's settled then. I'll make you breakfast, we'll go see your patient, and you can be a lady of leisure for the day. You'd better get lots of rest. You'll need it for tonight."

I lean over, cup his face, and press my lips to his. "Sounds good to me."

"Then you can have the pleasure of my company on a drive back to Copper Creek."

"This also sounds good."

He wiggles out of my grasp and backs away toward the kitchen. "My stomach's grumbling. I think I need to feed it."

As he fusses around, turning the element on with the frying pan and pulling the bacon from the plastic wrapper, I smile at our domesticity. I could get used to this; it's wonderful and scary. In that moment, I can't imagine being apart from him, but the reality is our time together will come to an end in less than twenty-four hours.

I have to make the most of it before leaving.

WE GET MORE curious looks as we walk through the hospital hand in hand. Drew doesn't start work for another half hour, and I've got the use of his car to drive around before I pick him up later.

I'm glad he knows where he's going. After the craziness of last night, I wouldn't be able to identify what corridors led to the maternity ward, let alone Julia's room.

"Here we go." He lets go of my hand and pushes the door.

Julia is sitting in bed, and she smiles as we walk in.

"Good morning. I brought you something to read." I drop the plastic bag with the magazines I bought on the way on the table beside the bed. There's a selection of Hollywood gossip and lifestyle books to give her some variety.

"Thank you."

"How are you feeling?" I sit on a chair beside the bed, and smile.

Julia's lips twitch. From her hazy gaze, she's obviously still tired. "Much better than I was. Thank you. You saved my life."

I shake my head. "Doctor Campbell did that. I just worked out what was going wrong."

"I still owe you a debt of gratitude. So does my community. I'm sure they'll all be very grateful."

Nodding, I'm not sure what to say in response to that, but I clamp my teeth together, remembering that I still need to return to collect my car.

"I'm glad they called you in. There was a lot of debate about it."

"What do you mean? It was clear you were in trouble."

She drops her gaze. "When I asked for help, the other ladies didn't want to bring in anyone from the outside. Ash made the decision."

I nod. "Okay."

"What he says goes, but they didn't like it. He must have looked you up just in case anyway, because he knew who to ring straight away."

I shiver at those words. Why me?

The baby grizzles, and I lean over the crib and stroke his fuzzy head. "Hey, don't give your mum a hard time. She's been through enough."

He lets out a bleat, and I nod. "I bet you're hungry."

I pluck him out, and rock him for a minute before handing him to Julia. It's awkward, but she puts him to her breast and he sucks as if there's no tomorrow.

"Thanks, Hayley."

"You're welcome. I'm going to get going now and give you some privacy, but I'll be back again tomorrow before I head home to Copper Creek."

Her eyes widen. "I never thought about how I'm getting home."

"We'll sort something out. You'll be here for the next few days at least, and even if I have to come and get you myself, I'll get it sorted." Not that I'd complain if it gives me an excuse to see Drew.

She smiles. "Thank you. I seem to be saying that a lot."

"It's no problem. Just let someone here know if you need anything. They have my details, so they can call me if you need me." I grin. "From the looks of it, I think you'll be just fine. Now, because I'm in the big city, I'm going to go and get some retail therapy."

Julia laughs. "It's been a long time since I've done that."

My heart hurts for her. She can't be much younger than I am, and she's given her freedom up for what? I know I shouldn't judge, but it can't be healthy.

"If I don't see you before, see you in the morning."

Drew's waiting outside when I come out, and he takes my hand and squeezes. "Everything okay?"

"Aren't you checking in on her?"

He nods. "I will. Just wanted to give you a few minutes with her alone."

"Her baby's doing really well, from what I can see. He's a hungry wee thing."

"That's good."

I reach into my bag and pull out my phone. There's a text waiting from Ash.

Thank you for letting me know. I look forward to your return.

My return? He must be referring to Julia, but she'll be travelling after I do. After her C-section and the complications, she'll be in hospital for a while yet.

Julia will have maybe a week in hospital recovering. I can update you when she's due to come back.

You need to come and get your car. I'll be waiting for your call.

A shiver goes through me. Maybe I'm just imagining things, but after those intense looks yesterday, his words take on more meaning than they should. It scares me.

"Hayley?" I raise my face to see Drew with his head tilted to the right. "Earth to Hayley."

"Sorry. I sent a text to Ash last night to let him know that Julia was safe. He's not showing much interest in her."

I hold my phone up to show Drew the texts, and he bristles. "Someone's got an admirer."

"It's not just me, right?"

He shakes his head. "Be careful around him."

"I promise."

Bending a little to kiss me, he lingers before pulling away.

"Here are the car keys. The house key is the silver one if you want to go home and rest." He waggles his eyebrows. "Totally understandable after last night."

I lick my lips slowly, his eyes never moving off them. "I'll need plenty of energy for later, won't I?"

"Something like that." He shoots me a killer smile that I hope no one else ever gets. How am I going to go all day without him after that? "Give me a call when you're ready, and I'll come and get you. If you're lucky, I'll cook you dinner."

"You don't have to. We can go out for dinner, or I can order something."

I take the keys from him. "It's the least I can do."

He grins. "I should go, but I'll see you later."

I walk out of the maternity ward with so many eyes on me, and it puts an extra sway in my hips.

He's mine.

I MAKE the most of being in the city.

Mum and Dad still send me money from time to time, and my bank account has enough in it to hit the stores and spend. When you live in a small town for long enough, you miss what the bigger places have to offer. It's nice to be surrounded by shops and able to splash out a bit.

Drew's car is soon filled with bags, and I have to stop myself because there'll be no room for me at the rate I'm going.

It's been a while since I've had my hair styled. The most I've done with it in forever is a trim at Fiona's Cuts, back home. This time I get to pamper myself, having it layered, but still long enough to tie up.

I float down the supermarket aisles, picking out things to cook for dinner, thinking only of this second and final evening with Drew before I go home again. If tonight is anything like last night was, it's going to be hard to leave.

My mobile rings as I drop the groceries in the boot, and I smile at Drew's name popping up on the screen. "Hey."

"Hey, princess. I'm knocking off now if you want to swing by and pick me up."

I grin. "I'll be there shortly. I'm still out shopping."

He laughs. "Good for you. See you soon."

Drew's waiting outside the hospital entrance when I pull up, and I step out of the car so he can drive.

His jaw drops. "Wow."

"I decided you were right. It was time to pamper myself. I can see you approve."

He wraps his arms around my waist and even slips me the tongue with his kiss. "You look amazing. I mean, not that you didn't before."

"You should see all the crap I bought."

Laughing, he lets go of me and takes the keys from my hand. "I'm glad you had fun."

"I really did. My reasons for coming here might not have been the best, but it was really nice to splurge a bit."

He grins. "Let's get home."

Home.

He says nothing as I bring in all my purchases from the car, and shakes his head with a smile when I return a third time.

I dump the last lot of bags on the floor next to the couch. "That's it."

"Are you sure?"

"It's been a long time since I've been on a shopping spree."

He nods. "I bet. At least now you have a second reason to come to Hamilton more often."

I place my hand on my heart. "You mean, now I've discovered all these stores I didn't know existed."

Drew rolls his eyes as he slides his hands around my waist. "I'm talking about me."

"Ohhh." I lick my lips. "I guess you're a good reason too. Maybe even the best reason."

His gentle kiss leaves me wanting more, and I forget about cooking dinner for the moment as he pulls me toward the couch. It's only just wide enough for us to lie on together.

It's a while before I come up for air, and then it's to make cheese on toast. Forget the potato bake and steak I'd planned. There's not time for much else before we go to bed.

We eat the food and then brush the bed down, trying to get the crumbs off the sheets. Drew laughs and pulls me down on top of him, and when his mouth finds mine again, I know I'm home.

"Can I keep you?" Drew asks.

"I love being here, but we both know I have to go back to Copper Creek."

He gives me that sly smile that gets my stomach doing cartwheels. "Guess I just have to convince you to stay."

"You could come home with me."

Drew sighs and shakes his head. "I'd love that. But there's no future for me in Copper Creek. I wish there was."

I shrug. "You could always work with me."

He gives me a wistful smile, one that tells me he's not lying. "If only it was that simple."

I reach for him, cupping his cheek with my palm. "It's okay."

He turns his head, kissing my hand. "You know I have to do everything in my power to convince you to move."

"You'd better."

We sit in silence for a moment, and I snuggle into him.

"Tell me how you ended up in Copper Creek. You said you didn't cope at the city hospital."

My stomach churns. I hate talking specifics about what happened, but of all people, Drew will understand. "I lost a patient in my second year of practice."

He frowns. "I'm sorry to hear that. It's a tough thing to get past."

"There was nothing I could have done."

Drew nods. "Sometimes, things happen that are just out of our control." He links his fingers in mine. "My third year, I had a mother have a coronary episode mid-caesarean. It was massive. She never stood a chance. The baby made it, but it still haunts me. I wanted to do better."

I squeeze his fingers. "It doesn't sound like there was anything you could do."

He shakes his head. "I'm sure yours was the same."

"It was a bit different. I tried to report my concerns to a doctor who didn't really give two shits. My patient had placental abruption."

His eyes widen. "Holy shit. And you got the blame?"

"He told everyone I hadn't reported it to him in time. I went through a review process and was put under supervision for six months."

Drew's face is tight. I swear if I looked closely there'd be steam coming out of his ears. "No one believed you?"

"I was a second-year midwife. He had much more experience."

"What's his name?"

I stroke his face. "It doesn't matter. Margaret needed another midwife and talked me into moving. I was shattered. So many of my own colleagues treated me like I had the plague. Leaving turned out to be the best thing I ever did."

"It matters because if I ever run into him at any conference, I might smash him in the face."

I shake my head. "It's not worth it. I'm in a good place now."

"A good place that's a long way from me."

"Drew …"

He sighs. "I'm sorry. Everything's just so fucked up. I had a shitty relationship with someone here, and now have a chance at an amazing one with someone who's miles away." Turning, he runs his fingers through my hair. "I miss you when we're not together."

"I hate it."

His eyelids flicker.

"As soon as I was old enough, I was in boarding school. Mum said she wanted nothing but the best for me, and apparently, that was living in another part of the country to my parents. I've spent half my life feeling like I've been abandoned by them." I fight back tears. "And then I get attached to the most amazing man I've ever met, and he's miles away."

I close my eyes as he leans in and presses his lips to my forehead.

"We make a great pair, don't we?" he asks.

I nod.

"Hayley, I want to try. The way I feel about you is overwhelming, and we've barely scratched the surface." His blue eyes are so full of emotion, it leaves me wanting to cry. "I want more."

"So do I," I whisper.

"If you hadn't ended up on my doorstep, I would be on yours. I haven't stopped thinking about you since that first night."

Tears roll down my cheeks, but they're tears of happiness. The thought of a long-distance relationship rips me up, but Drew's worth it. He's so worth it.

"I haven't stopped thinking about you either."

"Maybe I won't let you go." He rolls on top of me, spreading my legs with his own. "Why are you crying?"

"I'm not."

"So, what are the tears for?"

I take a couple of short, sharp breaths. "Because when I'm with you, everything feels right. Like it's meant to be."

He smiles. "That's how I feel." He cups the back of my head and pulls me in tight.

"I have this problem. I think I'm addicted to you."

He plants butterfly kisses all over my face as I giggle. "The feeling's mutual."

"Let's do something about that."

10

DREW

I TAKE HAYLEY UP TO THE HOSPITAL TO SEE JULIA AGAIN IN THE morning.

Julia's recovering well, and her baby's thriving.

In the car on the way back to Copper Creek, we talk and laugh and learn even more about each other.

That's how my head processes my day. Just one thing after another until we pull up outside Hayley's house and I know I have limited time with her.

The last two nights have been the best of my life. She fulfils me.

"Are you staying over?" she asks.

"Do bears shit in the woods?"

Hayley laughs. "I want you to stay. You're becoming a bit of a habit, Drew Campbell."

"I hope so."

I grab some of her bags and help her carry them inside.

Before long, there's a pile of parcels in one corner of the living room.

"I'll call Margaret to let her know I'm home, and then I'm all yours for a while."

"Just for a while?"

"Okay, the night. But I'm going to be on call, so if anyone needs my help ..."

I grin. "I'll help you and maybe it'll be quicker?"

She laughs. "If you have some magic trick to speed up labour ..."

"If only."

As she calls Margaret, I take a long look around her living room. Both times I was here, it was almost straight to the bedroom. Maybe now, I can take the time to look around and get to know her better.

There's a photo on the mantelpiece, and I pick it up. This must be Hayley and her parents. Her mother looks stiff and awkward. Her father is more relaxed, his arm around Hayley's shoulders. This is the couple who sent her away, and my heart aches that it still has an effect on Hayley. She wants us to be together, but I'm not sure how well she'll cope with the distance. It's not insurmountable, but it might just be enough to ruin everything.

She wraps her arms around my waist and buries her face in my shoulder. "That's my mum and dad on the day I became a midwife."

"Your dad looks happy enough."

"He's not so bad now. It's Mum who still has the stick up her butt."

"They seem similar to my parents. My mother can be such a horrible person, but my dad wouldn't hurt a fly. I don't know how he lives with her, but they seem to make it work."

She laughs. "Sounds familiar."

I place the photo back on the mantel and turn to her. "Let's not ever be like that. All bitter and twisted. Our kids will be able to do what they want for a career, and we'll support them."

"Our kids?" She clamps her lips together, and it's obvious she's suppressing a laugh.

I shrug. "Okay, my kids. With whoever decides to take a risk and have babies with me."

Hayley pecks me on the lips. "I think you'll make a great parent, then."

"Maybe. We still have half the day left. What else are we going to do?"

She lets out a sigh. "I need to go and get my car."

"If you want, I can grab one of my brothers and we can pick it up."

Hayley shakes her head. "It's okay. At least it'll be in and out. That place gives me the creeps."

She plucks her phone out of her pocket and taps on the screen. It takes seconds to get a response.

"Any time this afternoon."

I nod. "Did he ask after Julia?"

Her eyes roll. "No, just said that he's happy for me to pick up my car and is looking forward to seeing me."

"Is he now?"

She puts her phone back into the pocket of her jeans and licks her lips. "Are you getting jealous there, Doctor Campbell?"

I shake my head. "Nah. I know you're my girl."

"That confident, huh?"

Holding my hands out, I shrug. "Who else is going to give you constant orgasms?"

She grins, snickering and grabbing my arm. "Only you, I guess."

"You only guess?"

"A practical demonstration might be in order tonight."

I nod. "I don't think that'll be too much of a problem."

She raises her face to mine, and I give her the most tender kiss I can muster.

"Keep kissing me like that and I might just be able to give you a permanent job," she whispers.

"That's what I'm aiming for."

THAT DAMN MOUNTAIN.

When we were kids, that fence wasn't there. People still lived in seclusion there for the most part, but it wasn't like that. How Corey lives up here beside them, I'll never know.

A few years ago, they wanted his permission to put up the fence. He said he didn't care, but he wasn't paying anything toward it. They went ahead and built it. He says in some ways it's good; the wind used to howl up the hill when the weather was bad. Now there's a wind break on that side of his property.

I drive up to the gates and they open. It's not hard to see why this place intimidates people. The fence around it is massive. Once the gates close behind you, it's suffocating no matter how much space is here.

As I drive us toward the main building, Hayley points. "There's my car. I'll just grab it and we'll get out of here."

"Not wanting to stay and hang with your new friend?"

She screws up her face as I laugh. "I can't wait to get back out of here."

"Heads up. Is that him?"

A tall, dark-haired guy walks down the steps and toward Hayley's car.

"That's him."

I pull the car up, and she shoots me a quick smile. "I'll just get in the car and we'll go."

"Okay."

She steps out and takes a few steps toward her car. Ash's eyes are fixed on my car—not that he'll see much with my tinted windows. He walks toward Hayley and speaks to her as she presses the button and unlocks her car.

Screw this.

I get out of the car and walk around. "Everything good, princess?"

She smiles and nods. "Fine."

"I was just thanking Hayley," Ash says.

I nod.

"Drew performed the caesarean. He's the one who deserves the credit." Her eyes are so full of happiness as our gazes lock, and I give her a wink that makes her blush.

"Is that right? So you're here to drop Hayley back home?"

"I'm her boyfriend."

To his credit, he only lets his facial expression blank for a moment. Something's not right about this guy, and that just confirmed it. If he was any other guy showing interest in my girl, I could handle it. But with all the rumours about this place, I don't trust him one bit.

"Thank you for helping Julia," he says.

I nod. "You're welcome. Someone should give you a call about arranging transport home in a few days."

I shoot a smile at Hayley. "Let's get going."

Her expression brightens. All I want is to get out of here with her. This place gives me the creeps.

I wait for her to get in her car and start the engine before I give Ash a nod and do the same. Signalling for her to go first, I follow, leaving him standing watching us leave.

She's not coming back here again if I can help it.

SHE KNOWS there's something wrong.

We're cuddled up on the couch after dinner watching some home renovation show, and her body against mine just feels so right. Having her in my arms is everything.

"You okay?"

I nod. "Yeah."

"You're not saying much. That's not like you." Her lips twitch, as if she's unsure if she means it as a joke.

"Just thinking about today. That place gives me the creeps. I don't want you going back there."

She nods. "It's a tough situation. I want to work with them to make sure there's maternity care available or the next Julia might not be so lucky."

"I know."

I grumble, pulling her closer. "I'm not going to stop worrying."

"I'm not asking you to. I'd be more concerned if you weren't worrying. But it's what's right, Drew. Something needs to be in place to help them."

I nod because she's right. Of course her first care will be any mothers and babies, but it doesn't make things any easier. "Just be careful of him. There's always been all kinds of stories circulating in town about what goes on up there."

Hayley nuzzles my cheek. "Of course I will. And you don't need to be jealous. It's only you I want."

"Good, because the thought of you near anyone else drives me crazy."

"I really liked how you introduced yourself as my boyfriend."

I smile, gazing into her eyes. "That's what I am, isn't it? I mean, I know we haven't been together physically a lot, but frankly, I'm surprised my phone hasn't caught fire with some of the text messages we've shared."

She laughs. "It's easy to get carried away with you."

"Wanna go get carried away now?"

Hayley plants a kiss on my cheek and stands, pulling me to my feet. "Come on, then."

"Whatever you say, princess."

IN THE MORNING it's a lonely drive home to an empty house. I hate it when she's not here. We've known each other five minutes, but Hayley McCarthy has me wrapped around her little finger.

After two nights of Hayley being here, the house I'd found refuge in is empty. Even though she brought nothing with her, everything around me reminds me of her—the dent her body left in my mattress, the scent that leaves me remembering our bath together, the ache to hold her and touch her. Not even voicemails from Lucy demanding I call her can distract me.

She could take everything I own and I wouldn't care if I had Hayley.

I'm hers.

11

HAYLEY

One week later, the cove is quiet.

It's rare to find it like this. There are usually people about, and in the height of summer, it's teeming with life.

I pause and look out over the water. It's still, but for the odd splash in the distance. The fish must enjoy the peace too. Curling my bare toes in the sand, I take a deep breath.

This is what I love about my life here. Despite being on the go all of the time and the sometimes long hours, the tranquillity is hard to beat when I get a moment to enjoy it.

But today there's something missing. I think when I went to Hamilton a week ago, I left my heart there. This thing with Drew has come on so quick and strong, but at the same time, it worries me I'm reading too much into it.

But then a part of me is still laughing over Drew's comment about *our* kids. He's feeling the same about me, I'm sure.

"Hayley."

I freeze at the voice, and turn to see Ash Harris coming toward me. *Great*. "Uhh, hi."

He makes my stomach flip with that intense blue-eyed stare of his, but not in a good way. More in an I-want-to-recoil-and-run-away way. I can definitely see the appeal though. Those girls in his compound must be drawn to him. I would be.

"I had hoped that it would be quiet down here. I find the water calming," he says.

He draws level, and I nod. "Me too."

"I'm happy to see you. You caused quite the stir in our little community."

I hope so. You're all lunatics. "Just doing my job."

"You did it very well. I'm impressed."

I blush. I can't help it. After everything that happened early in my career, any compliment means a lot. Back then, I spent so many hours debating whether to go on or not, but my love for the job won out. "Thank you. How's Julia doing?"

He pauses for a second, as if he's surprised I've asked after her. "She's doing well. The baby's thriving."

"Glad to hear it. I hope she's being well looked after. That was a traumatic experience for her to go through."

"It was. She's getting plenty of rest."

"She needs it. Please give her my regards." I turn and walk the short distance to a nearby picnic table. I'm not concerned whether he follows me or not; I came out here for the fresh air and peace.

He sits opposite. "I want to tell you about our community."

I swallow. "Okay."

"Dad left me with a great responsibility, looking after his followers."

"So they're not *your* followers?"

He shakes his head. "No. I will lead when they need it, but they're all masters of their own destinies."

Stuck behind a wall and cut off from the world. "Julia needed antenatal care. The hospital had to take a few chances, given that I had no medical history for her. You can't take short-cuts like that."

Ash draws himself up. "It's better if we don't have outsiders come within our walls. They don't tend to understand us."

No shit. "That's all well and good, but situations like that need medical professionals. If you hadn't called me, Julia and her baby could have both died."

He nods. "I know. So, I have a proposition for you."

I swallow. I'm not sure if I'm interested in any proposition this man has. "I learned a big lesson with what happened to Julia. Maybe the ways of the past aren't the best ways. So, I'd like to invite you to join us."

My stomach drops. "Uhh that's very kind of you, but that won't be happening."

He smiles, showing off the perfect teeth that tell me he's probably seeing a dentist at least.

"If you want our help, then you need to speak to Margaret Joyce. She's my boss and runs the clinic which I work out of."

Ash licks his lips slowly. I know that move; it's meant to entice me, but it just leaves me aching to roll my eyes at him. "I mean come and live with us. You'd have a good life. I'm sure Julia will tell you how great things are."

I had thought he was about to suggest they use our midwifery service, but it's way more extreme than that.

Those piercing blue eyes fix on me, burning a hole in my brain. If this is how he gets followers, I understand.

Four years ago, when I arrived here, maybe I would have been a better target for him. I was broken and lost. Now, I have a job I love, friends, and Drew. I'm loved and wanted and cared for. "I'm not coming to live with you."

He smiles. "Maybe I can work on convincing you. I think you'd be a good fit."

"I'm happy with the life I have."

"And yet you're down here, de-stressing."

"Because I have a happy but busy life."

Silence settles over us, but he never drops his gaze. "Have dinner with me."

I shake my head. "I can't."

His eyebrows twitch. "Just to say thank you for saving Julia's life?"

"You don't have to thank me. Julia and the baby's survival are what's important."

He nods. "Of course. I'm so grateful, and I just want to show some appreciation."

I roll my eyes. "You're not going to take no for an answer, are you?"

He laughs and shakes his head. "Nope."

"I'll talk to my boss, but I might do it on one condition."

"Name it."

"That it's to discuss future care for any pregnant women in your community. The easiest way to avoid situations like Julia's is for us to get in and see them. Or for them to come and see us."

He gives me a short, sharp nod. "Deal."

"I can't stress how important this is."

He leans forward. "You don't give up easily, do you?"

"Never."

A smile spreads across his face. "I like a challenge."

I walk away, unsure how I feel about it all. A few weeks ago, and I probably would have just gone and got it over with. Now I think about Drew.

How is he going to feel about this?

THE AFTERNOON WEATHER IS COOLING, and I get the urge on the way home to make cheese toasties for dinner. It's comfort food, one that helped get me through studying.

Determined to stand on my own two feet, I did my best to support myself and live within my means. My parents were loaded, but I didn't want to rely on them—or at least I didn't want the fuss that seemed to go with doing so. All I ever wanted was a simple life, and this town has given me that.

I pull up outside the bakery. It's usually open until five, and I'll only just make it, but the bread's so good here. The supermarket stuff has nothing on it.

Owen smiles as I walk into the bakery. "Hey, Hayley."

"Hi."

"After some bread?"

I nod, and he grabs hold of my usual multigrain loaf. "It's on the house."

"Why?"

He grins. "I hear you're making Drew happy. That's a big plus in my book."

I chuckle. "He's making me pretty happy too. I still want to pay."

He slides the bread into a plastic bag. "Don't worry about it."

"What if things don't work out between me and Drew?"

Owen shrugs. "I'll make you pay for your bread again."

I can't help but laugh. He's been a bit flirty with me on a few occasions in the past, but I've just brushed it off.

"So, what else has your brother told you about me?"

He hands the bread over. "Not a lot. Well, about how amazing you are. All I know is that he's never been this happy. I think his last girlfriend sucked the life out of him, but you're good for his soul."

"I heard she'd moved onto sucking the life out of the landlord."

Owen throws his head back and laughs loudly. "I guess you could say that. Drew's got a big heart, and he deserves to be happy."

I don't know what to say to that. It's like we're being married off already. "Thanks for the bread, Owen."

He nods. "Any time."

The little bell above the shop door rings out as it opens.

Owen grins. "There's a surprise. Are you tracking her phone or something?"

I turn. Drew stands behind me, a big smile on his face.

Everything that's happened today is forgotten when I lay eyes on Drew. "What are you doing here?"

He grins. "I just thought I'd pop down for the night. It's been too long since I've seen you."

Owen laughs. "What's it been? A week?"

"A week's a long time when you've met the perfect girl."

I blush as Owen rolls his eyes.

"It's okay, Owen. I know you've met plenty of perfect girls. At least, that's what you tell them …" Drew winks at me. "Whereas I mean it."

I laugh. Owen shakes his head. "And to think I gave you a free loaf of bread."

"Well, I wasn't going to visit, but I saw Hayley's car outside."

"Oh, so you're just here to see her?" Owen's tone is harsh, but his amused expression tells a different story.

Drew nods, slipping an arm around my waist. "Sorry."

"I think I might be able to forgive you. Pop in before you leave in the morning and you can grab some food."

"Sounds good."

Owen smiles. "Get out of here, you two. I'm closing up because I have places to be."

"Places to be or people to do?" Drew laughs.

"You know me so well."

THE BREAD LIES FORGOTTEN for the moment on the kitchen bench. Drew and I have better things to do.

I close my eyes as he laces kisses down my torso, his lips burning a trail. This is what I want all of the time. Not just on the odd weekend, not just during these stolen moments.

Drew reaches my stomach, and tears well as he goes down on me. I can't help it. A mix of emotions leaves me sobbing silently, even as I shudder against Drew's tongue.

He's worth so much to me, but I don't know how to start telling him.

"You taste amazing." He torments me until I reach the peak before tumbling down. He kisses my thighs, taking big mouthfuls of flesh as if he can't get enough of me, and I can't get enough of him.

It's not until he emerges from between my thighs and starts a journey back up my body that he sees something's wrong. Concern fills his expression. "Hayley? Are you okay?"

I nod, but the tears continue to flow. Okay doesn't begin to describe how I'm feeling.

"Tell me what's wrong."

My heart stops as he asks and doesn't just move past it. I've had a lifetime of people ignoring my feelings. Not Drew. "I'm just so happy."

His expression lightens as he scans my face. "Tell me what the tears are for."

"I just … I'm a little overwhelmed that we're together again."

Drew strokes my cheeks and wipes my tears. "I couldn't wait until next week, or next month, or whenever we got a chance to see each other again."

I smile a little. I don't want to feel so needy, but since we started seeing each other, he's all I can think about. It's not fair being in the honeymoon phase of a new relationship with no groom.

"Thank you," I croak.

"There is literally nowhere else I'd rather be." He leans over and nips at my neck, leaving me gasping.

I bring my hands up and cradle the back of his head as he slips into me, filling me emotionally and physically as only he can. "I want to be with you, Hayley. I knew for sure the night we sat in that bath and I held you as you nearly fell asleep in my arms. All I've wanted to do since then is hold you."

He moves slowly, torturing me with his slow pace, but I enjoy it as he does. The longer he's inside me, the better.

He's all mine.

IN THE EVENING, we watch a movie after eating the cheese toasties. Sprawled on the couch in my trackpants and a loose T-shirt, I'm comfortable and relaxed. My head's on Drew's lap, and I'm only half-watching *Captain America*.

Drew's stroking my hair, and I close my eyes. "Going to sleep, princess?"

"Maybe." I yawn.

"Did I wear you out?"

"Maybe." I push myself off his lap and sit. "I love that you're here."

"Thought you might. I'll have to leave early, but you're worth it."

I sigh. "You're working tomorrow?"

"Yeah, but a later shift. I'll be fine. Work's crazy at the moment, but you're worth it."

He reaches over and hooks my hair behind my ear. "I was missing my girl and needed to see her."

"I needed to see you too, but I can't take off when I feel like it."

"Neither can I. I had to do some serious grovelling to get someone to swap hours with me."

I grin. "If you're working tomorrow, you'll need to get a lot of sleep tonight."

He waggles his eyebrows. "I had other plans. Are you even watching this movie?"

"No."

"I've got something for you. Not that you really need it, but I did. Lucy's still calling me wanting financial help, and I keep telling her to talk to her lawyer, but I don't think she's doing it because she doesn't have the money."

I frown. "I'm confused."

"The way it all ended bothered me. Not that I miss her, because I'm in such a better place now, but this was important." He reaches into his pocket and hands me a piece of paper.

I unfold it, and I smile as I recognise what it is. He's been tested for everything under the sun and come out of it with a glowing bill of health.

"I'm here, Hayley, and I'm all yours. Maybe my past will bug us for a while, but I want to try and put it behind us."

I smile. "Thank you for this. In some warped way it means a lot."

"For me too. I know we've been using condoms, but I wanted us to be safe. Given our respective occupations."

Laughing, I press my hand to his chest. "I agree. So, what else are we going to do today?"

"Let's talk."

"Are those *all* your other plans?"

He smirks. "No, but I like talking to you. We cram so much into the limited time we have together, and it can't all be sex. Even if I want it to be."

I nod. "Fair enough."

"Do you want to have children?" he asks.

The question catches me by surprise. He's sweet and funny, but sometimes so intense. It's not like we've been together that long. Still, I decide to answer honestly. I'd rather get it out in the open. "One day."

"I do. I want lots."

The grin on his face makes me laugh. "Define lots."

He shrugs. "I grew up in a family of five boys. We were all really close, at least until Adam left. I want that closeness for my kids."

I take a moment to respond. "I grew up alone. And then I was a terrible disappointment to my parents. I was never sure if I wanted to put a child through that. Not that I'd treat them that way, but I always wished I'd had a brother or sister to turn to. I had no one else. So, I don't know about lots, but I want more than one."

His eyes grow so sad. "That sucks. What on earth were your parents thinking? You should have been all the more precious to them." He sighs. "Though, I can't talk. Not after the stunt Mum pulled. Then again, if we'd all done more to make sure Adam knew the truth ..." He takes a deep breath. What did you do to disappoint your parents?"

"What did your mother do to Adam and Lily?"

"Lily didn't tell you?"

I shake my head and get a sigh in response.

"You know what happened to her, right? The abuse she suffered from her mother?"

I nod. All of Copper Creek knows about that. There are people who sympathise and see past what Lily's mother did, and others who don't like her, convinced she's turned out the same as the woman who gave birth to her. In the four years I've been living here, I've heard a lot of gossip.

"Adam left because he was a mess, and he'd fallen out with Corey over it. In trying to avoid hearing how happy Lily was, he cut all of us off. Mum fed him a bunch of lies about how well she was doing and who she was with."

I grip Drew's arm. "Even the town gossips knew she was raising Max by herself."

"Adam didn't know that. The stubborn prick was too hurt to come back and check for himself. They lost so much time together unnecessarily." He kisses my hand again. "I don't want to lose time with the right person, and I think I've found her."

"Drew ..."

"Back to you, princess. Tell me about your parents."

I bite down on my lips. "Have you heard of David McCarthy?"

"The name rings a bell."

"Brewery King."

His eyes widen. "I think I read something about him. Worth millions?"

I nod. "That's my dad. He wanted me to go into business. My mother wanted me to find my own rich guy and give her grandchildren. I decided to become a midwife and help other people with their babies."

Drew's eyebrows knit as he frowns. "How can that be disappointing?"

"It wasn't what either of them wanted for me. And then I had that patient die."

"It's a lot to deal with, especially when you're not long qualified."

I sigh. "I was on the verge of giving up I was that frustrated. Then Margaret and I found each other and she convinced me to come here. Best thing I ever did."

Drew bends closer and presses his lips to mine. "If only I'd found you four years ago."

"I needed to find me first. You got me at a good time." I grin.

"I'll have you any time."

12

HAYLEY

I DREAM OF HER SOMETIMES

She's not real, not yet at least, but I have a little girl who's so much like me. She snuggles into bed and I hold her tight, breathing in that baby smell.

I think I dream of her because she'll have everything I didn't have. I'll have no expectations other than that she grows up healthy and confident enough to make her own decisions. She'll be strong because I'll support her in whatever she chooses.

My eyes don't want to open when the phone starts chirping on the coffee table just as I get comfortable on the couch. Hopefully, it's Drew. We haven't seen each other for three weeks, and I'm climbing the walls a bit. This whole long-distance thing is awful when all I want is to be in his arms at the end of the day.

I fumble for it as my hand makes contact with the wooden surface, pulling it to me and opening one eye.

Shit.

"Hi, Mum," I mumble.

"Hayley, you sound tired. Did I wake you? It's the middle of the day."

I wipe the drool from the corner of my mouth. "I've been working most of the night. Just catching up on some sleep."

"If only your job was normal hours."

"Babies don't keep to rosters." I laugh, but it's hollow and tired, and I want to screw my eyes up and finish this so I can sleep. Conversations like this leave me wondering if I was ever a baby at all. I have no idea how my mother coped.

"Do you remember Courtney Jackson?"

I let out a loud breath. "Kind of."

"It's been a while since I've seen her, but her boy is back from overseas. Remember him? Although, when I say boy, he's a rather impressive man now. A lawyer."

I shake my head and roll my eyes. They ache. What I need is sleep.

"Well, Mum, I've got a boyfriend. I just haven't told you because I wanted to know where it was going first."

She breathes heavily. It's the breath of disappointment I've heard before. I haven't shared my private life with her in years, and she's annoyed right now that I haven't updated her. I can tell by the silence.

"What does he do for a job? Does anyone in that town have a job?"

I bite down on my bottom lip before I really upset her. "He's a doctor in Hamilton."

"A doctor?" Now she sounds upbeat.

"He's an obstetrician. His family lives in Copper Creek. That's how we met."

"Oh. So how much does an obstetrician earn?"

I slap my palm against my forehead. "I don't know, Mum. We haven't gone into salary specifics. It doesn't matter to me." I sigh. "We're getting to know each other, and we're happy. That's all that matters."

"I'm just looking out for you."

"I know, and I appreciate it so much. But I can't live the life you want me to. It has to be what I want."

She sighs, and for the first time it washes over me, as if it means nothing. Because that's exactly what it is. I'm doing what I need to keep myself afloat, financially and emotionally.

"Okay. I'll let you get back to sleep. Think about it, though. She was telling me he was asking after you."

"Who?"

"Courtney Jackson's son."

This is so vague it's worth testing her. "What's his name? Does he know me?"

There's silence again, and I slam my hand across my eyes in frustration. She doesn't even remember his name and yet she's all but married us off in her head.

"I'm going to sleep, Mum. I can barely keep my eyes open."

"Fine. Talk again soon."

The call ends abruptly, as it usually does.

We weren't always this way. This wall between us went up when I abandoned her and Dad's plans for me and did what I wanted, only to have them both doing the whole 'we told you so' routine when things went downhill.

I close my eyes and return to the dream of my child, the one who only exists in my head. She visits more often on days like this, almost like a premonition that my mother will contact me and make me feel inadequate.

Even when my life far surpasses any of my past expectations.

I DIDN'T KNOW what loneliness was until I met Drew Campbell. Not that I blame him for that. I'd suffocated in the city, yearning for peace and quiet, and found Copper Creek just when I needed it.

I've made friends. My colleagues are wonderful and supportive. Margaret and I are a great team. And I've dated from time to time. For the most part though, I'm content to be by myself, away from the expectations of my parents and the crowded big city.

Drew makes me feel whole and empty all at the same time. When I'm with him, my world lights up in a blaze of colour. When I'm not, it returns to the drab hues it was before I came here, and I've never felt so alone.

When he's not here, I ache for him.

Tonight is my dinner with Ash Harris to discuss the women in his community getting proper pre-natal care. My stomach rolls because he makes me nervous. Meeting him in public beats going into that community again, as that scared the crap out of me, but it's not much better.

I dress conservatively, with a deep blue high necked dress with long sleeves. My heart wishes Drew was here. Maybe I should have been more forceful and not let Ash talk me into this. I'm the queen of hindsight.

It's just a couple of hours.

Picking up the phone, I dial Drew again, but the call's not going through. I don't have a landline because I live on my mobile, but there are times when the phone coverage is a bit patchy out here. It always picks its moments.

He knows I'm going and isn't happy about it, but I just need to hear his voice.

At the sound of a tap on the door, I throw my phone into my handbag and open it.

The dark eyes of Ash Harris drink me in, and I shrink back. His lips curl, and I have no doubt he thinks it's because he has some sort of magnetic effect on me. I've seen that effect in practice on some of the women in his community. That's not what causes my reaction. He scares me.

"You look incredible," he says in that smooth-as-silk voice.

I smile, but it's in the knowledge that my overwhelming attraction to Drew overrides any potential interest in this guy. He came into my life at exactly the right time. I'm far from vulnerable now. "Thank you."

"Shall we go?"

I nod, and follow him out to his car. Margaret might think this is a good idea, but I'm still not convinced. Maybe because Ash makes me so nervous.

He drives the short distance to the poshest restaurant in town. It's not open all year-round, but it is during the spring and summer when tourists are more likely to be in town.

My head's in a whirl as we're led to our table. The most important thing about tonight is getting a foot in the door. The last thing I want is to have to go through what we did with Julia a second time. With proper care, it would never have gone that far or been the emergency that it was.

"Heineken please," he says to the waitress. "Hayley?"

"Just a glass of water, thanks."

"Would you like to order food too?" the waitress asks.

He nods. "May I please have the scotch fillet with peppercorn sauce? Medium-rare."

"Can I get the same?" I ask.

My skin crawls when he smiles at me, as if he's pleased with my decision. I guess he's used to people following his lead. The thought never crossed my mind. I just like the steak here.

I lean forward, ready to talk shop. "So, we need to talk about the situation that happened with Julia and how that can be avoided going forward."

Ash leans back in his seat. "You really want to talk about business straight away?"

"That's what I'm here for."

He nods. "The easiest way to fix it is for you to come and live with us. Live with me."

"That's not going to happen."

The drinks arrive and break the tension between us. He never removes his gaze from me, and it's uncomfortable, but I don't let him know that. I get the feeling he'll be looking for any vulnerability, any way to get under my skin and convince me to do what he wants.

"There are two community midwives, and we basically share the load between us. There'll always be someone to take care of pre-natal visits, births, and after-birth checks between us."

"I want you." His tone suggests that he means more than just for me to be a midwife in his community, but I choose to take it that way.

"I work for Margaret Joyce. We have a roster."

He shakes his head. "No, Hayley. I want *you*."

There's no mistaking it now, and I swallow hard. "Well, that's impossible."

"Is it?" His lips curl into a smile. "You'd have everything you ever wanted. I would make you my queen."

Princess. Drew's voice is in my head, and I draw strength from it. "I'm not interested. Like I've already told you, I have a good life, a job, and a boyfriend."

Disappointment flickers in his eyes. "I could give you more."

I hold my palms up. "This isn't going to happen."

For a moment, we stare at each other.

"Excuse me for a minute. I need to go to the bathroom." Ash gets up and walks away. Has he given up, or is he just taking a moment to work out a new strategy? Maybe he really just needs to use the bathroom. Leaving is an option, but I don't want to cause an even bigger scene in a town that's so prone to gossip. *Shit*. My stomach churns at the thought of Drew's family finding out about this dinner. No matter how innocent it is, it doesn't look appropriate.

Ash wants me, and his intensity terrifies me. He's just offered me his whole world, whatever that is. I've had a glimpse behind the curtain, and I can see how impressive it could look.

"Hayley."

I look up. Owen Campbell's walking toward me, and anger's written all over his face.

"Owen?"

"What the hell are you doing?" he hisses.

"I'm having a business dinner."

"It's *who* he is, Hayley. I don't trust him. And I thought you were with Drew. Doesn't look like it."

My jaw drops. "Drew's my boyfriend. This isn't a date. Plus, Drew knows about it."

"That's what it looks like to me."

"You're wrong."

Ash walks back toward the table, raising an eyebrow at us. Owen rolls his eyes. "Enjoy your evening."

"Are you okay?" Ash asks.

I nod. "He was just saying hi. He's my boyfriend's brother."

"Not a nice hi from the look on your face."

Shrugging, I turn back to my drink. "We don't know each other that well."

"And he's upset seeing you with another man?"

"Something like that."

He gives me a smile. "I'm sorry. I understand your reluctance to leave your life and live with us. With me. I'll just say thank you for everything you've done, and we'll have dinner."

"We still need to work out future care for any pregnancies that might eventuate in your community."

"That can wait."

I've been put in my place.

Ash licks his lips slowly. "Is this going to cause trouble between you and your boyfriend?"

"No. Drew knows how I feel about him."

Across the room, Owen keeps his eyes on me. His date also has her gaze focused in my direction, but she's glaring. God knows what she thinks.

I'm relieved when dinner arrives as it kills the

uncomfortable silence between me and the man across the table, who's probably not used to anyone saying no to him.

At least tonight is nearly over.

WE REACH MY HOUSE, and I can't wait to get inside. This guy plays games, and even if I'm refusing to play, it's exhausting. There must be people who just give up fighting it because he's so intense.

I slip my key in the door, and turn back toward Ash. "Thanks for dinner."

"Thank you for coming with me. Maybe we could do it again sometime." He flashes that vibrant smile and before I know it, his lips are on mine, his tongue pressing for entrance into my mouth.

"Get off me." I push, my heart pounding with panic.

He runs his hand through his hair, his eyes piercing me. "I thought ..."

"You thought what? I said no." All I want is Drew—all I need is Drew. If I ever doubted how strong my feelings were, there's no more doubt.

Ash reaches for my elbow. "I want you to come and join us."

"Don't touch me." I pull back.

He licks his lips and nods. "I'll leave, but please consider it."

"I told you, I'm happy with my life the way it is."

Taking a step back, he doesn't take his eyes from me. In another place, another life, maybe I could fall for this guy, but not this way and not here or now. "Think about it. I know you'll change your mind."

He turns and walks down the path toward the road. I shove the door open and stumble inside, closing and locking it behind me.

Drew.

I reach the couch and sink into it, retrieving my mobile before I throw my bag on the floor. It's after ten, but surely he'll still be awake. I can only hope I can get a signal.

The line rings and rings, and just as I give up hope of him answering, there's a noise in the background.

"Drew Campbell's phone," a tired woman's voice answers, and my stomach climbs into my throat.

"Is Drew there?"

"Doctor Campbell's in surgery and it's a complex one so he's left his phone at the desk for emergencies. Can I take a message?"

I let out a breath and close my eyes. "Umm, can you please tell him that Hayley called?"

"Are you a patient of his?"

"No. I'm his girlfriend."

"I'll let him know. You're the midwife who brought that girl in the other week, aren't you?"

"Yes."

"I've worked with Drew since he was a trainee doctor. It's nice to see him with a smile on his face. That last girlfriend he had just made him miserable." She pauses. "I hope I haven't spoken out of turn."

"Not at all," I croak. Her words touch my heart.

"I'll pass on your message. I'm not sure how long he's going to be."

"I understand. Thank you."

Hanging up the phone, I burst into tears. While her words were lovely, all I want is to hear Drew's voice. It might have been easier to get his voicemail.

I'm a mess. Carrying my phone with me, I drag myself to the bedroom and strip off my clothes. I pick up Drew's T-shirt from the bed and tug it on over my head. It doesn't smell of him, but it's the closest thing to the man I'm falling for I have.

Curling up under the sheets, I tuck the phone beside the pillow. *Drew.*

I don't even realise I've fallen asleep until the phone chirps beside me. My eyes are raw from crying, and it hurts just to open them and see Drew's name on the caller ID.

"Drew." I cling to the phone.

"Hey." His soft tone tells me he's concerned, and the relief just from hearing his voice slows my racing heart. "I'm sorry I took so long to return your call. I was in surgery for a really long time."

I sniff, and despite my tired eyes, hot tears spill down my cheeks.

"Hayley, you okay, babe?"

"No," I whisper.

"What's wrong?"

I lick my parched lips. "Tonight, I did something dumb, and I really need to tell you about it before you hear it from your brother."

"What? Which brother?" There's panic in his voice now. I don't think I worded what I just said very well.

"Owen. He saw me at dinner, and I think he got the wrong idea."

"Wrong idea about what?"

I bite down on my bottom lip. Hard. "I went to dinner with Ash Harris."

There's silence for a moment. "I knew this was a bad idea. Especially when he gives you the creeps."

"All I want is to help those women. I thought it'd be easy to get through."

He lets out a breath. "And Owen saw you?"

"Yes. He had a go at me because he thought it was something it wasn't. I swear I didn't think about that, Drew."

"I see."

"Ash dropped me off at the door, and then he …" Tears overtake me as I take big gulps of air.

"What the hell did he do?" The anger in Drew's voice is clear. Exactly who it's directed at, I'm not sure.

"He kissed me," I whisper.

I hear him swallow. "What are you trying to tell me, Hayley?"

Oh God, he thinks I'm breaking up with him. "I pushed him away, and I told him I was seeing someone else. He already knew that, and he was pretty insistent, but I got rid of him."

"Shit," he yells. "And then you couldn't get hold of me. Do you need me to come? I'll get in the car if you need me."

I let out a loud breath of relief. "I'm okay, but I thought you would be angry with me. I wanted to tell you before anyone else …"

"You thought I'd be angry with you for what someone else did? All I want right now is to wrap my arms around you and tell you it's going to be okay."

My heart explodes. My fear all but evaporates, and I close

my eyes. "I wish you were here, but I don't want you driving. Not if you've been in surgery for hours."

"I want to be there too. I'll see what I can do, and I'll call Owen, tell him to back off."

Sighing, I nuzzle the phone. "There's no need. I know you want to protect me …"

"Damn right I do. I know you have issues with doing this long distance, but, princess, I'm in this for the long haul if you are."

I sniff, wiping my nose. "I am too. I want this to work with us."

He lets out a small laugh. "Since you were here, all I can think about is you. You wearing my shirt, you in the bath, you and I having breakfast together … Everything."

"You're all I think about too. I don't know what to do about the distance." I roll over and onto my back.

"Me either. We'll work it out. I'll be there on my next day off, and we can spend a couple of nights together. If that's what you want."

"It's all I want." I stop short of telling him I love him, even if I'm feeling it. One step at a time. I don't want him freaking out.

"No more having dinner with that freak. Margaret will have to find another way in."

"You're so hot when you're bossy."

He chuckles. "I'm gonna be bossy when it comes to you." He pauses. "Shit, I just love that we get each other. We can talk work and both understand it. I can talk shit and you still listen."

Laughing, I roll back over. "Speaking of work, I know you had a late one, so you'd better get some sleep."

"It'll be hard to sleep without you after this call."

"I miss you. Goodnight, Drew."

"Night, princess. I'll call you tomorrow. Don't worry about Owen; I'll take care of him. In fact, I'll ask him to keep an eye on your place just in case that weirdo gets any ideas."

"Thank you," I whisper.

"Try and get some sleep. I'm going to go and have a shower before bed and think about you."

I let out a laugh. "Are you thinking about me before or after the shower?"

"Before, during, after—all of the time."

When I put down the phone, I can breathe again.

I should have known Drew would be on my side.

13

ADAM

Ben.

I can only assume the extra stress and exhaustion that a new baby brings has brought on my dreams again.

When we first moved in here, I put together a lighting system so that we were never in the dark at night. It helped Lily sleep easier, but some nights it makes no difference to me. These days, I envy her sleep, even if she's cramming it in between feeds. I won't feel sorry for myself, though; she did this once before without my help. If anything, thinking about my past feeds my guilt for not being here when she needed me the most.

Instead, I slide out of bed. Rose woke a short time ago and after a scream, a feed, and a nappy change, she's fast asleep. I don't know how long it will last, but I can't get back to sleep. Not after the horrors I've seen in my dreams.

Sometimes, my eyes are still fuzzy when I wake, and I see

the blood. I'm covered in the scarlet liquid, and no matter what I do, I can't get rid of it.

I bypass our en suite and head down the other end of the house toward the main bathroom. Stripping off, I run the shower until it's as hot as I can bear, and I stand under it, letting it drown my bad feelings.

Lily and Max shouldn't have to deal with this, but then I know from previous experience that I need to talk and not bury my past. This is what nearly did me in before.

I grab the soap and loofah, and begin to scrub. I shower every day when I finish work, but when I'm like this, I'll never be clean enough. None of it was my fault, and yet I feel responsible. I was sent back to the US for the funeral of my friend afterward, nursing my shoulder injury. Ben had a wife, and a kid on the way.

I knew what it was like to lose the person you loved more than life itself.

When I returned for his funeral, it was the first time I used alcohol to numb the pain. Now, here with Lily, I've slipped into the easy routine of having the odd beer with dinner. Getting together with my brothers might mean a barbecue and a couple of dozen beers between us. We don't have anything stronger in the house, but in this shower, it's all I can think of.

Lily, Max, and now Rose have filled a gap in my life I never knew existed. That I'm in the shower scrubbing away imaginary blood in the middle of the night, when everything I ever wanted is under this roof with me, fills me with shame. How can it not be enough to chase away the demons of the past?

I don't want to disturb Lily, so I wrap a towel around my

waist after drying off and head into the living room. Lying on the couch, I flick on the television.

"For three easy payments of only 39.95 …" The TV drags on, and it seems that infomercials are the only thing I can find. For a moment, I consider turning on the Xbox and playing, but Max knows exactly where we're at in every game we own, and if I interfere with that, he'll be unhappy. I love that kid, and the last thing I want is to upset him. As he grows older, he understands more, and he's matured a lot since we've moved here. But there are still things he obsesses over, and that makes life a little hard at times.

It was Max who convinced me to finally get a Facebook account. Some of the kids at school already have them, even though they're too young, according to the Facebook rules. Max isn't allowed one, so he'd decided the next best thing was for his dad to be on there.

I move to the computer in the corner and turn it on.

There's a friend request. So many people have crawled out of the woodwork these past few weeks to send me them. I've been reunited with people from my childhood, and other former servicemen, plus some still serving. I freeze as I see the name on this one.

Jenna McLean.

My finger hovers over the mouse button. Sure, I'm curious about what's happened to my ex-girlfriend, but is this a good idea? Lily will have my balls if she thinks anything dodgy's going on.

I'll just be upfront and tell Lily. Can't hurt to have a look. Things didn't end well with Jenna, but then, looking back, we maybe never should have been together. I just didn't realise until I had the love of my life back what a good relationship was. Lily and I argue like any other couple, but there's always the love, the overwhelming emotion that comes with your heart being melded to someone else's.

Now I look back on our time together and realise that's the way it always was with us. Since we were fourteen.

I click accept and go to Jenna's page. There's a million selfies, and she looks good, really good. The smile on her face in most of the pictures is bigger than any she ever had when she was with me. It seems she's found true happiness, too.

My mouth goes dry when the message window pops up. This isn't anything I ever considered happening.

Long time, no see.

I pause. I have a sudden urge to crawl into bed with Lily and wrap my arms around her.

Sure is.

Maybe I can keep it brief.

You're in New Zealand?

Licking my lips, I take a deep breath. I'm half a world away and with the people who really matter to me now. I guess I can have a simple conversation.

I am. Came home about a year and a half ago.

Wow. Never thought that'd happen. You were pretty determined not to go there again.

I close my eyes. We started with so much promise, but things with Jenna didn't stay happy for long. I made her miserable so many times while I struggled to start a new life. When we'd met, I was on the verge of leaving the army.

My mother has cancer. I came home for her.

And I ended up with everything I ever wanted. My heart warms at that thought.

I'm sorry to hear that. I have to admit, I Facebook stalked you before I sent the friend request. Not that I could see much. How's everything else?

My profile picture is Max and me. We're standing out on the deck of the house, his dog, Lucky, sitting next to him. Lily took the photo, and in it, Max has his arms slung around my waist, and mine are around his shoulders. He has the biggest, silliest grin on his face, and my gaze is full of love for the boy beside me, and the lady taking the photo.

Well, I'm back home and back with Lily.

Every other time I've replied, those little dots have appeared to show she's replying. Not this time. It takes a full minute before they appear.

Really? I thought that was all behind you.

So did I, once.

How do I word this without making it sound like I regret having been with Jenna? I take a breath and type.

I did too. Turned out we had some long unfinished business. I have a son.

Another pause.

Is *that the boy in your photo?*

I smile; I can't help it. Every time I think of Max, all I want to do is smile. I went from being empty to my heart overflowing because of him. He makes every day better.

It is. His name is Max.

He looks very happy. You both do.

Thanks. We are happy. Things were complicated for a while, but we're a family now. Lily and I just had a baby girl a few weeks ago.

There's another pause.

Congratulations. I'm really happy for you, Adam. I knew you never thought it would be a good idea to go home, but it's obviously been the best thing for you to do.

Thanks. I hope things are going well for you too. If you scroll down the page, there are photos of the four of us together when Rose was born.

When she doesn't reply, I take a look at my newsfeed. As much as I love catching up with old friends, I love the life I have now. The garage is always busy, and we make a good income from it. Enough to keep us living comfortably, anyway.

You have a beautiful family.

Thank you.

I scroll down for myself and smile at the photo Jenna would have seen. Lily's in our bed, cradling the baby in her arms with me beside her and Max in front of me. It's taken after I talked him down. Drew took the photo, and the love in it beams from the screen. It captures one of the best days of my life, and it shows.

You're up late. What's the time there?

I look at the computer clock.

2.10 a.m.

Nightmares keep you awake?

I woke up when the baby did, but couldn't get back to sleep.

"Adam?" Lily's voice comes from the hallway. Her twisted ankle healed quickly with rest, and a month later I need to find some help still, but she's forgiven me. I'm still not sure about Corey.

I gotta go. Lily needs me.

Goodnight.

I stare at the screen for a moment. Jenna might not have

been the right one for me, but she helped me through the early days when I was dealing with PTSD.

Maybe I should be asking for her help now I'm struggling with it again. Moving back here, setting up the business, and having my family together has been a big distraction. Being busy doesn't work to shut the darkness out completely, and too much is seeping into my world right now.

Shutting off the computer, I turn around to see Lily walking in the door. "What are you doing? It's the middle of the night." Her eyes are so tired, but she has that hazy smile on her face. The one she's had since the baby was born.

"I couldn't sleep, and I didn't want to disturb you." I swivel on the chair and she sits on my lap, leaning her head against mine.

"The bed's cold and lonely without you." I plant a kiss on her neck, and she sighs. "Another week or two and that can turn into something more. Especially when you're only wearing a towel."

Chuckling against her skin, I wrap my arms tight around her waist. "I'm looking forward to that."

"So am I."

I look into those beautiful blue eyes, the eyes filled with so much love that it warms me all over. "Let's get to bed. I'm sure once I have you in my arms, I'll sleep like a baby."

Lily laughs. "I'm not sure if that's such a good comparison right now."

"You're so right. Is she asleep?"

"For the moment."

I run my fingers through her hair, pulling her closer for a kiss. "I love you."

"Love you too. Let's go and make the most of the quiet

while it lasts." She stands, grabs my hands, and pulls me to my feet. "Come on, Campbell."

For a moment, I take in her face. Her eyes are tired, but they no longer have the dark circles they did when I came back. For her sake and the sake of the baby, she ate better than she had done in years, and her once gaunt figure filled out. She's radiant, and the glow emanating from her leaves me smiling. This is the happiest I've seen her. Do I pull her into my darkness, or let her bask in the light for a while?

"What?" she asks, a smile playing on her lips.

"I'm just thinking about how much I love you. I'll give you a hundred babies if it leaves you with that happy smile on your face."

She laughs. "The one we have now is enough for me for the moment, and we'll see."

"Two."

Nodding, she squeezes my hand. "Two. Of all the things we've done, I think they're what we can be most proud of."

"I agree. I'm glad we've got our shit together."

I pull her into my arms and breathe in that baby smell that Rose leaves behind.

"Speaking of having our shit together, you had better get some sleep if you've got more overtime ahead of you."

"The things I do to keep my lady in the manner to which she's become accustomed."

Lily licks her lips. "I swore once I'd live in a tent if you asked me to. That still stands."

I lead her down the hallway toward the bedroom. "A tent would be no good."

"Why's that?"

"I can't imagine all four of us in a tent. When would I get you alone?"

She laughs as I slip my arm around her waist. "That's a good point."

We pause at our bedroom door, and she sighs as I pull her in for a kiss. I love kissing Lily. Her soft, warm lips always bring me comfort and reassurance. Maybe I should stay in bed and kiss her to make myself feel better. Even the thought leaves me feeling selfish when she's struggling with lack of sleep.

"Come on," she says, in a tone so soft and loving.

Everything else is forgotten as we go back to our bed.

Even the blood.

14

HAYLEY

It's early when I wake to knocking on the door, and I pick up my phone to see it's just a little after six. Too tired to think straight, I stagger to the door and pull it open. Breathing a sigh of relief that it's Owen Campbell on my doorstep. I lick my lips.

"Aren't you a sight?" He casts his gaze over me, and I look down in horror as I realise I'm wearing Drew's shirt and nothing else. For once in my life I'm thankful I'm not that tall, and that Drew's long shirt more closely resembles a nightgown than a T-shirt on me.

"It's too early. What are you doing here?"

"Are you okay?" He studies me closely. My eyes are still sore from crying the night before, and they're probably red.

"Yeah. I was, once I could speak to your brother and make sure we were good." I shoot Owen a glare, and his expression grows sheepish.

"I'm sorry about last night. Can I come in? I brought breakfast."

"I'll put the kettle on."

He follows me into the kitchen and sits at the table, tearing open the bag. "Cheese and bacon croissants. They're freshly cooked. I hope you're not vegan or anything."

Yawning, I shake my head. "That sounds good. How do you take your coffee?"

"Milk, no sugar." He sighs. "I wanted to apologise for last night. Drew called and tore a strip off me."

I pluck two mugs from the cupboard and flick the water on to boil. "He said he was going to talk to you."

"He's just a crazy man in love. I'll forgive him."

Spooning the coffee into the cups, I smile. "You think so?"

"He's crazy about you. He said you had some trouble with that weirdo."

I sigh as I pour the milk. "He tried to kiss me. I don't know if he's used to people saying no to him."

"That's not a good thing. I'll leave you my number and if you need any help, give me a call."

Placing the cups on the table, I sit opposite him. "Are you always this helpful?"

"Why wouldn't I be? If you're Drew's girl, you're practically part of the family. Better than the last one."

He pushes the paper bag into the centre of the table. Four croissants sit on it, and the scent wafting from them is amazing.

"From what Drew's said, that's not difficult." I pick up a croissant. It's soft and warm, and I can't wait to sink my teeth into it. "Thank you for breakfast."

"It was the least I could do after being so rude last night.

Drew deserves better than what he had with his ex, and it sounds like he's got that now. I feel bad."

I take a bite and close my eyes as the melted cheese and bacon taste fills my mouth. After the stress of the night before, it's heaven. "I really appreciate you making the effort. This is so good. You can bring breakfast any time."

He grins. "I wouldn't tell Drew that."

"That's not what I mean, and you know it."

Laughing, Owen leans back in his chair. "You don't have to worry about me. It's not going to stop me flirting shamelessly with you when Drew's around. He torments Adam like that."

"I noticed. He has a nickname for her."

"Lily-Belle?"

I nod.

"He used to call her that when we were kids to get a rise out of her because she hated it. After all the shit that happened with her mother, he stuck with it because it was familiar." He leans over a little. "She's like the sister we never had, so don't ever read too much into it."

I laugh. "Okay. I won't."

"So, what are you guys going to do?"

"What do you mean?"

He takes a sip of his coffee. "It makes no sense for Drew to come back here, so I assume you're moving to Hamilton."

I shrug. "We haven't got that far yet, but it's the only thing that does make sense."

Owen nods. "Are you okay with that?"

I finish my last bite and pick up my mug, cradling it in my hands. "I love this place. It's been my saviour in so many ways, but I want to be with Drew. I'm not really sure what I'll do."

"He really is smitten. I don't think I've ever seen him like this."

"Did you ever meet his ex?"

Owen rolls his eyes. "Once, when I went to Hamilton to check out a new supplier. She's a real piece of work, that one."

"What do you mean?"

"She was just so whiny. Drew came out for a drink with me, and she decided to tag along only to complain that where we were going wasn't nice enough. She wanted somewhere fancy where the drinks were probably twice the price. All she did was sit in the corner and whinge the whole time."

I shake my head. "I'm trying to picture Drew putting up with that."

"I'm pretty sure he only did because he felt guilty finishing things. She quit her job five minutes after moving in without speaking to him, and I think he felt obligated to look after her."

"That's the kind of thing he would do. He's such a softy."

Owen nods. "Yeah, he is. That's why I reacted the way I did last night. I've seen enough of his kind nature being taken advantage of." He sighs. "I should have known you weren't like that."

"To be fair, how would you have known? It's not like we're close friends. I just buy bread from time to time."

He laughs. "Maybe we should remedy that. My flat is useless, but I'll talk to Adam about having a barbecue at his place. We'll have a family get-together."

"Does that include your parents?"

"Have you met them yet?"

I shake my head. "No. Drew hasn't met mine either, so I think that's fair enough. I've heard a bit about your mother."

"Then you'll know why they won't be invited."

"I guess. She sounds a lot like my mother to be honest."

He rolls his eyes. "You and Drew will be perfect together then. Just stay away from all of the parentals."

I grin. "My mother wants to hook me up with a man of her choosing. I'm sure she'll like Drew, though. He ticks all her boxes."

Owen smiles. "Why do you think I'm still single? It's so I don't have to deal with all this shit. As if you don't have enough to deal with too. The last thing I'd do is hook up with someone in a different city. Screw having to travel for sex."

I know he's just chatting, but that hurts. Every day, I feel the distance more and more. It's not as if we're in different countries and unable to see each other, but our distance still reminds me of the years I spent in boarding school, abandoned by my parents.

When I first went there, I cried every night for weeks. I only got to go home during the school holidays. I even spent long weekends as a boarder and learned for the first time what loneliness was. When I let my mind still and relax, it's what I feel now.

"Shit, Hayley, that was insensitive. If it works for you two, that's awesome."

I shrug. "I'm not sure if it is. Drew means everything to me, but I hate the time in between, you know?"

He nods. "If I know Drew, he hates it too. He's such a nice guy, and he gives his heart away way too easily. But I think he's found something special with you."

"It is special."

"So you two will make it work somehow. I can guarantee that if he's sleeping with you, there won't be anyone else in his life."

I smile. "I hope it'll work. He's a nice guy, your brother."

"Yeah, he is. And that's from the brother who had to put up with sharing a room with him for the first twelve years of my life."

That brings a grin to my face. "Tell me about you guys growing up. Was Drew always so sweet?"

"Always. Corey was the one who constantly got in trouble. Adam followed in his shadow until he met Lily."

I nod.

"Drew would bring home stray animals and pretend to be a doctor."

His memory makes me smile. I could just picture Drew doing that, he's so caring.

He tilts his head. "At least you're smiling again. I thought for a bit I'd put you off a long-distance relationship with my brother."

I can't pretend it doesn't still bother me, but I don't want to talk about it anymore. "What about you? What were you like?"

He shrugs. "I just never wanted to settle down. Still don't. I have my bakery, and that's enough for me."

"Really?"

Owen shifts in his seat as if he's uncomfortable. "Really. I'm not the type to get tied to someone forever."

"Maybe the right person is out there for you."

"It's okay if they're not." He nudges my arm. "Drew's

never sounded the way he does talking about you. That's love."

Glancing at the clock, his eyes widen. "Shit. I told Mel I'd be back in twenty minutes. It's nearly half past."

"Do you need a hand in the bakery? I'll help."

He grins. "I bet you would too. You're as nice a person as Drew is. That'd be why you're so sickly sweet together." He lets out a loud breath. "We'll be fine. Mel complains a lot, but she's turning out to be such a great baker. I hope she stays with me when she finishes her apprenticeship."

"For your sake, I hope so too." I stand, taking the paper bag and scrunching it into a ball. "Thank you for visiting, Owen. It means a lot."

"You're welcome. Pop by for a chat whenever you need to. I'll give you my number, and I mean it—call me if you need anything."

"I will."

He stands and hugs me.

"Be good to my brother and he'll worship the ground you walk on. Promise."

I nod.

"I should go before you realise I'm feeling you up. Give me your number and I'll text you mine."

Laughing as he lets go of me, I tell him my number.

He leaves me with fresh croissants and a smile on my face.

I know I've found a friend.

15

DREW

I MISS HER.

Hearing her so frantic on the phone didn't help. This distance is coming between us, even if we're happier than ever. It's such a screwed up situation, and I hate it as much as I love her.

And I do.

Every time I close my eyes, I see her. She's so full of life, and the thing I've come to love most is making her smile. Why did I have to fall for a girl who lives back in Copper Creek and not here?

It's dark when I get home, and my phone rings just as I get to the front door. I pull out my brand-new iPhone and roll my eyes at the name on the screen. What did I ever see in Lucy?

My curiosity gets the better of me. I don't want a confrontation, but why the hell would she still be calling me?

My lawyer hasn't heard from hers, although I prepared him and did the groundwork just in case.

"Lucy."

"Drew. We need to talk. I need money."

"You need to sort that out for yourself."

"You owe me."

I shake my head, memories of the past few months filling my mind.

"Drew, I hope you don't mind, but I quit my job." That was a week after moving in.

"Drew, I bought some new clothes today. Your credit card declined at the third place. You might need to do something about that." That was often her refrain as I dropped the limit bit by bit to stop the spending.

Yeah.

Life was fun with her, but I have so much more money now she's not a part of my life. Plus, I have love, actual love. The kind of love you want to scream from the rooftops. Even if it is a long-distance love.

"Ahem."

I roll my eyes.

"I'm pretty sure you owe me. It's over, Lucy, but you already know that. Go home to your parents if you need money."

"I'll talk to my lawyer."

I sigh. "That's what I keep telling you to do. Do whatever you want. Just leave me alone."

Hanging up the phone, I slide my key into the front door and turn it. When I first moved in, living here felt like the right thing to do. Plenty of space, and lots of time to just be me. But

I'm selfish now. I want to come home to Hayley. I want her sweetness around me every day, that gentle demeanour I love so much. She's everything I ever needed and more.

The house is quiet, and it's missing the one person I want here.

I dial her and lie back on the couch.

"Hello?"

Immediately, I regret my timing. Her voice is thick with sleep, but a little husky, which stirs something in me. "Hey."

"Drew? Your number didn't come up. I didn't know it was you." There's joy in her voice, and my heart warms hearing her.

"I got a new phone, and I've been playing with it. I'll have to work out how to turn the caller ID back on. I'm sorry if I woke you."

"It's okay. It's been a long day, but I'm not going anywhere else tonight."

I smile and roll onto my side. "I wanted to hear your voice. I miss you so much."

"I miss you too. Wish you were here."

My heart pangs at her words and her sad tone. She's as empty without me as I am without her. It's ridiculous that the distance between us isn't that big, but when we're apart it might as well be a million miles. "I do, too. I'd love to curl up in your bed with you and just sleep. I had a busy day. What have you been up to?"

"Mostly ante-natal checks. I stopped in to see Lily. She's doing so well, and that baby of hers is just the sweetest."

Before this, I never got homesick, but just the sound of her voice makes me long for Copper Creek. More specifically, her little cottage.

"She's got the Campbell DNA—that's why. We're all sweet."

Hayley laughs. "You are, anyway. I don't know your brothers well enough to comment."

"The diplomatic answer."

"You're the one I want to spend time with." She sighs, and I know that feeling. "Was your day long too?"

"The longest."

"I hate this," she whispers. "It's my birthday on Thursday and I wish you could be here for it."

My heart breaks when I hear her sadness. I did this by calling her when I could have let her sleep. It's such a tough situation to be in. I just want my girl with me. All I can think about is what she told me about her relationship with her parents. They abandoned her in boarding school, and this must be a similar feeling for her, even if it's not me sending her away. "I hate this too. We'll work out what to do, I promise." I sigh. I just want a distraction—anything other than just thinking about the miles between us. "Tell me about my niece."

Hayley takes a deep breath. "I think she's going to be a lot like Lily. She's got the same blue eyes, although you know they could change at some point. That dark hair is disappearing, and there's some fair hair coming through."

"Max was like that when he was born. Then it all fell out and he was bald and looked a lot like my grandfather."

She laughs, and even though it's accompanied by a sniff, it brings a smile to my face. "How's Max coping with his sister? Any better?"

"I think so, but it's a gradual thing. He's impressed by the way she burps."

I chuckle, picturing my nephew and how he gets hung up on all kinds of things. "It's a big change to his world."

"He seems to be adjusting."

"I'm glad."

I don't let the phone call go too long. She sounds tired, and I'm a dick if I keep her awake when she needs her rest.

It's driving me up the wall that she's not here resting with me.

I'M LOST IN THOUGHT, standing at the reception desk in the maternity ward the following day.

I need more time with Hayley, but travelling back and forward is tiring with my work schedule. It'd be easier if there was another midwife in Copper Creek. Margaret and Hayley depend on each other, and I can't expect her to pop up and see me at short notice.

"Everything okay?" Caitlyn asks, shoving a customer chart in my face.

I smile. "Yeah."

"How's Hayley doing?"

"She's good. Working hard. Seriously, country-town midwife life is just like running a farm. There's lambing season, and there's baby season. She's busy."

Caitlyn nods. "I wouldn't mind going somewhere a bit more remote. Less stress than this place, I'm sure."

"Yeah and no. Hey, do you remember a story about a midwife in Auckland about four years ago? Lost a patient to placental abruption and got put under supervision?"

Caitlyn narrows her eyes as if she's concentrating. "It

rings a bell. The doctor involved said she didn't tell him in time or something." She frowns. "It's not often things like that happen, so they stick with you."

"Do you know who the doctor was?"

She shakes her head. "I can probably look it up and see if I can find out. Where was it?"

"Auckland."

"I'll take a look." She licks her lips. "Why?"

"Hayley was the midwife."

Her eyes soften. "Oh, Drew, I'm so sorry for her. I can't remember the details, but I have a feeling she got hung out to dry."

"She did." I shift my gaze to the ceiling. "I know it's probably pointless chasing anything now because it's so far in the past, but I'd like to know who to avoid working with."

Caitlyn grimaces. "Tell me about it. Why do you think I like working with you? At least I know you listen to me."

My chest tightens with emotions. Just for her to say that means a lot, and I'm glad she feels that way. I'd never ignore what Caitlyn has to say.

When I think of how much Hayley would have fought for her patient, how much she fights for patients now, I know the loss must have devastated her. It's a testament to her strength that she's stayed in the job.

Toward the end of my shift, Caitlyn comes looking for me.

"I found it," she says quietly.

"Found what?"

She passes me her phone, and there's the judgement in black and white. Hayley's reprimand when she did nothing wrong. I don't even know this Doctor Marcus Johnson, but I know I believe in her.

"Thanks."

"She was in her second year. That'd be tough when you haven't been doing it that long. It's good she's still practicing."

I nod. "She's tough. I watched her with my sister-in-law, and she's good. She even put up with me being a distraction."

Caitlyn laughs. "I bet you were a right royal pain in the butt."

"You know me so well."

She rolls her eyes. "I don't know how she puts up with you."

"Well, I think she might love me."

She's still laughing as I leave the hospital for the night. As much as I'm looking forward to going into private practice, I'll miss this place. I'm not sure how often Caitlyn and I will work together when I leave. She started here the same year I did, and we've grown in our jobs together. Her husband's an occasional drinking partner of mine, too.

If only Caitlyn was the only woman problem I have to fix.

I have to convince Hayley that moving's the best thing for her. That she'll be welcomed here with open arms, even if she doesn't get a hospital job.

I have to.

16

HAYLEY

I SMELL.

Today has been a long day full of bodily fluids, and no matter how much you scrub, it's impossible to get rid of lingering scents. I'm going home to stand in the shower until all the hot water is gone, and after that I'll probably stay in the cold. Today of all days, I should be relaxing and enjoying myself, but when Margaret was ill, I had to stand in to work for her. That's what happens when you're a team.

I pull into my driveway before noticing there's a familiar silver car parked on the street. *Drew.*

My heart leaps at the realisation that he's here on a day when I usually feel so alone and neglected. My mother is far more interested in who she sets me up to marry than the day she gave birth to me.

He steps out of his car, grabbing a sports bag from the passenger seat before walking toward me. On his face is a grin a mile wide, and I realise he has a bouquet of flowers in his hand.

"This is getting to be a habit. What are you doing here?" I ask, breathless with joy.

His dimpled smile lights me up. "I needed to see you, so I swapped shifts. I've got tonight off, but I'll have to go back tomorrow evening because I have an early shift to make up for it."

"One night is plenty." Despite his bag and the flowers, I fling my arms around his neck when I grow close, and he drops what he's carrying as he pulls me up off the ground and spins me around.

He buries his face in my neck. "God, I've missed you. Even if you do smell a bit funky."

I laugh. "No births today, but I did do a couple of newborn checks and got a bit of baby poo on me. Twice. I know it's not stinky, but it's got that aroma I need to wash off."

"That's a great hit rate. Congratulations."

I close my eyes and breathe him in. He has no such aroma issues. "You, on the other hand, smell good."

"Doesn't mean I can't join you in a shower."

He picks up his bag and the flowers. Laughing, I grab his hand and pull him toward the house. Not that he resists. His body slams into mine from behind as I get to the front door, and I giggle as I slide the key in.

As I push the door open, I turn and jump into Drew's arms, hooking my legs around his waist. He chuckles, dropping his things just inside the door, but for a moment, I lose focus. There's a dark blue car slowing across the road. I blink slowly, wondering if I'm seeing things. If I'm not mistaken, that car belongs to Ash Harris.

The wheels spin as it takes off, and Drew takes two steps inside the door, dropping me to the ground. "Hey. Are you okay?"

"What?"

"The colour's gone from your face."

I shake my head. "I thought I saw ..."

"What?"

"Ash's car."

"Ash?" His eyes narrow, and he turns to look out the door.

"It's gone now. It might not have been. I'm just being paranoid." I push the door closed.

He cocks his head. "That man worries me. Especially after the last dealings you had with him."

"I know." I press my palms to Drew's chest. "The last thing I want to do is think about him while I get so little time with you."

Drew nods. "Must be shower time, I reckon."

"I think so too."

He bends, his mouth covering mine. I love kissing Drew. He's home.

"Shower."

This time he leads me, and as he fiddles with the mixer in the shower to get the temperature right, I let my clothes drop to the floor.

He turns toward me, a wistful smile on his face. "That view was totally worth the trip."

I laugh.

"Get in the shower and I'll join you in a second."

The water's at just the right temperature, and I raise my face to let it wash over me for a moment.

His body presses against mine, with only the water running between us. I'm tired and having him to lean against isn't helping me stay awake.

He grabs the shower gel and loofah, giving a generous squirt before rubbing my stomach.

"Are you washing me?"

"Do you mind?"

"Not at all."

I lean my head back on his shoulder and close my eyes as the water dances down my body. He draws circles on my skin, looping around my breasts and then dropping the loofah to run his hand over the same spots to remove the bubbles.

"That bit's clean."

I laugh. "Thanks."

He runs a finger down my back. "I think I could do this all day."

"There's only so much hot water."

"Let's not waste any more time, then." His hand snakes around me, and those long, skilled fingers find my clit.

I reach up, clasping my hands behind his neck. "This is exactly what I needed today."

He nuzzles my ear. "I want to be everything you need."

It doesn't take long, his left hand gently squeezing one breast, his fingers between my legs. I'm aching and needy and wanting, and I don't know what day or time it is anymore. I love this.

"I need you," I cry.

"You have me."

"Don't worry about the condom."

His hot breath is on the back of my neck. "Lean over."

I cry out as he slams into me, and I brace myself in the corner of the shower. It's raw and brutal, but it's what we both need. He grips my hips and slides out only to come back in just as hard. My head bumps the wall, but the slight discomfort doesn't matter when he's inside me.

"I didn't mean to do that. Are you okay?" His voice is filled with concern, and my heart flutters.

"I'm fine."

"I'll make it up to you later."

I have no idea what that means, but I'll take everything he gives me, and my whole body shudders as he slows and cups my breast.

"Hayley, I'm so close."

When he says my name, I shift my feet, bringing my legs almost together. He groans and squeezes my nipples.

"You feel so …" Drew doesn't finish his sentence as he gives one last thrust, pulsing inside me. He's perfect—this is perfect. I could live my life being loved by him every single day.

My legs wobble, and he supports my weight, washing me down with a sponge. I turn and meet his soft, warm lips that tell me he's feeling the same way I am.

I shriek as the heat disappears and is replaced by ice-cold water running down my back. Drew laughs. "I guess we were in here a while too long." He reaches for the mixer and flicks it off, pushing open the shower door and grabbing a towel.

"You first," he says, wrapping it around me before grabbing another one. He ties it around his waist, and I cry out in surprise as he scoops me up and into his arms.

"Aren't you cold?"

He shrugs. "Pretty sure you'll warm me up."

I grin.

"Are you hungry? I'll make us some cheese toasties if you've got the ingredients."

I snuggle into his chest as he carries me to my bed. "It's all in the kitchen."

He places me gently on the sheets, and drops his towel, slipping into bed beside me and pulling up the covers. In his arms, the cold of the shower is forgotten. His skin is warm, and I burn all over, waiting for him to touch me. I wriggle out of my towel and drop it to the floor now I'm under the duvet.

His fingertips are on my cheek, and he runs his thumb across my bottom lip. "It's obscene how much I've missed you."

I laugh, and tears well in my eyes at the thought that we'll only get a single night before he leaves.

"What's wrong?"

My stomach churns. I don't want to bring it up again, but we promised to be open and honest with each other. I hate the way I feel, and then I feel guilty over it. "I'm struggling with this distance. I just want to be with you."

"I want to be with you too. I'm sorry things are the way they are. I wish they were different."

"Can we skip the food? I know it's early, but I just want to cuddle up and sleep."

Drew curls around me, enveloping me with his body. "Tired?"

"Very. Even more so after all that hot water and exercise."

He presses his lips to my neck. "Happy birthday, Hayley."

"You remembered?"

"I do pay attention. Even if I'm far away. I didn't get the chance to say it when I arrived, given you pouncing on me."

I roll onto my back and find myself gazing into his eyes. They're so full of emotion.

"Today wasn't just about showing up to get laid. I wanted to spend your birthday with you." He cups my cheek, and I close my eyes. He's everything I wanted, and having him here eases the pain of us being apart. "I've got a present for you in my bag."

My eyes fly open. I go from being sleepy to being too excited to nod off.

"I'll grab it."

I admire his bare arse as he walks out of the room. Drew's a thing of beauty, even if he doesn't know it. The view from the front as he returns leaves me sighing.

"Here." He hands me a flat black box with a bright red bow tied around it and climbs back into bed.

I tug at the ribbon, and Drew laughs as I throw the lid of the box off the bed.

Inside is the most delicate fabric, and I pick up a piece of the clothing. It's the softest black G-string I think I've ever seen.

"I love it. But it's so random. You know what underwear I usually wear." My drawer is full of cotton briefs. The most exciting I get is that they're different colours.

"Well, I thought that you might like something to wear when we're together. Although to be fair, you could wear granny knickers and I'd still want to get them off you."

I laugh. "They're lovely."

"There's a matching bra in there too. Lily helped me with

the sizing. If it doesn't fit, we can exchange it. Gives you another excuse to come and see me."

"I'll try it on. You're so thoughtful. Thank you."

He grins. "I'd be a pretty poor excuse for a boyfriend to not be here for your birthday."

I place the G-string back in the box. "I'm so glad you came. The gift is perfect. How did you get to be so good at picking pretty underwear out?"

"According to my credit card statements, Lucy shopped there a lot. She was such a clothing snob, I knew it had to be pretty high quality."

I let go of the box. "Let me get this straight. You bought me lingerie from a store you know about because your ex used to wear this stuff?"

He blanches. "I was going through the statements because my lawyer told me to in case she stopped talking about it and actually tried to get any more money out of me. I saw the name and went to the website." His gaze drops. "I wouldn't have a clue about what she wore. All I knew was when I saw the things I thought how great they'd look on you."

My heart thuds watching him. All the excitement in his face faded when I got angry, and he's done nothing wrong. "I'm sorry." I palm his cheek, and he raises his face to look at me again.

"No, I'm sorry. I should have thought that out better than I did. You deserve better." His words melt me inside. He cares. I know that much. He's come all this way just to spend time with me when he's supposed to be working.

I love him.

My chest clenches at the thought, but there's no other way to describe how I feel about Drew Campbell. We dance this dance around it, but that's my reality right now, and I think maybe it's his, too.

"Do you want to know why there are five G-strings in that box and not just one?" he asks, his husky voice telling me how much he wants me again right now.

"Enlighten me." I lean closer.

"I figured there was a good chance they wouldn't last long. The sight of you in one of those? Well, it might take everything for me not to rip it off you."

If he was any other man I might have laughed at his words, but if Drew does feel the same intensity I do, he might just mean it.

"Drew," I whisper.

"You're the best thing that's ever happened to me, Hayley. That's why I'm here, despite the distance."

Hot tears spill down my cheeks, and he shakes his head. "Don't you ever cry with me. I don't know how much longer you'll put up with this, and I want our time together to be happy."

"It hurts." My voice breaks before I can say anything else.

Drew nods. "I know it does. For me, too." He reaches up and wipes my tears away. "I'm sorry about the stupid underwear. All I wanted was to see you, to be with you. This is driving me crazy, and I can't do a damn thing about it."

He reaches for the box in my hand, and throws it to the floor. "I'm such a dick. Here we are with limited time together, and I'm making you cry. I'm sorry."

I shake my head. "It doesn't matter. You're here. That's what's important."

"Yeah, but it's your birthday." He pulls me into his arms, and I flop in his embrace, letting him hold me. "I miss you every second I'm not here, and I don't know what to do about it."

"I miss you too," I whisper.

Drew closes his eyes. "How are we doing this to each other? This is supposed to be a happy day."

"It's no different to any of my other birthdays." I wriggle out of his grasp and lie back on the bed. The G-string I took out of the box is still in my hand and I stretch it between my fingers. "Think I can use this as a slingshot?"

Drew laughs, lying next to me and sighing. "You can do whatever you want with it. I'm sorry."

"You bought me a gorgeous present. There's not really anything to be sorry about."

I drop the G-string to the floor and snuggle into his arms. "Thank you. It means a lot that you're here."

"Where else would I be?"

17

DREW

HAYLEY'S STILL ASLEEP WHEN I LEAVE HER BED IN THE morning. I think I wore her out, but at least she had the best birthday I could give her.

Anger boils in the pit of my stomach that I seem to be the only one who cares for her. Mum can be a crotchety old bitch at the best of times, but she'd never forget my birthday.

What would Hayley have done without me being here? Showered and gone to bed early, alone in that big bed of hers? I know she says she likes the solitude of living in a rural town in comparison to the big city she came from, but surely it's been isolating.

I reach the kitchen, and open the fridge to see what there is to eat. The least I can do is make her breakfast. My stomach grumbles, and I'm reminded that neither of us ate last night. The more food, the better.

But first, coffee.

Flicking on the kettle, I pick up the flowers discarded by

the door and find a large glass to set them in. At least she'll have these to remind her of my visit. To get some sun, I walk to the big window at the side of her cottage.

Lost in thought, I jump when the knock comes at the door, and I look at the microwave. It's only seven-thirty a.m. Who could be visiting now?

I tug open the door, grinning at the sight of Owen standing there, brown paper bags in hand. He laughs. "I spotted the car this morning when I was on the way past."

"You live behind your shop."

Owen winks. "I didn't spend the night at my place."

I roll my eyes, and step back to let him in. "So you brought me breakfast?"

He nods. "I grabbed a few things. Have you got the jug on? I'm parched."

"I just made a coffee, but I'm happy to make you one too."

Owen looks around as he walks toward the dining table. "Hayley not up yet? If you hadn't answered the door, I was gonna leave your food on the doorstep."

Shaking my head, I return to the kitchen bench and pull another coffee cup from the cupboard. "She had a big day yesterday. I was about to make her some breakfast in bed."

"Things pretty serious between you guys, then?"

I smile as I spoon the coffee into the mug. "Yeah. They are. I really like this one."

"I'm glad."

His words catch me by surprise. He's been a player for as long as I can remember, and it shocks me a little he hasn't had a crack at Hayley in the past. He won't get that opportunity if I have anything to do with it.

"I mean, you had some bad luck. Including that last great

catch."

Rolling my eyes, I pour the water and grab the milk out of the fridge, turning his coffee a light brown shade. "She seemed alright, at first."

"It's not like you ever let us spend much time getting to know her."

I place the coffee on the table and sit. "You should be glad of that. She probably would have found a way to pick your pocket and fleece you, too."

"That bad, huh?"

I nod. "My own laziness in calling off a relationship that was wasn't really one bit me in the arse. It might have been fun at the start, but that didn't really last long." Smiling, I take a sip of my coffee. "What I've got with Hayley is nothing like that. She's amazing."

"When's she moving to the city?"

My heart sinks. It does every time I think about it because I feel as if I'm being unreasonable not wanting to move. But the reality is that there's nothing in Copper Creek for me other than Hayley, and if we're in the city, I can give her the world. "I don't know about that. It's a big move, and she's happy here."

"From the looks of the smile on her face, you make her happy."

I let out a sigh. "I hope that's enough."

"She's a great girl. I did try to chat her up, but she's not interested in me."

Frowning, I glare at my brother. "When?"

He shrugs. "Quite a few times during the past four years. She's not a hermit, and you know I flirt with anyone who comes into the bakery."

Rolling my eyes, I take a sip of my coffee. "She knew better than to go near your dick. It's been around the block a few times."

Owen chuckles. "That just means it's more experienced."

"You keep telling yourself that while I get the perfect girl."

"Am I interrupting something?" Hayley emerges from the living room with a smirk on her face, clad in that T-shirt of mine she stole and never gave back. With her tousled hair, she's still got that just-fucked look about her, and it makes me want to throw Owen out and start all over again.

"I was just telling Owen if he didn't overshare, he might have a chance with someone like you."

She waggles her eyebrows as she leans over to kiss me. "I'm not making that call."

"See? Hayley knows the deal." Owen laughs.

"I wasn't complimenting you," she says as she sits on my lap and grabs my coffee cup out of my hand. I loop one arm around her waist and pull her tight against me.

"If you're up for it today, we could go and see Mum and Dad," I say, resting my head on her back.

"You're brave." Owen snorts and takes another sip of his coffee.

"Dad's alright. Mum I can deal with."

Hayley takes a sip of my coffee. "They can't be any worse than my parents."

"Wanna bet?" Owen grins. "Drew's right. Dad will love you just because you're you. Mum will treat you like you're the devil's whore."

"Owen," I growl.

"It's true. I'm just warning her."

Hayley shrugs. "I guess I have to meet them sometime. Now's as good as later."

Introducing Hayley to my parents is something I feel I need to do, given how serious I am about her.

At the same time, it scares the shit out of me.

"Drew."

Dad's in the backyard when we get to the house, and he beams the biggest smile ever at me.

"Hey, Dad."

"I didn't know you were home." He flicks a look at Hayley, and his eyebrows twitch, like she looks familiar.

"I'm going back tonight. I just wanted to bring Hayley to meet you before I left."

He smiles again and holds out his hand to her. "Hi, Hayley. It's nice to meet you, but I get the feeling I've seen you before."

"I live in Copper Creek, so I'll have been around the shops from time to time."

"That must be it."

"Is Mum about?"

He sighs. "She's inside. The last few days have been rough. We need to go back to see the oncologist again, and we're not expecting good news, but don't you dare tell her I told you."

"Oncologist?" Hayley asks.

I lick my lips. "Mum has breast cancer. She had a mastectomy maybe eighteen months ago, if that, and chemo, but it looks like it's come back."

"Oh. I'm sorry to hear that."

Turning to catch her gaze, I see the hurt in her eyes. My girl is such a big sweetheart, and I love her for it. "Let's get inside and see her."

Mum's sitting in a recliner in the living room, and she keeps a straight face as she looks Hayley up and down.

"Mum, this is Hayley."

"I thought you were with that other one," Mum says.

"Lucy and I broke up a while ago. I met Hayley at Adam's place."

She nods, still not giving in to a smile.

"It's so nice to meet you." Hayley's already won Dad over; the warmth in his eyes makes that obvious. Mum was always going to be a tougher nut to crack.

"How about I make us all a coffee?" Dad nods toward us, and I follow his lead and guide Hayley through to the couch. Mum watches, her judgemental eyes fixed on Hayley's back.

"Are you from the city?" Mum asks as we sit.

Hayley nods. "Originally. I was born in Auckland and grew up there, but I've spent the last four years living in Copper Creek."

"What brought you here?" Mum's almost being pleasant, but she's still in interrogation mode. Hopefully it won't be long before Dad interrupts.

"I'm a community midwife."

"And you enjoy living here?"

Hayley smiles. "It's lovely."

"My son works in the city. He'd stagnate in a place like this. Are you moving to be with him?"

I roll my eyes. "Mum, that's a work-in-progress. We haven't been together that long."

"Long-distance relationships never succeed. That's why I'm asking."

Hayley links her fingers in mine.

"Well, Mum, we both want to make this work," I say.

She shakes her head. "It's all well and good wanting it. I don't want to see you hurt."

This was a mistake. Why did I ever think bringing Hayley here was a good idea? Sure, she had to meet my parents sometime, but the worse Mum's health is, the more bitter she gets.

Hayley shifts slightly, and the tension's clear in her face. She already has issues with the distance. Mum's not exactly helping.

"Dad says you need to go and see the oncologist again," I say, trying to steer the conversation in another direction.

"I'm not discussing that right now." Mum shoots a pointed look at Hayley, and I cringe inside.

"Coming here was a mistake," I say.

"Here we go." Dad arrives in the doorway with a tray of mugs, a bottle of milk and a bowl of sugar. He places it on the coffee table and sits in the recliner next to Mum. Maybe he can rescue this. He beams at Hayley. "So, Hayley, is your family in Copper Creek?"

Hayley shakes her head, and it gives me a sense of relief that Dad's at least keeping the conversation going and upbeat. "My parents are in Auckland."

"What do they do?" Dad asks.

I reach for her hand and squeeze it, and she shoots me a smile. "Dad's a businessman. Mum does all kinds of things."

Dad smiles. "What brought you here?"

"Work. I had enough of the pressure of the big city, and

Copper Creek is the pace I need."

Mum snorts. Dad wriggles in his seat.

"There's no future for Drew in this town. He spent too many years training to give up his work," Mum says.

"I know," Hayley says quietly.

"I'm sure Drew and Hayley will do what they need to do," Dad says.

Mum glares at him. "And when it all falls apart? Drew always was the sensitive one."

"I'm right here, Mum." No wonder Adam has nothing to do with her. I can't let her treat Hayley like this.

"Just stop it. We're adults and we're working through the complications that come with a long-distance relationship. Hell, when it comes down to it, it's not like we're living in different countries."

Hayley grips my hand, and I long to see the light back in her eyes. My mother appears to have extinguished it.

"I'm just looking out for you," Mum says.

"I can look after myself."

Dad sits there silent. He's useless sometimes, but I guess he cops the worst of it, especially now she's ill.

My family is so screwed up.

HAYLEY'S quiet all the way back to her place, and my chest aches at the thought that I'll be leaving shortly.

"Hey." I pull her into my arms as soon as we get in the door, and she leans her head on my chest. I stroke her face until hot tears roll down the back of my hand. "Don't cry."

"I don't know if I can do this," she whispers. "What if your mother's right, and it all falls apart?"

I lace my fingers in her hair, running a thumb over her cheek.

"We'll cross that bridge if and when we come to it. Don't overthink it, babe. Let's make the most of the times we are together and just have phone sex in between."

She gives me a small smile, not the laugh I'd hoped for. For a moment, she closes her eyes and tears roll down her cheeks again. "It's the in-between bits. I know you haven't pushed me, but I'm feeling the pressure of needing to move for this to work. It took me so long to feel like my life was sorted, and now it all seems to be up in the air again."

"It doesn't have to be. The distance is driving me insane, but I'll put up with it for as long as I have to."

She licks her lips and swallows hard. "I don't know if I can."

She's breaking up with me. "I'm sorry about my mother. She can be awful at the best of times, and her illness isn't an excuse. She was like that before."

Hayley shakes her head. "It's not your mother. I'm sure sometimes she's perfectly lovely."

"Then what is it? I know the distance is getting you down, but we'll work that out."

More tears spill down her face, and she focuses blue eyes filled with sadness on me. "I can't take the distance, Drew. It's not fair that the one person I want to be with, that I want to love, is so far away, and I can't do anything about it."

"Then move in with me," I whisper.

"Your mother's being protective of you. I never had that luxury. This is where I found my peace, and I don't know if I can give that up, for my own sanity."

I gulp. "So, what are you saying?"

"That I don't think this is going to work. I'm already dealing with abandonment issues, and you're three hundred kilometres away."

"Is this you saying it's not you, it's me?"

She nods, and my heart shatters into a billion pieces. "I met you right after you broke up with Lucy. What if this is just a rebound thing for you? Do I give up everything I worked so hard for?"

"No. This is not a rebound thing. What I feel for you is bigger than anything I've ever felt for anyone."

"Maybe."

I want to tell her I love her, but I also want her not to feel pressured into committing to something she can't deal with. I've never been in this position before, and I have no clue what to do.

"I'll go." I say the words quietly as I don't want to make a scene. She's in agony, and I can't relieve her pain. I knew from the start this would be tough for her, but we tried, and now this hurts so much.

Hayley nods, and I bend to kiss her cheek, breathing her in one last time.

"Call me if you change your mind."

Her eyes are full of tears, and I'd give anything to throw my career away and stay with her. But I can't. Not if I want to build the future we might still need.

With my heart breaking, I grab my things and make my way out to the car. I look back at her little house, but there's no sign of her at the window, and for a moment I grip the steering wheel to stop myself shaking.

It can't be over.

18

ADAM

I THOUGHT THE WORST WAS BEHIND ME.

It's not.

I gave in two days ago and stashed a bottle of bourbon in a kitchen cupboard. Lily has enough on her plate with Rose not sleeping well. She doesn't need the stress of me struggling. And I am.

Ben visits me more at night as it gets closer to the anniversary of his death. I just hope that after that date, it eases off.

Maybe it's guilt that drives the dreams. I spent so long wishing it was me who died that day instead of him. Me, who had nothing to live for at that stage while he had everything.

Maybe it's that now I have the life he longed for—the steady love of a good woman, and children. He was so close to being a father for the first time, and that was a role he couldn't wait for.

Maybe it's just because I miss him.

He would have had so many words to say about me being back here. Ben was my person, the one I poured my soul out to. He knew how much pain I was in when I thought Lily had left me, and he knew how hard I fought myself to stay away from town.

My heart's in my throat when I think about him and how much he would have loved this place. He would have adored Lily and Max, and been happy for me.

The thought of that leaves me feeling even guiltier.

This time it's a little after midnight, and I seek Jenna out. She was the first person to help me; maybe she can do it again.

I hesitate as I hold my mouse over the message button. This feels like a betrayal, even if I'm not up to anything. Lily would be hurt. But I also don't want Lily to have to worry about me when she's still dealing with having a new baby.

Rose isn't the best sleeper, and I help as much as I can, but the days are as long as some nights for Lily. The garage is so busy, it's hard to find time to help her as well.

I click the button.

I need help.

The reply is almost instant.

What can I do?

I'm having more dreams again, and I'm worried it'll impact my relationship with Lily. I've already hurt her by mistake.

Those little dots appear, and my stomach clenches at the thought of turning to my ex for help.

Hurt her how?

My brother shot a possum and the gunshot caught me by surprise. I pushed her to the floor to protect her.

Shit. Okay. Do you have someone to talk to over there?

I sigh.

I don't know if there's anyone close who can help. That's the worst part of living in a small town.

It's not a good idea to talk to me.

I know.

Where exactly are you? I know I'm far away, but maybe I can find someone.

I let out a loud breath.

I'm in Copper Creek. There's a slightly bigger town about fifty kilometres away called Carlstown.

Okay. I'll see what I can drum up. I'm not sure if I can help, but you know I'll try.

I nod. Of course she will. I might have hurt her deeply, but Jenna's a good person.

"Adam?"

I turn. Lily stands behind me. "What are you doing?"

"Catching up with an old friend." I should tell her, but I'm worried about upsetting her unnecessarily.

"Come back to bed. I've got something for you."

I grin. "What's that?"

She peels back her bathrobe, revealing her naked body underneath. Her breasts are full and firm, having grown in size during pregnancy. Lily's never been more beautiful.

"Are you sure?"

"It's time."

I lick my lips, more than ready to reacquaint myself with her body, but there's something I need to do first. "I'll just finish this. I'll be two seconds."

"What is it?"

I swallow. "I'm asking Jenna for help with something."

"Jenna? As in, ex-girlfriend Jenna?"

I nod.

Lily's eyes convey her hurt.

"Lil, she has contacts, and she might be able to find someone here I can go to for help."

"You didn't think you could talk to me?"

I run my fingers through my hair, and she crosses her bathrobe again, tying it closed.

"You've just got so much on your plate. Having a baby, then I lost it in the kitchen. She friend-requested me on Facebook one night and messaged me, and we've had one conversation."

She swallows hard, and tears run down her cheeks. I've hurt her.

"It hurts that you would keep this from me."

"I never intended to."

Shifting her gaze to the ceiling and away from me, she sniffs. "I told you we needed to trust each other, but it feels like you broke that promise."

I shake my head. "Lily, I wouldn't do anything to make you lose your faith in me. I swear. We had one conversation, and she asked me about my family and saw my photos. That's it."

"And then she's the one you ran to when you needed help."

I close my eyes. It's true. Lily should be my first port of call, no matter what. "You're right. I'm sorry."

When I open my eyes, she's taken a step back. I reach for her, but she pulls away. What the hell was I thinking? Lily's so much stronger than she realises, but I've hurt her at a time when she's particularly vulnerable. She's just shown me that vulnerability in coming to me and revealing her post-birth body, which, knowing how self-conscious she can be, must have been tough, and I admitted to turning to someone else for help.

I love her with all of my being.

"How long have you been messaging Jenna on Facebook?" Lily's tone is pained, and I can't bear to hear it.

"She messaged me. And I replied to be polite. Not for any other reason."

All Lily's insecurities surface. She's fought so hard for everything in her life, and here I am wanting to make her life easier in some ways, but just making things worse. "Are you sure?"

"Lily, I love you. I only want you." I let out a loud breath. "I only ever wanted you."

"You left me once before." Her voice cracks.

I shake my head, my eyes searching hers, but all I see are her tears. "No. It wasn't like that."

"It was. You didn't even hang around."

Boom. There it is. The thing that's never been said, but has been simmering at the surface since we got back together. The worst part is that she's right. "No, I didn't. And I'll regret that for the rest of my life."

I stand and reach for her, pulling her into my arms despite her resistance. "You're right. I didn't hang around, and I should have. I should have trusted in us more, and known you wouldn't leave me. And then I stayed away far too long."

She sobs, going limp, and I hold her tight.

"I was young and stupid, and I hate myself for what I did.

You didn't do a single thing wrong, and you spent years suffering for it."

"You didn't wait for me."

I shake my head. "I made the biggest mistake of my life. All I can hope for is that you let me make it up to you."

"So talk to me. Tell me. *I* need to know how you're feeling."

"The last thing I want to dump on you is what's going on in my head."

She sniffs. "Please, Adam. Do you know what it was like being in my mother's sewing room all those months? Drugged, slowly starving, terrified of the dark? The only thing that kept me going was the thought of being with you at the other end. Now, I have you back, but I need all of you."

"You have all of me. I swear."

Her arms wrap around my waist, and I close my eyes. I'd do anything to go back in time and right my wrongs, but with no other option to do that, all we can do is move forward.

"I'll never leave you again, Lily. I swear."

"Having a baby isn't going to stop me worrying about you."

I press my lips to her temple. "I'm sorry to make you worry. You and Max and Rose are all I need. I just want to be the best man I can be for all of you."

She lets go of me, and her eyes search mine. "Don't you get it?"

"Get what?"

"You already are."

I shake my head. "That's not true."

She lets out a loud breath. "You've given us everything.

Most of all, your heart. I know you'd do anything for us, and that's what we need."

"I'm worried that I'm broken. That I'll screw up and hurt you again. Hurt the kids somehow."

Lily places a firm hand on my chest. "We're both broken. But I know we're each other's glue. I'll hold you together if you hold me."

My heart stills. She's right.

"Rose is still new, and I'm suffering some sleepless nights with her. That doesn't mean I'm not here for you."

"I know," I whisper.

"Stop treating me like I'm made of china. I've been through the worst that life could throw at me, and I'm stronger than I've ever been right now. So much of that is because you came back, and I have the other half of my heart again."

I nod, pulling her into my arms.

Everything she says makes sense. We'll get through this together.

In the morning, there's a simple message from Jenna with a name and phone number. Lily's with me this time, and she smiles as I type back.

Thank you.

I open another tab and Google the guy. Great. He's in Hamilton. I can't complain, but it would have been better to get someone closer.

Lily lets out a sigh. "Guess you'll be doing some travelling."

"If this works out, are you going to be okay at home without me when I go to see him?"

She smiles. "I'd rather get you help now than wait and make things worse for you."

The browser dings, and I flick back to Facebook.

You're welcome. I hope it's useful.

"Tell her I say thanks too."

Lily says thank you, too.

I'm glad to help. Having a broken you is no good for her or your babies. Take care, and let me know if I can do anything else.

Standing, I slip my arms around Lily's waist and hold her tight. "God, I love you."

"We should have known there'd be bumps in the road with two damaged people being together. But we have one thing going for us that a lot of people don't."

"What's that?"

"When we're together, we're whole. I don't think we'd have ever been as good with other people. You and me, Adam—this was always meant to be."

I reach behind me and flick the computer off.

"Are you going to call that guy?"

"Well, I could, but Max has gone to school, and Rose is asleep. Wanna make the most of it?"

A smile spreads across her face. "You might be onto something there. But there's something I need to do first."

"What's that?"

She takes my hand and leads me to the kitchen, heading straight to the cupboard I stashed the bourbon in.

"How did you …?"

"I've not been as preoccupied as you thought."

I open my mouth to protest, but the lid's already off, and the amber liquid is being tipped into the sink.

"This is about the last thing you need. We're going to stop this before it starts."

I nod. "You're right."

"We're in this together. You and me. The way it always was." A smile spreads across her lips. "Now move your arse and get into that bedroom."

I laugh as she leads the way, dropping her clothing as she goes. Following her lead, I slip into bed beside her, and pull her into my arms. Naked Lily is my favourite Lily.

Her skin's so soft, and as I pepper her neck and shoulder with gentle kisses, I run my hand down her back. We've shared what intimacies we can since Rose's birth, but most of the time she's been so tired, and I haven't pushed my luck. Now I get to indulge in my favourite girl.

"I wasn't sure if you'd like my body anymore," she whispers. When we got back together, she was quite self-conscious at times, given how thin she was. Over time, she'd grown more relaxed around me.

"I've always loved your body. Still do. You had a baby, Lily, and if anything, you're even more beautiful."

Her cheeks flush red.

"Just being able to touch you again is all I need." I slip my fingers between her legs and stroke her gently.

She reacts, her eyelashes fluttering as my index finger plays on her clit. "Adam, I'm a bit nervous about this."

"I'll be gentle. You know I will. If anything hurts, tell me and we'll stop. Okay?"

She nods. "I love you so much."

"I love you too. With everything I have." I drop my head

to her breast and run my tongue around her nipple. She sucks in a breath, and I chuckle. "It's okay. I know those belong to Rose for the moment."

Lily laughs, and her body relaxes. "I don't want to leak all over you."

I shrug. "It is what it is. It's still you, Lil. Doesn't make me love you any less."

Moving down her body, I marvel at the changes in it. When I returned, she was all skin and bones.

I kiss her stomach, and she sighs as my tongue hits her clit. "This. So much this."

I laugh against her skin. "Miss me?"

"Yes. I mean, I haven't been in any state for this, but I missed how close I feel to you."

I take a bite out of her thigh with my lips. "Maybe this is the therapy I need."

"It's got to be a good start, right?"

She bucks her hips against my face, and I take her over the edge. Grasping my hair, Lily moans, and the sound's music to my ears. I know her body so well, and I know what's waiting for me.

Slowly sliding into her grounds me. It's Lily and only Lily I'm supposed to be joined with. No one else will ever do.

She's breathless as I thrust, gentle at first and speeding up as I get closer. This will be no sex marathon. I want and need my girl so much; it's not going to take long.

"Adam," she whispers, and it's enough to take me there.

I close my eyes when I come. Lily's my heaven, and I'm back where I belong. Maybe it'll help me get through the night without the bad dreams. That might be wishful thinking, but today we've reconnected on more than a physical level. Telling her about Jenna has closed the gap between us.

Rolling to her side, I pull her into my arms. "Are you okay? I wasn't too rough?"

"You're always gentle. I'm fine."

I slide my hand down her back until it rests just above her arse and kiss her temple. "I love you, Lily. I'm just so worried I'm going to screw this up."

"You're not alone. If anyone understands this, it's me. Don't shut me out. We'll work it out together."

I don't answer at first, and I cover her mouth with mine to taste her sweet lips again. She always got me better than anyone else, always understood.

We will work it out.

19

HAYLEY

I ROLL MY EYES AS ASH HARRIS'S NAME COMES UP ON MY caller ID. I've been trying to work out my next move when it comes to getting midwifery care into that damn place, and I guess I need to take this in case there's some other situation that's come up.

"Ash."

"Hayley, I need you."

"Look—"

"I've got a girl here in the early stages of pregnancy. She's in a lot of pain, and I need you to look at her."

I take a deep breath. "Bring her into the clinic."

"She says it hurts to move. Can you please take a look at her?"

Shit. Margaret was up all night at a farm thirty kilometres away. I can't ask her to go in my place.

"Sure. I'll be there soon. Maybe I can get a follow-up visit in with Julia, too?"

"Anything."

The gates open when I drive up to them. There's still no sign of anyone opening or closing them, and I can only assume they're controlled remotely. It's creepy.

More than anything I wish Drew was with me. I miss him more than anything and his reassurance would help get me through this. I'm still grappling with my decision and will be for a long time to come.

I reach the main building, and Ash is there with a big smile on his face.

"Hayley, it's so good to see you."

"Where's the patient?" I cut to the chase. No point in wasting time with small talk.

His expression grows serious. "Right through here."

There's a young girl waiting for me. She barely looks legal, and she's pregnant. What the hell is going on in this place?

"This is Christine," Ash says.

"Thanks. Can you wait outside?"

"I want him here." Christine sounds a little panicked.

Ignoring him, I focus on the woman. "Hi, Christine, I'm Hayley. I'm a community midwife."

She nods.

"You're in pain?"

"I was. It's not as bad now."

My body tenses. If she's feeling okay, why am I here? "How far along are you?"

"About fourteen weeks."

I nod. "I'll do some basic checks, if that's okay? Listen for the baby's heartbeat."

She glances at Ash before nodding.

"Lie down on the couch, and I'll take a look."

With her lying on her back, I lift her shirt to feel her stomach. I swear I feel Ash's eyes on the back of my head, but I push away the feeling of discomfort he gives me to focus on her.

Grabbing my stethoscope and Doppler out of my bag, I close my eyes for a moment to focus while I grasp Christine's wrist. Her blood pressure is up a little, but nothing to worry about.

The baby's heartbeat comes through loud and clear on the Doppler, and Christine smiles as the sound of the rapid beat fills the room.

"Everything looks fine. It's time to organise your midwifery care."

Her gaze goes straight to Ash, and he gives her a short, sharp nod. "Okay."

"I'll leave you some information. You give me a call when you've read through it, and we'll sort out your first appointment."

"Thank you."

I turn to Ash. "Now, can I see Julia?"

Julia's baby has already grown so much. Andrew gives me a big grin as she passes him over. It takes everything in me not to react to the fact that he's a lot like the man I suspect is his father, Ash Harris.

"That's a big smile, little man. He's growing so fast."

She reaches for my arm. "He is. Thanks to you. I can never thank you enough for everything you did."

"You're so welcome. He's a beautiful, healthy baby, and I'm so glad you're both well."

Another woman in one of those drab, grey dresses arrives

with a drinks tray. "Tea or coffee?" she asks.

"I might just give it a miss, thanks. I've got to get home soon." I don't have anything to do, but screw hanging around here longer than I have to.

"You're not going so quickly?" Julia asks. "You're like a baby whisperer, the way he's so calm in your arms. He's a bit up and down at the moment."

"Sure." Surrounded by people, she seems desperate for some company. I turn to the woman. "Coffee please. Milk and two sugars?"

The woman gives me a smile, and I turn back to the baby in my arms. "You're just growth-spurting, aren't you? How's your feeding going?" I look up at Julia.

"Good. He's so hungry, but I'm still resting after everything that happened. I'm in here most of the day, if I'm not sitting out and getting sun."

I nod. "That's good. Happy baby, happy mum."

"Here you go." The coffee's placed on the bedside cabinet, along with Julia's drink. I pass the baby back and grab the mug. Better to get this over with, and I just have to take a couple of sips to look as if I'm enjoying the hospitality. Seeing Julia is good, though. She's clearly doing much better, and the baby's thriving.

It doesn't take long for whatever's in my drink to hit me.

Shit.

"Something … something's in my …" I can't even finish the sentence, and Julia stares at me. I've had my drink spiked before, and this feels exactly the same.

The cup crashes to the floor, and I push myself to my feet, stagger, and lean on the bed.

"Hayley?" Julia's terror registers with me. She doesn't

know what's going on any more than I do. I can hear the panic in her voice.

My ears close in as if they're being stuffed with cotton wool. Julia screams and leaps out the other side of her bed, her baby in her arms. My vision's blurred, but I make her out as she heads toward the French doors leading to the deck. I try and follow her, but my feet are made of concrete.

An eternity passes.

Strong arms lift me, and I'm looking into the eyes of Ash Harris.

"Let's get you somewhere comfortable."

No.

I want to go home. I want Drew.

"Drew." I say his name out loud because it's all I can manage, and because I need him so badly. I'm shaking because I don't know where this is leading, and this is the last place I want to be.

"Everything will be okay," Ash says softly. He takes me down a corridor and into another room. There's a large bed, and he lowers me onto it. I fight the urge to go to sleep with everything I have, but any energy I had is gone.

"Drew's not here, Hayley. I know you broke up. I've been watching."

I let out a pained moan.

"You're meant to be here. With me. You'll get everything you ever wanted." He presses his hand on my midriff, and my stomach rolls in revulsion.

"No." I manage to get the word out, but the fight is ebbing out of me. My heart's racing, and I try and push myself up, but sink back down.

He lies beside me, stroking my hair. "It's okay, Hayley. You don't need anyone but me."

I let out a sob.

There's a loud knock on the door.

"Ash, I need your help." Julia's voice fills me with hope. She must know where I am.

"I'm busy, Julia."

"It's Andrew. I don't think he's well."

He sighs. "He was fine earlier."

She lets out a sob. "He won't stop crying. Please come and see him. He's so good with you."

"Holy shit. I'll be back." He sweeps his hand down my side, his thumb grazing my nipple. I want to scream, but let out a groan instead.

"That's what I like to hear."

And then he's gone, and I'm left in the room by myself.

What the hell can I do?

20

HAYLEY

The door opens, and I squeeze my legs together as tightly as I can manage. I've fought as hard as I can, and I'm losing. Terrified of what I'm going to wake up to, I open my mouth to try screaming again.

"Let's get you out of here." A gruff voice and a blurry face I don't recognise are in front of me. I'm lifted into huge arms, and I struggle to protest. "It's okay, Hayley. You're safe."

I don't know why, but I relax, although that's probably the drug's work. I'm desperately trying not to fall asleep, but it's so hard.

"I'll get you to safety. I think I know just the place."

A familiar smell fills my senses. It's like coming home, and I give in to the temptation to close my eyes as I'm placed on the back seat of my car.

"You are so lucky Julia was looking out for you. God

knows what he would have done," the gruff voice grumbles, but I'm in no position to respond as everything sinks into blackness.

MY HEAD THROBS, and I open my eyes.

I don't know where I am.

Panic grips me, and I look down to see I'm fully clothed, but under a duvet. My mind's fuzzy, and nothing clears as I look around the room.

Apart from a chest of drawers in the corner, the room is bare. The bed I'm in is massive. It must be a king at least. The curtains are a deep blue and pulled over.

I rack my brain for memories, but nothing's forthcoming. Pulling my aching arm out from under the covers, I take a look. There's a Band-Aid about halfway up my bicep, as if I've given blood.

"Hayley. You're awake."

A tall man I recognise from the photos at Drew's parents' house stands in the doorway. I might have been in town for four years, and generally everyone knows everyone in Copper Creek, but I don't know the elusive Corey. I'd recognise him even without seeing him in the photos, however; he's so similar to Drew.

Shit. What happened?

"Corey?"

He gives me a forced smile. "It's a shame we didn't meet under better circumstances. I'm glad you're in one piece though."

"What happened?"

He sits on the end of the bed. "Do you remember anything?"

I shake my head. "I got a call to meet with one of the girls in the community. I remember going there, and seeing Julia …" I clap my hand over my mouth. "My drink was spiked."

"What makes you say that?"

"When I was seventeen, some arsehole spiked my drink at a club. I remember thinking that's what it felt like."

His eyes narrow. "Seventeen?"

"I shouldn't have been there, but I had friends who realised what was happening and got me out."

"Well, you had a guardian angel this time, too."

Another familiar face appears in the doorway. It's Graham Taylor, the senior sergeant at the Copper Creek Community Police centre.

"We need to talk," he says.

I nod.

He approaches the bed and sits. "What can you remember?"

"Uhh, I got a call from Ash, who said there was a girl in the early stages of pregnancy in a huge amount of pain. I tried to talk him into bringing the girl to the clinic so I could take a look at her, but he said she was in too much pain to move. She was fine, so I went to check in with Julia. I helped her a while ago when she needed an emergency C-section. Someone made me a cup of coffee."

"And after that?"

I close my eyes. "It's messy. I remember realising I'd been drugged and thinking it was too late to do anything. Then I remember being in my car. I woke up here."

He nods. "When Corey called, I took the liberty of bringing Doc Paton up here. He drew some blood. I should have waited until you were conscious, but …"

"Time is of the essence when someone's been drugged. Of course I don't have a problem with it. You need to get in there, find out how many others didn't get away."

Graham's got this sheepish expression on his face, and I let out a low moan. "You're not doing anything, are you?"

His eyes dart about, as if he's got something to hide. "I'll go and have a chat with him."

"They're already under investigation. Aren't they?"

He lets out an exasperated breath. "Not that I'm supposed to tell you. When the old man ran it, they were a bit odd, but there was nothing sinister going on. That Ash Harris, he's bad news, Hayley. You need to stay far away from him."

"I don't intend to go anywhere near."

"We have a couple of guys undercover. They're the ones who got you out. You were bailed into your car and it was driven here. It's right outside. This is the first time they've caught this happening to someone, but they've suspected shit like this went on for a while."

I lick my lips. "He asked me to go and live there. Said he realised they needed a midwife, but he wanted me."

"Wanted you?"

I nod. "Yeah. Me. Said he would make me his queen."

Corey rolls his eyes.

"When?" Graham asks.

"After I air-evacuated Julia to have her baby. I made it clear I wasn't interested."

Graham lets out a loud breath. "Apparently it's not the

first time he's taken things into his own hands. He wants you there, make no mistake."

"Taken things into his own hands?"

"I hear he can be very persuasive. Even more so when he's working on a vulnerable woman."

I frown. "I wouldn't class myself as vulnerable."

"You are if you're drugged."

My head spins with this information. "You think he's done this before?"

He nods. "Think about it. You're young, and you're in desperate need of help. Along comes this man who sweeps you off your feet and offers all the answers. If there's a tiny bit of doubt, he'll convince you with some help that you wanted to be with him."

"I had a feeling about him. Like he was the type to manipulate the situation if he could. But I still had no idea how far he'd go."

My stomach rolls. My parents might not have always been that supportive, but if I was desperate I could turn to them. How many young girls out there didn't have that option?

"Not just girls, either. The little community his father started has grown a lot since junior took over.

"But why?"

"That's why they're under investigation. We need to get to the bottom of what's going on. All we know so far is that it all seems above board, except he's got a little harem of women he sleeps with. That, and there's something going on that our guys haven't quite earned his trust enough to get into."

I nod. Graham doesn't have to tell me any of this, but I'm glad he trusts me enough to tell me.

"Julia's baby. He resembles Ash."

"It's very likely he's the father. Julia doesn't trust him as much as he thinks. She made contact with the police when she was in hospital. It's amazing what a bit of freedom and a whole heap of resentment does. There's a lot she doesn't know, but she's gone back to learn what she can. You were lucky today, Hayley. You need to stay far away from that place."

I gulp. "I will, but what do I do if any of those girls need help?"

"Get Margaret to do it. From what you've said, he's developed an unhealthy interest in you."

"What if Margaret's not available?"

Graham sighs. "Then call me, and I'll come with you. You are not to go into that compound alone."

I nod, but it doesn't make me worry any less.

"I'm here most of the time too," Corey says. "I'm happy to be your shadow."

Hot tears spill down my cheeks as my frustration erupts. All I ever wanted was to help people, and all it's taken is for one nasty person to shatter my faith in this town—the town I was so desperately scared of leaving because I'd found peace here.

Do I have to watch my back from now on? Is it just entering the community in the hill that should make me afraid? My little house has always seemed so safe, but is it?

"Hey." Corey sits beside me and pulls me into his arms. I don't even know him, but he's a member of Drew's family, so I trust him. "Want me to call Drew?"

I shrug. It should come from me, but I don't know how I can find the words. Drew will freak out, even if we're not together. "Drew and I broke up." My voice is tiny.

"He'll still want to know. You've got my brother in such a spin already, but it's up to you if you want me to tell him."

"I don't know what to do."

Corey leans back. "Stay here the night if you want. Sleep off whatever Ash put in your system. I've got a spare room I can bunk down in so you don't have to move."

"Or I can give you a lift home," Graham says.

"Honestly, I can't even think right now. All I want to do is sleep."

Corey smiles. "Then go back to sleep. If you want to go home later, I'll drive you. You might be close to those weirdos, but you'll be safe here. I don't like the idea of you being alone."

"Agreed," Graham says.

"Besides, then I get to ring my brother and tell him I've got his girlfriend in my bed."

I roll my tired eyes. "I'm not his girlfriend."

"It's still gonna bug the shit out of him. You've got a lot to learn about us Campbell boys. Now, do you want a proper cup of coffee?"

"I really want to sleep, but I'd kill for one."

Corey gets up and leaves the room to make a coffee, and Graham pats my hand. "I'll check in with you in the morning. We need to make sure your home is secure, too. I don't trust Ash Harris and his minions any farther than I can throw them."

"Thanks, Graham."

I'm left by myself for a moment, and my head is awhirl

over what's happened. How quickly things changed, and what the hell is happening behind those walls?

"You can use my property." Corey's speaking to Graham. They're in another room, but his booming voice carries.

"This is a big step. What changed your mind?"

"Her. No one fucks with my family. You can set up whatever you need to monitor that arsehole. Just don't get in my way."

"Understood. I'll go have a chat with Mr Harris now."

"Good luck."

The aroma of coffee fills the room, and I look up to see Corey walking toward me. For a moment, I hesitate. The last time I accepted a cup, well—I don't know what could have happened to me.

"It's okay," Corey says softly.

"I know." I accept the coffee and take a sip. He's made it black with no sugar, and I grimace, but it's still soothing.

"Let me guess. You take milk. Sugar?"

I nod.

He scratches the back of his head. "I don't have either. I'm terrible at keeping the cupboards stocked."

"It doesn't matter. I really appreciate this."

"Anything you need. If you really want me to go and get milk and sugar, I will."

I smile. "Really?"

"If Adam coming back taught me one thing, it's that family comes first."

"But I'm not—"

His mobile rings, and he plucks it out of his breast pocket. He smiles as he answers, "Bro."

My breath catches.

Corey hands me the phone. "It's for you."

I let out a loud breath as I take it. "Hi."

"What's going on? Are you okay? Do you need me to come?"

My eyes sting as tears well. "I'm fine, thanks to Julia and your brother. You don't need to worry."

"Like hell I'm not going to worry. I want to drive there and bring you home to me right this second. This break-up is killing me as it is, and now I hear you're in danger?"

"Drew ..."

He sighs. "I know how hard this has been for you. It's hard for me, too. I still need to know you're safe."

I close my eyes. It breaks my heart to hear him, but I made my choice for my own sanity. Do I go back to the way I was before? Deliriously happy for us to be together and miserable when we were apart? "I'm safe. Corey's taking care of me for now, and then I'll go home tomorrow. I'll be fine."

"You mean the world to me, Hayley. I want you back."

I run my fingers over my scalp as the tears fall. "I know," I whisper.

"Why is this so hard with us? I understand the distance and how much you hate it. I hate it, too, but I still want to try." He sighs. "Stay safe, and I'll make sure Corey and Owen look out for you. If that man comes anywhere near you, you call for help."

"I will," I whisper.

The call ends, and for a moment, I stare at the phone.

"I knew he'd freak out if I didn't tell him."

Nodding, I hand the phone back to Corey. "I know."

"Are things really that bad between you? He sounded pretty frantic."

I shake my head. "It's not him. I found peace here, Corey. My life fell apart, and this town helped me put it back together. There's nothing here for him, and I'm scared of moving back to the big city."

He sits on the bed. "Want my advice?"

"Do I have a choice?"

Laughing, he shakes his head. "I've known Drew his whole life, and he's in way deep with you. I'm pretty sure if he had to, he'd give it all up. He might think there's nothing here for him, but the truth is that you're here. I bet anything you're worth it."

I roll my eyes. "Why did I have to fall for the brother who doesn't live here?"

"Now I've met you, I'll be asking that question every single day."

I laugh so hard I snort, and cover my nose in embarrassment.

"Told you I'd flirt just to piss him off. At least you're laughing now. Drink your coffee, and you're welcome to turn the TV on. There're some DVDs there. You might find something you like."

"Thanks, Corey."

"Any time. That lot next door need to be taken down."

He leaves me alone with my coffee and the remote control. All I can think about is Julia still inside. If she was disturbed enough to call the police, why the hell did she go back? And what's Ash Harris up to?

I place the mug on the bedside cabinet, and nestle down under the covers.

It doesn't take much to drift off.

When I wake, I don't know where I am.

For a moment, panic rushes through me, and I sit up, my heart pounding as I look around the room.

You're safe. You're with Corey.

"About time you woke, sleepyhead." Drew's voice comes from the doorway, and my breaths come sharp and fast as I look at him. "I came down as soon as I finished work. How could I stay away?"

I want him to hold me so badly, but that scares me. Walking away from him has been the hardest decision I've made in my life, and probably the worst. "You didn't have to come."

He crosses the room and sits on the bed, still not touching me. "Of course I did. I love you, Hayley. There might be this physical distance between us, but my heart's always here with you."

He loves me.

My heart explodes.

"Give me one good reason for you to stay here," Drew whispers.

I swallow hard. "My job."

"There are jobs in Hamilton."

"You know this has been my sanctuary."

He leans over, pleading with his eyes. "Let me be your sanctuary."

Everything he does melts my heart. There is nothing Drew wouldn't do for me. I know that. I've never been so conflicted.

"I can't leave you here knowing that Ash Harris has his twisted heart set on you. And he's not afraid to use illegal methods to get to you."

I shake my head. "He'll never win."

"Even if he doesn't, he's obviously prepared to fuck with your head, and maybe even your body to get what he wants."

Everything he's saying is true, and all it does is make me feel more trapped than ever. When I was in Auckland, the walls closed in around me, and now I'm feeling it again. I'm already torn between the place where I found freedom and love. All he wants to do is love me. All I do is complicate things. "I'm so confused."

He nods. "Do you want me to take you home? Your car's here, but I don't know if you should drive."

"I'm still so tired."

"You were drugged, sweetheart. It'll take a while to work its way out of your system. I would prefer it if you weren't doing that in my brother's bed."

I laugh. "Corey was keen on calling to tell you that."

Drew's lips twist into a smile. "That's not surprising." He reaches out and wraps his hand around the back of my neck, pulling my forehead to his forehead. "I don't want to lose you, Hayley. Not now, not ever."

"I'm doing what I need to do."

He sighs. "Get ready, and I'll take you home. Corey will sort out returning your car. If I was you, I'd take a couple of days off work to get back on your feet."

My heart aches as he lets me go.

He drives me home, and I feed on his calmness. It's what I need.

I need him.

Drew Campbell is my sanctuary.

My stomach churns as he leads me inside, and I collapse on the couch.

"You okay?"

"It's just good to be home."

He stands in place beside the couch and watches me. It's as if he's waiting for an invite to join me, and he probably is. I didn't think it was possible for things to get harder.

Eventually, he shakes his head and sighs. "Now I've made sure you're alright, I'll get going."

My heart hurts, and I nod.

"Whatever happens between us, I'll always be there for you, Hayley. Everything I am and everything I have is yours for the taking."

I push myself up and pat the couch. "Come here?"

He lets out a breath of relief and sits beside me. He doesn't touch me, and I love him all the more for respecting my feelings.

"I'm so confused. Not about you. I know how I feel about you. I'm sorry about the way I handled things. It was all wrong. But I don't regret what I've done. I need time to work out what I want."

Drew nods. "Take as much time as you need." He leans closer and reaches up to brush hair out of my eyes. His lips touch mine in the sweetest, softest kiss we've ever shared. "I meant what I said back at Corey's place. I love you, Hayley, and that's not changing anytime soon."

With another kiss, he stands, and I watch as he reaches the door.

As it closes, fresh tears roll down my face, and my heart aches.

I love him, too.

21

HAYLEY

MARGARET JOYCE IS ONE OF THE MOST IMPORTANT PEOPLE I'VE ever had in my life. She's my boss, my mentor, and one of the best friends I've ever had.

When I first arrived in Copper Creek, I stayed with her family during the first few months, and we bonded. Our working relationship has worked well these past few years because we know each other so well.

And she's suspicious about why I'm here to talk to her.

Like I said, she knows me so well.

I sit in her living room, nervous as I was the day I first arrived. Maybe because I never foresaw telling her I was leaving.

She smiles.

I take a deep breath. "Well, it's like this …"

"You're moving to Hamilton to be with Drew Campbell." Of course, Margaret knows; she always does. She took this injured little bird under her wing and nurtured her until she was well and able to fly again.

I blush. "I might. We broke up because I couldn't handle the long-distance thing." Tears prick my eyes.

"You can't live without him." She pats my right hand.

"I don't want to. As much as I love being here, and I could keep on doing it, I love him. Maybe it's just time for me to move forward."

Margaret nods. "If you want to know what I think, you've grown as a person while you've been here. The space and peace have done you well, but perhaps finding Drew is the next step in your journey."

"I need to go and see him, and smooth things over. I'm such an idiot."

"You're no idiot. Relationships can be hard as it is, and I'm sure long-distance ones have challenges all of their own. I'm happy to see you following your heart. Plus, I think there's a lot more for both of you in the big smoke."

Tears roll down my cheeks as I throw my arms around her neck and hold on tight. She's done so much for me, and now she's happy to see me on my way, even if it leaves more work for her.

"Thank you for everything," I whisper.

"Thank you for coming here. You have such a good heart, Hayley, and you've been dedicated to this job." Margaret pulls back and looks me in the eyes. "I think it's good you're going. For your heart, and for your safety."

I lean back, and stare.

She smiles. "I know, Hayley. Graham Taylor came to see me. He was worried that you might put someone else's needs over your own safety. If I know you, and I think I do, if you'd got another call to go to that damn place you'd go whether you had anyone with you or not. You care so deeply."

I drop my gaze, and she raises her fingers to my chin, pulling my head up. "It's not a bad thing. You take good care of the mums and babies so well. I'll just have to find another stray to take in."

"I'm so sorry."

She shakes her head. "Don't be. I know what it's like to find the right man. It's mine and Tom's twenty-fifth wedding anniversary next week, and I still kinda like him."

I smile and let out a sigh. "I'm going to miss this place. I'm going to miss you."

"I'll miss you, too. But Drew's family's back here, and you'll come for visits. And when you two make your beautiful babies, I want to know all about it."

"He does want a few."

"I'm so happy for you, love. You deserve it."

She envelopes me in her arms, and I breathe a sigh of relief. It doesn't make me feel any less as if I'm letting her down, but at least I haven't lost her friendship.

"So, if it's okay with you, I'll head to Hamilton for the night. Drew might be working, but he gave me a house key ages ago and I want to surprise him." I bite my bottom lip. "To tell you the truth, I'm a little scared. He told me a week ago that he loved me, but what if he's changed his mind?"

She smiles, her eyes full of warmth and understanding. "You know Drew better than anyone. Do you really think he's not waiting for you?"

I shake my head. "I just need to see him."

"Then go. If I need help, I'll call for it. Carlstown isn't that far away."

My heart squeezes at the thought of seeing Drew again.

Now to go and sort things out with him.

IT'S late afternoon by the time I get to Hamilton.

I need to see him face to face. Sure, I could have called him on the phone, but when I tell Drew that I'll move to be with him, I want to be in his arms.

Truth is, I just miss him.

He's been there for me, even when he thought there might be no hope. When he came to me at Corey's place, my heart felt not quite as empty as it had been after I broke things off. That sealed the deal.

His car's in the driveway, and the living room light is on. There's another car parked behind his that I don't recognise, so I stop out on the street and head toward the door.

I knock, and after a few minutes of not getting a response, I take a deep breath, slide the key into the lock, and give a silent prayer that he wants me here.

"Drew?"

There's no sign of him in the living room, and I drop my bag on the couch and move to the big bay window. My breath catches as I see him, standing beside the pool. He's clearly been swimming—water drops all over his back, and I smile as I turn and start toward the door.

On the other side of the fence, there's a blonde standing by Drew. She's fully dressed, including six-inch stilettos that look out of place by the pool. Obviously, she's not been swimming with Drew, so who is she and why is she here?

Shit.

It's not actually any of my business.

We broke up.

But I have to know one way or another. I push open the door.

"Hayley?" Drew's eyes don't lie. He's confused, but in them I see all the tenderness I saw a week ago. He's not upset that I'm here.

I swallow. "I need to talk to you. I'll just ..."

"Yeah, you need to get out of here." The blonde speaks, and my eyebrows twitch in response.

"She's not the one leaving." Drew glares at the woman, and my skin prickles at the tension between them. I've interrupted something, but it's not romantic.

"But, Drew," she whines.

"But, nothing. You weren't invited here, and I already told you to leave. I suggest that's what you do."

She looks between us. "So, this is my replacement?"

The penny drops. *Lucy*. I take a step toward Drew. What I want right now is to be in his arms and to show this woman just who he belongs to.

"No. I love Hayley. I don't think I ever loved you."

She's in my way, so I open the gate and head toward Drew, stepping around Lucy. In an instant, I feel her hands on me and I'm falling, hitting the water with a splash. *What the hell?*

She's not that far from the edge, so with my nostrils flaring in anger, I reach for her legs and tug at them until she loses her balance, falling in behind me.

Drew roars with laughter, approaching the pool and holding his hand out to me. "Want some help getting out?

I'm sorry. Apparently, life with the landlord isn't really working out that well for Lucy."

"You bitch. Drew, I just want what's fair."

I turn to see her in the water behind me, her hair hanging limp around her face.

"Then tell your lawyer to speak to mine. They can sort it out. I've got better things to do, and I'm so sick of you harassing me. It's been over for months, Lucy. Leave me alone or I'll get a restraining order."

I take his hand, and his gaze switches back to me. "I hope you're here for the reason I think you are."

"Couldn't live without you. Is that what you want to hear?"

His mouth spreads into a wide grin, and that tells me everything I need to know.

He really does love me.

LUCY SLINKS OFF, and when I hear the sound of a car starting I breathe a sigh of relief.

"Are you okay?"

I shrug. "I'll be fine. It's just water."

"Why are you here?"

"I told you."

He shakes his head. "I want to hear it."

Tears well, and I don't even know why. He takes my hands in his. "I love you, Drew. And I should have listened to my heart. I can't imagine life without you."

He smiles, his eyes searching mine. "It's about time you caught up."

I laugh, and his mouth claims mine. We're a tangle of lips and tongues, and I'm lost in Drew's love. The way it should always be.

"You know, it's probably a good idea to get you out of those wet clothes," he murmurs.

"I can't believe she pushed me in."

He shrugs. "I don't know how she tracked me down. She keeps threatening me, but never following through."

"What will you do if she does?"

"Get my lawyer to deal with it. I'd much rather pay all my attention to you. How about a shower?"

I grin. "Now you're talking."

The shower warms me, and Drew turns up the heat as he towels me off and leads me to the bedroom. I've missed him so much.

I laugh, jumping up and hooking my legs around him. We tumble backward onto the bed, and Drew's hands are all over me, rediscovering what I made him think he lost.

The truth is that it was him all along. My heart was with him all the time.

His lips are on one breast, his tongue flicking over my nipple. Drew's laying claim to me again, and I'm loving every second. He's the man I want to spend the rest of my life with.

I cry silently as he covers my body in kisses, burying his face between my legs and worshipping my body. How did I ever think I could leave this behind me? How could I ever give this up? My fate with Drew was sealed the day we met, when he gave me that first soul-burning kiss.

My body jolts as he forgoes teasing for the immediacy of sex, sliding up my body and into me. Two months ago, he was right. We are pieces of the same puzzle.

"This is so right," he murmurs, his lips brushing my neck.

"I know, and I'm sorry."

Drew raises his head, and his eyes scan my face. "You did nothing wrong."

"I hurt you."

"You hurt yourself, too. I don't care what my mother says, or your mother thinks, or what anyone else wants. It's been you since the day we met."

He moves slowly, and I spread my legs a little wider to let him in farther. He groans. "You'll be the end of me."

His kisses fill me with joy. I'm surrounded by his love, by him, and I wouldn't want to be anywhere else but here.

I'm where I need to be.

"Hayley." He calls my name when he comes, and gives me a deep kiss that leaves me swooning.

I can't give this up.

When he lies beside me, I curl around him. "Why didn't you just tell me you love me before I broke things off?"

His nose twitches. "You were at breaking point. I didn't know if it would make it better or worse." He swallows. "When we didn't make it, I hated that I hadn't told you, but I was glad because I knew it'd make things even harder for you. When Corey told me what Ash did, it nearly ripped me in two that I hadn't told you."

I sniff as tears stream down my cheeks. "The last time I saw you, I wish I'd asked you to stay."

Drew reaches for me, and his lips brush mine as he wipes the tears from my chin. "You're here now, and that's all that matters. I know you've found it hard, but I'll do whatever it takes."

"I want to be with you. It's just hard to say goodbye to

Copper Creek, and the last thing I want is to work in a hospital again."

"Then don't." His voice is gentle, and his eyes convey the emotion behind them.

He lets out a breath. "Being with you, well, I could give it all up and come home. Maybe I could work as a GP. But I'm in a position here to offer you a life, to give us both everything we ever wanted. It's all I want. You're all I want."

"You don't have to give it up," I whisper. "I'm ready."

"Ready?"

"Copper Creek was there when I needed it to be. Now, I need you."

His lips twitch. "What are you trying to say?"

I blink away fresh tears. "I'll move. It won't be overnight, but I'll find a job and come here to be with you. If you want me."

"Do you really need to ask?" He smiles. "Maybe I won't let you go."

"I have to sort things out back home, but I want this, Drew. I want to sleep in this bed all of the time. I want to sit in that huge bathtub with your arms around me." I lick my lips. "I want you."

His smile grows to be a grin. "Let's make it happen. There's nothing more I want right now."

I nod. "Me too."

IN THE MORNING, I wake to Drew draped over me. The sun streams through the bay windows, and I lie naked on the bed, bathed in sunlight. This is how I want to live.

My heart sinks a little at the thought of going home. But I have work to do and need to figure out plans for my career so I can make the move. I'm going to make our dream a reality.

The distance will be hard to deal with again, but now I have a plan, and it'll all be worth it when I can move here permanently. Drew's given me more than anyone else in my life ever did, and in such a short time.

"Don't go back." His soft voice is in my ear, and it'd be so easy to give him what he wants.

"I don't want to. But I have to be a grown-up."

"We could run away and never be grown-ups again."

I laugh and shake my head. "I kinda like being a grown-up with you. We get to do adult things."

"Now you're talking."

I shiver, and he pulls the bedding up. "Don't. I'm nice and warm here. The sun coming through is gorgeous."

"Only because I forgot to pull the blinds. Someone distracted me." He plants a kiss on my cheek.

"Are you working today?"

"My shift starts later."

I lick my lips and roll toward him. "I'm going back in a few hours."

"You just got here." He raises his head and leans over to kiss my shoulder.

"I wanted to talk to you face to face. I've done that, and now I have to go home and start packing up my old life."

He grins. "I'm glad. I just want you all to myself."

"You have me. I'll start looking for a job today. And Margaret says it doesn't matter, but she needs someone to replace me, too."

Drew nods. "I know, I know. A guy can hope, can't he?"

"I'll be here soon. And we can wake up like this every day."

"I like that idea."

After Drew cooks us breakfast, I get ready to go home. Not that I want to. If I could, I'd stay right here and wake up tomorrow in that big bed with the sun bathing me in warmth.

But I have a house to pack and a job to sort out.

"Do you really have to go?"

I press my forehead to his. "You know I do. It won't be for much longer, though. We'll work it all out, and I'll be back before you know it. Complete with all my things."

"I have to make room for your stuff?"

Chuckling, I let him go. "I plan on taking over your house with my girly things."

Drew grins. "I wouldn't have it any other way."

He gives me one last lingering kiss, and I sit in the car seat before I change my mind. "Be safe."

I nod. "I'll call you tonight?"

"I'll look forward to it. I love you."

"Love you, too."

He leans in the window. "I'm gonna make you say that every day when you come and live here."

"You won't have to make me do anything."

I feel empty as I drive away. Living without him was never an option.

I have no idea how I thought I could.

22

HAYLEY

EVERY SINGLE KILOMETRE OF THE JOURNEY HOME IS HARD. THE farther I get from Drew, the more I hate it. I love Copper Creek, and what it's meant for my life, but right now I don't want to be there.

I want to be with the man I love.

The sooner the better.

There are a couple of cars parked near my place as I pull into my driveway. The neighbours are quiet and rarely have visitors, so it's something that catches my eye. I shrug and grab my bag from the back seat, getting out of the car.

I'll miss my little house. There's always been something quite special about it. It's the perfect size for one person, one person who wants to be alone. Now, I look forward to the space of Drew's house. That's a real family home.

I'm so wrapped up in my little world, I don't hear anyone behind me at first.

"Hayley."

My blood runs cold as I recognise the voice, and my hand shakes as I try and slide the key in the lock. I lose my grip on the key and it drops onto the doormat with a dull thud. "What do you want?"

"I just need to speak to you."

By the time I've turned, he's on the doorstep behind me. There's no way out. I take a step back, as far as I can get.

"I want to know if you've considered my offer."

"What offer?"

"To come and be our community midwife."

I swallow, clasping my hands together to stop them shaking. He hasn't spoken to me since I got away from him, and he seems to be pretending nothing happened. "You need to leave."

"Not until I've got an answer."

I swallow. "You already had one."

He leans over, taking me in with the cool blue of his eyes. "I don't think you really want to say no. We'd have a good life, Hayley. I'd give up the other women for you. You must be lonely here. I can help you. Plus the others get the best midwifery care around."

I tremble, knowing if I open my mouth I'll stammer out something when I want so desperately to sound confident. I know how far he'll go to convince me, know what he's done to others. Ash Harris doesn't scare me. He terrifies me.

"I think you need to fuck off and leave her alone."

My eyes widen at the sound of a familiar voice, and I turn my head to the left to see Owen Campbell emerge from behind my house.

Ash's brow wrinkles, and his eyes narrow. The two men

are pretty evenly matched, and I wouldn't want to take bets on either one of them in a fight.

"What he said." To my right, Corey Campbell appears. Tears well in my eyes that these guys are here to protect me. Summoned by Drew, I guess.

Ash holds his hands up. "I believe I was having a conversation with the lady."

"I don't believe the lady invited you onto her property." Alongside Corey, Adam shoots me a smile.

"I doubt you're invited either."

Corey grins. "Hayley's family. I suggest you get out of here and don't come back."

Ash straightens and glares at Corey. "I'll leave when Hayley tells me to."

"I already did." Bolstered by Drew's brothers' presence, I stop trembling and face him.

He backs away down the garden path. "Fine. I'll talk to you later."

As I step down from the doorstep, Owen moves behind me, slinging one arm around my shoulder. He calls after Ash. "I don't know if that'd be very good for your health."

I lean against him, my heart bursting from the actions of these three. They make me feel like part of their family.

"You are so not getting all that action, Owen. Shove over."

In an instant, Adam is at my other side, his arm around my waist and tugging me toward him.

"You two will pull her in half if you keep that up. Save some for Drew." Corey winks, and I laugh, surrounded by people I can depend on. They don't make me feel like part of their family. They *are* my family.

Tears erupt from me, a combination of feeling safe and loved.

"As long as you're here, we won't let him get near you," Owen says, pressing a kiss to my temple.

"We've got you." Adam nods.

"Are you okay?" Owen asks.

"I am now. How did you guys know to be here?"

Corey laughs. "Drew called us. We wanted to be here when you got home to give you a proper welcome home and let you know we're all here if you need us. When that dirtbag showed up, we thought we'd have a bit of fun if he bothered you. He didn't disappoint."

"Neither did you guys. I appreciate it so much."

Owen smiles. "If you ever need me, I'm just down the road. I know I've said it before, but, just call me any time of the day or night."

I nod. "I will."

"Welcome to the family, Hayley," Adam says.

My heart sings at the brothers' acceptance of me. Just as I'm about to leave, it's as if I've been adopted. I love this town.

If only my heart wasn't a three hundred kilometres away.

MY LITTLE HOUSE is full of chatter and laughter.

We spend the next couple of hours drinking coffee, with the boys telling stories of their childhood. Of course, most of them include Drew. The four of them are so close, and I think they all have some regret James isn't older so he could have shared more with them.

"We hated coming here," says Corey. "Hated it. We thought we'd be living in this tiny town and that there'd be nothing to do."

"How wrong was that?" Owen says.

"I said nothing to do, not *no one* to do."

Even I laugh at Corey's words. Owen's reputation isn't without merit.

My phone buzzes.

I'm at work and thinking about you. When are you moving?

I smile.

"Drew's ears burning?" Adam nudges my arm.

"Something like that."

"I'm really happy for you two. I'm glad Drew found someone who I know is going to be good to him, and vice versa."

"Thanks."

As soon as I can sort out work. I'm spending the afternoon with your brothers, btw.

Don't believe anything they tell you about me. So jealous I'm not there.

I look up from my phone and at Adam. "Thanks for introducing us."

"Lily wasn't impressed I asked him to come, but I'm glad I did."

I smile. "Me, too."

When there's a knock on the door, my eyebrows shoot up.

Corey reaches over and squeezes my hand. "I'll get it."

I nod.

He opens the door to Graham Taylor.

"Hayley?" Corey asks.

"Let him in."

Graham takes in the sight of me with Drew's brothers and smiles. "Good to see you've got lots of support."

"Support? The guy's a creep, but it's not like he …" Owen pauses, looking between his brothers. "What's all this really about?"

I swallow, meeting Adam's gaze. His frown tells me he doesn't know the full story either. Clearly Drew and Corey have kept this to themselves. "I had a run-in with Ash Harris."

His eyes widen. "What? I told you to call me if you needed me."

I nod. "I know, but Corey was there for me. And Drew."

Owen frowns. "What happened?"

"That's what I'm here to speak to Hayley about. My visit to Mr Harris," Graham says.

"He was here today," I say.

Graham's eyebrows rise. "Really?"

"Still going on about the offer he made me." I nod toward a chair. "Take a seat."

Graham sits and lets out a loud breath. "Well, he said you were there, but that you left of your own accord. But he's even more paranoid now. He knows someone betrayed him, and he's trying his best to find out who was involved in getting you out. Julia's completely on the outer now. He won't even speak to her."

"Wait. Get you out?" Adam asks.

"He … he …"

"He couldn't convince Hayley to be with him so he drugged her and, well, Graham's guys on the inside got her out before anything happened." Corey sits on the couch beside me and slips his arms around my shoulders.

Graham growls. "I'd prefer you not tell the world about our operation."

Corey chuckles. "Adam and Owen are entitled to know. Hayley's part of our family, and once Ash dragged her into this, it became personal."

"Holy shit." Owen's eyes meet mine.

"What the hell?" Adam says.

"We think that's part of his routine for convincing young women to join him. Seduction with a little bit of help." Graham shifts his focus to Adam.

"How has he not been arrested?" His eyes are wild with confusion.

"They're after him for something much bigger than what happened to me," I say.

Corey's grip tightens. "I tried to make sure we had evidence, and that Hayley knows she has our support no matter what."

"I don't even know what came back in my blood test yet."

"It was faint, and I think we got the blood just in time. There were signs of Rohypnol in your test."

My stomach rolls at the ease with which I was drugged. If Julia hadn't turned against Ash, if Graham's men had taken longer ... How would I have felt waking up and thinking I'd slept with Ash?

"He changed his pattern with you; I'm sure of that. He tried talking you into it, but you resisted. He's worked out who to target, and when to back off. You're different. You would have woken up and known something was wrong."

I nod.

"So, the question is, what the hell is he doing behind those fences?" Owen asks.

"I've narrowed it down to two things," Graham says. "He's either building an army or a workforce."

"A workforce for what? They might have those fences, but there's nothing obvious going on beside growing food for themselves," I say.

"I'm not sure, but there's something deeper. Our guys haven't got close enough yet, but the day is coming when we'll unravel everything."

I nod.

"My immediate concern is you. If he's got the balls to show up here knowing someone helped you leave, what else could he try?"

"I'm leaving town."

"When?"

"As soon as I can find a job."

Graham leans back in the seat. "I hope he's not driving you out of Copper Creek."

I shake my head. "No, I'm moving to be with Drew."

He smiles. "At least then I'll know you'll be safe."

I hope I am.

23

ADAM

"TELL ME WHY YOU'RE HERE."

This is my first visit to see Paul Jacobs. After I got his details from Jenna I looked him up, and colour me impressed. He's not cheap, but dealing with PTSD, particularly in veterans, is his specialty.

"I'm struggling, and I need help."

Paul smiles. "That's half the battle right there."

Over the next hour, I tell him everything—Ben's death, my injury, my difficulties that Jenna helped me through. And Lily. Like everything else in my life, it always comes back to Lily.

"You're scared you'll hurt her again."

I nod. "I'm not stupid. She's given me another chance she never needed to, and I made the most of it. Now we've got a successful business and a new baby, and she's been through so much herself."

"From what you've told me, there are things from both

your pasts that you've skimmed over. If you want to move forward together, you both have to be honest with each other."

I swallow. "I've always been scared. She feels like I abandoned her, and I did. No matter what I do now, I'll never be able to make up for that."

"Maybe not, but that you've started opening up to each other is a good thing. The past is painful, but it's what you do with that pain to make the future better that's important."

I let out a loud breath. "I just love her so much."

He nods. "She's the last person you want to hurt, but you hurt her, and while that's not a good thing, it's brought you here. Have you had any other instances of reacting to sounds like that?"

"Not that extreme. A couple of times my ex found me curled up in the corner of the room, but the recent one was the scariest. I was back there, tasting the sand, smelling dead bodies."

His eyebrows knit. "And it was a gunshot that set it off?"

"My brother shot a possum. My actual memory of what happened is pretty hazy, but Lily twisted her ankle when I shoved her to the floor."

Paul sits back in his chair. "How much treatment did you have back in the States? Did you get counselling?"

"A bit. My ex works with veterans. That's where we met. But I always wondered if it was enough, and if my seeming to be mostly okay was just because I lived with her and she'd been around people like me before. She knew how to talk me down, and what signs to look for."

He nods.

"She taught me some relaxation techniques, and that

works when it's not too loud or when an attack is coming. But the other day I didn't have time to try anything."

Paul leans closer. "It's called an exaggerated startle reflex, and it's very common in veterans with PTSD."

"I remember Jenna calling it something like that. What do I do to stop it?"

"There are medications that can help, and I would recommend you keep coming to see me. I know you have to travel, so we could even talk via Skype or phone."

Nodding, I breathe a sigh of relief. "Whatever it takes. The most important thing to me is to keep my family together, so I need to do everything I can."

"What kind of counselling did Lily get after her trauma?"

I grin. "Angling for business?"

He laughs. "Caught me. No, it just sounds like there are open wounds on both sides. She went through an incredibly traumatic experience, too."

"I'm not sure, but she still has a fear of the dark. I set up a night-light system for our bedroom. Have to admit, it's helped me a little too when I wake up from the dreams."

"Well, Adam. Apart from this, it sounds like you have a healthy relationship with each other. That's going to help you."

I nod, and for the first time in a long time I don't feel quite so agitated about the past. It's time to let Ben go and move on with my life.

My life with Lily.

It's a long drive home, but I can't wait to see Lily. She's not expecting me until tomorrow, and I spent some time doing some shopping before I started the journey.

The plan was for me to stay at Drew's place, but I couldn't wait to come home. Copper Creek is a quiet town, but leaving my family alone for the night doesn't sit right with me. Besides, I miss them.

As I drive into the yard, Lily appears at the back door. She beams as I step out of the car and walk toward the house.

"How did it go? I thought you'd stay the night at Drew's."

I let out a loud breath as we walk into the kitchen. "It was good. I stopped off to see Drew, but I just wanted to come home. I think I'll sleep better with you."

Her lips curl into a smile. "There are leftovers in the fridge if you're hungry, and you just missed Max. He grumped about you not being here, but he went to sleep pretty quickly once he was in bed."

"Dad?" Max appears in the doorway.

She rolls her eyes. "Speak of the devil. I thought you were asleep."

"I was, but you two make *so* much noise." Max wraps his arms around my waist. "Where have you been?"

"I had to go and see a special doctor."

His blue eyes fill with concern. "Are you sick?"

"No, bud. I've been talking to him about my days in the army."

"Can you tell me, too?"

Lily meets my gaze, her eyes so full of love.

"Sure, but not tonight. You need to go and get some

sleep." I bend, and press my lips to his forehead. "Love you, Max."

"Love you too, Dad. I knew you'd come home tonight."

"Of course you did."

He turns and disappears toward his room, and I drape my arms over Lily's shoulders. "Want to go to bed too?"

"Maybe after we know for sure that Max is asleep."

I laugh. "I've got a present for you. Go sit in the living room."

A confused look crosses her face. "A present?"

"Something special for my girl."

I go to the table and open my bag. Sitting right on top is the small velvet box, and my stomach clenches as I take it out.

How's Lily going to react? Things seem to be okay between us again, but does she trust me enough for this?

I don't know how I'll take it if she says no.

"Ready?" I call.

"I don't know. It might help if you tell me what it is."

Taking a deep breath, I walk into the living room. She's sitting on the couch, and her eyes are wide as I cross the room and drop to my knees in front of her.

"What are you doing?"

"Something I should have done a very long time ago." I open the box, and her mouth drops open.

"Adam," she says softly.

"You're it for me, Lily. You always were. I asked you once before and everything went wrong. But everything's going right for us, and I'm hoping we can try this again. I know we need to be more open, but I want to be more open with you forever. I want to promise that in front of our friends and family. Will you marry me?"

Tears roll down her cheeks, and she nods. "Of course I will."

I remove the gold ring with the teardrop diamond from the box. "I picked this out because I think I've caused you enough tears. This is the last one."

She laughs, wiping her face with her fingers. "It's beautiful."

The old ring I bought the first time around still sits on her finger. She's told me it carried her through the months her mother abused her, and it brought her comfort for all the years we were apart.

"I don't want to take this off," she whispers.

"Then, don't. I'm sure there's enough room for both. Something old and something new."

I slide it on her finger. It's a little loose, but nothing we can't get fixed up.

She throws her arms around my neck and I hold her tight.

"Are you two getting married?"

Lily laughs at the sound of Max's voice, and she plants a kiss on me before letting me go and nodding. "Yes, baby. Your mum and dad are getting married. Come over here."

Max rolls his eyes. "It's about time."

He's right. It is about time.

24

HAYLEY

The first week back sucks. I've arranged a trip for the weekend to see my parents and introduce Drew. If I can deal with his mother, he can deal with mine. The important thing is that we're together, and we're strong.

I've seen no sign of Ash, but Margaret tells me he's approached her about providing maternity care for the community. I wonder if he knows I'm leaving and won't be involved. At least he's making an effort.

Driving to Hamilton, my excitement grows the closer I get to Drew. I've put out feelers for jobs, and there are a couple of opportunities. All I can do is hope one of them pans out and that I can move soon.

Drew's waiting at the door when I get there. For some reason, he's excited about going to see my parents, even though I've given him plenty of warning. The thought of seeing Dad again warms my heart. Mum leaves my stomach sinking.

"Hey, princess." He greets me warmly, pulling me in the door and into his arms. I take a deep breath, inhaling him. His lips press against mine, and I open my mouth to let his tongue in.

I giggle.

"What?"

"You had bacon for breakfast. I have no idea where you put all that food."

He grins. "It makes those little soft pockets in my abs."

"There's nothing soft about your abs."

Drew hooks his arm around my neck and pulls me closer. "If you want, we could just hang out here and you can check out that claim."

I sigh. "I wish. But we have to get going."

He nods. "I do have some news I want to tell you, though."

"What is it?"

"I put in an offer for the house, and I think Daryl's going to accept it."

My breath catches. "You're buying a house? This house?"

Drew raises a hand to my face, using his fingers to push a lock of hair behind my ear. "I want a home. For us. I mean, if you want to."

"Drew," I say softly. "It's such a big place."

His lips twitch. "I thought we might need the space. You know, for when we make some babies of our own."

Everything I ever wanted is right in front of me. He's offering me the whole world. This time, I'm not so scared.

"Did you just say …"

A grin spreads from ear to ear as he keeps playing with

my hair. "You're the only person I've ever seen a future with. I mean, one with marriage and babies."

"You're real keen on that baby thing, aren't you?"

He licks his lips. "Maybe."

My heart explodes. I'm already so in love with him, and yet I think I just fell a little deeper. "I love that idea."

"I can't wait for you to move."

"Neither can I."

25

DREW

Hayley's parents' place is impressive. The house and grounds are huge. Hayley's breathing deeply beside me. It shouldn't be this hard for her, but I get it. As much as she says she doesn't care, I hope her mum and dad like me, for her sake.

"You okay?" I ask as I stop outside the front of the house.

She shrugs. "Ready as I'll ever be. Once they meet you, they'll love you." She says it, but there's uncertainty in her tone.

"Whatever happens, I love you. That's what matters."

A smile spreads across her face. "I love you too. Nothing that happens this weekend is going to change that."

"I know."

She reaches for my hand and squeezes. "Come on, Doctor Drew. Let's go get this over with."

I lean over and brush her lips with mine. "I'd follow you anywhere, princess."

We step out of the car, and I walk with her to the front door. This house just screams money, and I glance at Hayley. She's so grounded despite all this, and it makes her all the more appealing to me. She couldn't be fake if she tried.

"Mum, Dad, I'm here," Hayley calls as we walk in the front door.

I suck in a breath as a tall brunette who Hayley strongly resembles comes toward us. We make eye contact and she looks as if she's forcing a smile. Although Hayley warned me she might not be welcoming, I thought she'd be happier for her daughter.

"Hayley." The smile warms as she lays eyes on her daughter, and the two embrace, with Hayley's mother eying me with obvious suspicion over Hayley's shoulder.

Hayley pulls back. "Mum, this is Drew. Drew, this is my mother, Sonya."

Sonya nods and holds out a delicate hand with red-painted talons. I suppress my smile over the difference between the two women. One of the things I love about Hayley is that she's not afraid to get her hands dirty. It's clear her mother hasn't done so in years.

"I'm so pleased to meet you," I say.

"You too."

A tall, dark-haired man approaches, and the difference between him and Sonya is like night and day. This must be Hayley's father. He has such a wide, genuine smile on his face when he sees his daughter.

"Dad." Hayley wraps her arms around his waist, and he closes his eyes as he holds her tight.

"It's so good to have you home, sweetheart." He kisses the

top of her head and shifts his gaze to me. "This must be Drew. I'm David."

"Glad to meet you." He lets go of Hayley as I hold out my hand, and he takes it with a firm grip. The firmness of the shake tells me he's taking everything in. I've never hoped to make a good impression more in all my life.

"It's nice to finally meet the man who's swept my daughter off her feet."

I grin. "It's good to meet you, too."

He slaps me on the back. "We're just about to have some lunch. Come through and we'll talk."

As David and Sonya make their way farther into the house, Hayley and I trail behind. She grabs my hand and squeezes, and as I shoot a glance at her, all I see is adoration in her eyes.

I hope I don't let her down.

LUNCH IS MORE relaxed than I anticipated. Sonya spends the whole time eyeing me up, and while I think it makes Hayley uncomfortable, I can handle it.

David's the chatty one. He asks about my family, my work, and avoids the topic of my relationship with Hayley. I'm not sure if it's intentional or not, but it means the time passes without any trouble. If only visiting my parents had been this easy.

"Let me show you around," he says after lunch, and I look to Hayley. She nods and smiles, probably happy that the two men in her life are getting on well.

I lean over and peck her on the lips before standing. "That'd be great."

He leads me out the back of the house. There's what looks to be a small orchard on one side, and a swimming pool and tennis court on the other. It's magnificent.

"You have a gorgeous property."

David nods. "We're very happy with it. It seems a bit empty at times without Hayley, but it's home." He looks wistful. "Sometimes I miss the little house we had when Hayley was born. Lots of good memories in that place."

"Hayley told me how proud she is of you. Self-made man and all."

He grins. "She used to spend hours sitting with me in the garage while I brewed beer. I'd create a recipe and she'd help measure out the ingredients."

"That's awesome."

"It was." He takes a deep breath. "So, you're serious about my daughter?"

"Very. She's everything to me."

He nods. "She's my only child, so you had better take good care of her."

I smile. "I promise. I'll do whatever it takes to make her happy."

A wistful smile appears on his face. "I'm glad she seems to have found someone good. Her mother always had this idea that Hayley would marry someone she picked, but she forgets that wasn't the way with us. I always wanted Hayley to follow in my footsteps in business, but she's forging her own path, and I'm so proud of her."

Licking my lips, I make a move that'll either cancel all the work I've just done, or bring him and his daughter closer. "Can I ask you something?"

"Sure."

"Can you tell her that?"

Her father's eyebrows dip as he stares at me. "What do you mean?"

"I don't mean to disrespect you, and I can see how much you love her, but she feels like she disappoints you. Both of you."

He gulps. "Why would she think that?"

I shrug. "All I know is that she's told me she thinks you're disappointed that she's ended up with the job she's in, and living where she does."

He hasn't bitten my head off yet, and his strained facial expression tells me he's racking his brain for anything he might have said to give her that idea. "Well, it's true I was disappointed she didn't study business, and she went through that horrible time when that patient died, but she's happy now, and that's all I ever wanted for her."

My heart aches at the thought of Hayley and how hurt she's been at the way her parents have acted in the past. "I don't know if she understands that."

He licks his lips. "Her mother is a whole other story. She loves Hayley, but Hayley wants to live her own life. Sonya sometimes can't let go."

I nod.

Smiling, he claps me on the back. "Thanks for your honesty. It confirms for me that Hayley's found a good man."

"I only hope I can give her everything she needs. The distance has been hard on her, but once she moves to Hamilton, I think she'll be much more settled."

His smile grows. "I didn't know she was moving. That's wonderful. It brings her that little bit closer to us."

"She still wants to find a job before she resigns formally, but her boss knows she's leaving. I'm happy for her to move and worry about the job later, but I'm sure you know how independent your daughter is."

He chuckles, moving his hand to my shoulder and gripping it. "I sure do. You're the first boyfriend she's brought home in a very long time. I knew when she told us you were coming that it was serious."

"I love your daughter a lot."

Hayley and her mother are waiting at the door when we arrive back, and Hayley's nervous smile gives way to a grin as she meets my gaze.

"I hear you're moving to Hamilton," David says as we approach.

Her cheeks pale. It's clear he makes her nervous. I can only hope that my being honest with him will help bridge the gap between them. "Once I sort a few things out."

He opens his arms and hugs her tight. "I'm looking forward to you being closer to home. When I travel on business, I can come and see you."

"I'd like that," she says softly as he kisses the top of her head. I smile as she closes her eyes, embraced by her father.

"You found a good man, sweetheart. Someone who loves you. I'm so happy for you."

Her eyes open again, and she meets my gaze before shifting it to him. "Thanks, Dad. It means a lot."

"I'm so proud of you."

Tears prick her eyes, and she smiles.

"Oh, Hayley. Hamilton? That's no better than that pokey little town you're in now. You need to come home."

Hayley reaches for my hand and squeezes. "Wherever Drew is. That's home."

"She's happy, Sonya. We need to support that."

Sonya's eyes widen as her husband speaks. "I just want Hayley to make a good marriage. To be able to live a life where she's not cleaning up after people."

"I love my job, Mum, and I'll find a good one in Hamilton."

In that moment, it strikes me. Her mother is just like mine—bitchy because she can't control everything. *We need to keep them apart as much as possible.*

"Mrs McCarthy, I can provide for Hayley, for both of us. In a year or so, I'll be going into private practice, and I've already set things in motion to buy a house." I wink at Hayley. "To buy us a home."

Hayley reaches for my hand and squeezes.

"But Hayley said she'll need to find a job."

I grin. "Because it's important to her. She needs a career just like I do." Meeting Hayley's gaze, I think I fall in love all over again at the expression on her face. "But I'll always be there to catch her if she falls."

"Like I said, Hayley, you've got a good one there." David speaks up as Hayley leans over and brushes my lips with hers. I don't care what anyone else thinks. She and I are going to spend the rest of our lives together. I'm positive of that.

"I know I do." Hayley snuggles into me, happy and assured.

"Drew seems like a very nice person. I'm just not sure if he's the right one for you."

The second her mother speaks, I watch Hayley's self-confidence shatter into a million pieces. She goes limp in my arms.

"Leave him alone, Sonya," David says.

I squeeze her hand, and she takes a deep breath. "Hayley and I are both sure we're right for each other. I'm not sure what I have to do to prove it to you, but Hayley will always come first."

"She's our only daughter. I'm allowed to be protective."

"There's protective and there's overbearing. Right now, you're being the latter."

Hayley stares at her father, and I bite down a smile. From what she's told me, it's not often David speaks up. It seems her parents' relationship echoes my parents'. We have even more in common than we ever realised.

It's just one more reason that we're a good fit.

DINNER'S a whole different story to lunch. Sonya's clearly decided to ignore me, and Hayley's agony at how her mother's treating me is obvious.

We sit in silence and watch evening television, but through it all, Hayley never leaves my side, snuggling up to me on the couch. It's awkward, but I'll put up with it knowing what she went through visiting my mother.

"I think it must be bedtime," Hayley says. I take the hint and stand. The sooner we're alone together, the better.

"Your room is ready as always, Hayley, and Drew's is

right across the hallway," Sonya says, standing.

I bite down on my bottom lip, and Hayley's dad rolls his eyes.

"Really?" Hayley says.

"Is that a new rule?" David asks, and I suck my bottom lip in to avoid blurting anything out.

Sonya turns on her heel and walks away without another word.

I suppress a smile. "If it's any consolation, Hayley, I'm pretty sure my mother hates you."

Her and David both turn to me with open mouths.

"She never did like any of our girlfriends. No one will ever be good enough for her sons." I place my hands on Hayley's arms. "What I'm trying to say is that I understand."

David laughs. "I think you've hit the nail on the head there, Drew. If you two will excuse me, I think it's time to get some sleep."

He leaves the room and heads up the stairs first, leaving us at the bottom.

"Thanks, Dad. Have a good night. I think it's time for bed for us, too." Hayley wraps her arms around my waist.

"Us? We're not sleeping together."

She grins. "Wanna bet we're not?" Taking my hand in hers, she leads me up the stairs, pausing at a door. "You're sleeping in here with me."

"But your mum—"

"It's okay. Don't worry about it. Seriously, if you were Courtney Jackson's son, you'd be in my bedroom already."

"Courtney who?"

Hayley laughs. "Never mind. Come on, Drew. I promise not to bite." She grips my hands and swings them.

"What if I want you to bite?"

Raising one of my hands to her lips, she nips at my index finger. "That could be arranged"

"Hayley McCarthy, you're trouble. I don't want to disrespect your parents."

She tiptoes, her lips pressed against my ear sending shockwaves through me. She whispers, "My mother's hardly respecting you. So you can come in and disrespect me."

I chuckle. "I've got your dad on my side, though."

"He won't care. It's Mum who has the problem. It's not even a problem with you. She just likes to think she can run my life."

She grabs my hands and pulls me into the room, turning us so my back is to the bed.

When she flicks on the bedside lamp, the room lights up. This entire room is pink. If the way this room is decorated is any indication, it's no wonder Hayley's mother treats her like a child at twenty-eight. The walls are pink, as is the shelving against the wall. Even the canopied bed and linen are shades of magenta. It's like a pink bucket of paint exploded. The only thing that isn't pink in this damn room is the lilac carpet.

"Uhh. What the hell is up with the decor?"

Hayley rolls her eyes. "My mother's attempt at making me feel like a princess. I told her to redecorate when I left home, but she likes it like this."

I reach forward and cup her breasts. "I'll feel you, princess."

"That's what I'm counting on."

My calves hit the bed as she shoves me backward, and I chuckle. "I feel like I'm desecrating this room."

As I flop back, her hands are on the waistband of my pants, and she flicks the button open and slowly slides the zip. "Well, you are the first boy I've ever had in here."

"I'm not surprised."

My pants and underwear are pulled down to my knees, and my eyes roll back in my head as she takes me in her mouth. "Oh, the ceiling's not pink. There is a God."

Hayley laughs, the vibration in her mouth leaving me groaning.

Her hand pumps, and my cock responds. It's easy to feel at ease around Hayley; there's such a gentle calm about her.

But there's nothing calm about the way she's touching me.

She speeds up, and I give myself over to her completely. I already know I want to spend the rest of my life with her. Nothing and no one will stand in my way. Not even her mother.

I open my eyes and push myself up on my elbows. Her head bobs, her tongue lashing the tip of my cock. I'm so close, but now I'm taking charge.

"Get undressed," I growl, and she pauses, looking up at me with wide eyes.

"Drew ..."

"Now, Hayley."

As she stands, her chest rises and falls with rapid breaths, and I kick off my pants and reach for my shirt. The buttons flip open one by one as I keep my eyes focused on her. There are times when she's so self-assured, and then times when she retreats. The colour rising in her cheeks, I hold her gaze while she fumbles with her clothing.

I turn, pulling back the duvet and top sheet on the bed.

Standing, I make my way around the side and beckon her with a crook of my index finger. The last of her clothes discarded, she climbs into the bed, and I slip between the sheets, our naked bodies making contact.

Short, sharp breaths come from her, and I dig my fingers through her hair, pulling her into a kiss. My tongue finds a gentle rhythm with hers, and we're in sync, beautiful melodious sync.

"Drew," she whispers as I detach my lips from hers and drop them to her neck. She gasps as I lay a trail of kisses down to her shoulder before disappearing under the sheets to return the favour. "I didn't make you come."

"I've got something to take care of first."

"What?"

"You."

She giggles as I part her legs and plant kisses on her thighs. Her body tenses as anticipation builds, and she sighs loudly when my tongue makes first contact with her clit.

I want things to always be this special between us. I've loved other women, but none so much as Hayley.

I probe her gently with my tongue. Her hips flick toward me, and it's all I can do to hold myself together. She undoes me every single time. A rush of emotion overwhelms me.

She cries out so loudly that the people living in the next property over could probably hear her, let alone her parents.

"Roll onto your side," I say, positioning myself next to her.

Hayley's eyebrows shoot up, and I grin. I slip one arm beneath her and spread her legs with my other hand. From behind, I guide myself into her, and she gasps as I push.

"I love you," she says, leaning her head back.

Raising my free hand to her face, I run my index finger down her cheek. "I love you, too."

I hold her tight, thrusting hard. I'm buried so deep inside her, but it could never be deep enough. She's mine, and I want her to miss me when I'm gone.

She moans.

Hayley's the past I wish I had, the present I need, and the future I long for all in one.

"Marry me, Hayley," I whisper.

Her eyes flicker open, and she stills. "What did you say?"

"I want you all the time like this. Not so far away I can only imagine it."

"Drew," she whispers.

"I need to be able to touch you. Not just talk about it. I need you."

Tears form in her eyes, and I slow my pace. My whole heart is in her hands, as it has been from the start. Once we were together, it was only ever her. No one else can compare.

"I need you, too."

"So?"

The tears drop from her eyes and roll away. I bend my head and tenderly kiss each temple until they're gone.

"Yes. Yes, Drew, I'll marry you."

My heart breaks free and soars. Everything I've ever wanted is right here. We'll build our life together as husband and wife, and screw everything and everyone that came before. Hayley's my everything forever.

"You make me so happy," she says.

With our gazes locked, I come. I let out a strained groan, emotion overwhelming me.

My lips crash onto hers as I claim her mouth. I'm greedy, and want every tiny piece of her. She'll never have to worry about anything again, not have to deal with shitty situations alone. I'll always be there for her, no matter what.

She sighs as I pull out of her, roll her onto her back, and hold her tight.

"I think we should have a baby too."

Hayley laughs into my chest. "One thing at a time."

"Of course. We'll get the wedding out of the way and then we'll start on making babies," I say. She looks up to meet my gaze. "That's if you're interested."

"You know I am. You're just in mega-speed mode."

I nod. "You're twenty-eight, so we have seven years to get the baby-making out of the way before our chances start decreasing."

She slams her palm into her forehead. "I don't believe you just said that. Here you are being all romantic and sweet, and we're now talking about my biological clock?"

"Given my occupation, don't you think I'm always thinking about that?"

Laughing, she pulls me down to kiss her. "I'm not surprised, but can we talk about the serious stuff later?" Love radiates from her smile. "I will make babies with you. But one thing at a time."

"I want everything with you."

She turns off the bedside lamp. Curling up around her, I close my eyes. When she's in my arms, I don't worry about anything.

"Drew?" she whispers.

"Yes?"

"I want everything with you, too."

26

DREW

SHE'S RAVENOUS IN THE MORNING, AND HER MOTHER RAISES an eyebrow, presumably at the amount of food Hayley's eating. It's good to see her this way. I know from personal experience that when you have a busy schedule, it's easy to neglect yourself. This break has done us the world of good.

"What are your plans for the day?" Sonya asks.

Hayley's mouth is full, so I decide to speak up. "I don't come this way often, so we thought we might take a drive around, maybe do some shopping."

She nods. "I'm sure Hayley's wardrobe needs a refresh."

I shoot a glance at Hayley and pat her on the back as her eyes bulge. She needs to swallow her food before she has a rant and chokes. "Hayley can go crazy with whatever she wants."

Hayley swallows and wraps her arms around my neck. I turn my head to plant a kiss on her nose.

"You must have a good income to buy a house, provide my daughter with everything she needs."

I smile at Hayley's eye-roll. "I do alright for myself. Enough for both of us."

Sonya sits back with an unsatisfied look on her face.

David smiles as he sits at the table. "Good morning, you two. Have a good sleep?"

I nod.

"I had a great sleep," Hayley says. "It's nice to be home."

"Maybe you can come home more often." He shares a smile with her, and she moves her chair closer, leaning her head against mine.

"I've got some calls to make." Sonya leaves the table, and David sighs.

"I hope she wasn't giving you two too hard a time."

Shaking my head, I smile. "No more a hard time than my mother gave Hayley."

"It's hard to say who's worse," Hayley says, but I disagree. Visiting my mother left Hayley crying and breaking up with me. This is nothing. "If we're going shopping, I'm going to go and get changed." She kisses my cheek. "See you shortly."

My eyes are on her all the way into the house.

"Sonya wasn't that bad, was she?" David asks.

"She's fine. I know she's just looking out for Hayley. I'm just waiting to be asked for my bank balance."

David laughs. "She's been preoccupied with finding the perfect man for Hayley for a long time. Hayley's gotten it right, I reckon."

"Me too. Speaking of that, there's something I need to talk to you about."

His brows knit. "What?"

"I asked Hayley to marry me last night."

A smile I'm not expecting crosses his lips. I'm not sure how much of a stickler he is for tradition, but I guess I'm about to find out.

"That's wonderful. I'm assuming she said yes?"

I nod. "I've just done things a bit back to front. I should have spoken to you about it first."

He chuckles. "I figured things were heading this way. I'm not that surprised."

"It was a bit of a spur-of-the-moment thing. It's been on my mind, but I didn't plan it."

He grips my shoulder. "Thank you for talking to me about it. I'm over the moon, and maybe now you'll distract Sonya with wedding plans."

I grin; I can't help it. The thought of Hayley walking down the aisle toward me sets my soul alight.

"I hope so. I'm taking her out ring shopping today."

"Great." He presses his lips together. "If you don't mind me asking, are you okay to get her what she wants?"

For a moment, I blank, and then it clicks. *He's asking me if I have enough money.*

I nod. "I'll be fine. Knowing Hayley, she'll want to get something small and subtle, but I want something big enough to show the world she's mine."

"Good for you. I didn't mean anything by it. What I want is for my girl to get everything she deserves."

"That's what I want too."

He grins. "I think you're good for her, Drew. It's been a long time since I've seen her so happy."

"Are you ready to go?" Hayley stands in the doorway, a huge grin on her face. It's fair to say it's been stuck there since I proposed last night. I hope I always make her smile that much.

"Someone's eager," David mutters.

"Very."

"I hope you find something you like," he says to Hayley, waggling his eyebrows.

Her eyes widen. "You told?"

"Well, I kinda didn't ask for his permission first."

David stands and crosses the room, taking Hayley in his arms and kissing her cheek. "Congratulations, sweetheart. I think you picked the right one here. I won't tell your mother; I'll leave that to you."

As he sits back at the table, she rolls her eyes. "Chicken."

"I'm the one who has to live with her. I've got to be the good guy." He winks, and the love he has for his daughter is clear to see.

At least we have his approval.

IT TAKES three stores and a lot of other shopping along the way, but she finally lays eyes on a ring she falls in love with. My heart dances at the joy in her eyes, and I slide it on her finger in front of the counter. Hayley flings her arms around me, and I hold on tight, closing my eyes as I breathe in her excitement.

This is the woman I'm going to spend my life with.

It's not the biggest ring in the store, but it's simple and classic and what she wants—white gold with a single diamond. Her eyes sparkle as much as the stone does as she takes a step back.

"It's perfect, Drew."

"You're perfect."

Not caring who sees us, I slide my hand around to brace her head and kiss her. My heart bursts with love for her, and I can't get enough of this. I break a little thinking that after this weekend, we'll go our separate ways again, even if it's only for a short amount of time.

"Don't wait to find a job," I whisper.

She screws up her nose. "We talked about this."

"I know, but I don't want to wait anymore."

Hayley slips her arms around my waist. "I don't want to either."

"So remind me what we're waiting for then?"

She chuckles. "I don't want anyone thinking I'm with you for any other reason than I love you."

"I blame your mother for you thinking that way. You're not going to be an ornament in my home, Hayley." After another quick kiss, I smile. "You won't just be my wife—you'll be my partner. That's what I want."

"It's what I want, too.

"Then, let's do it. You just have to work out your notice, right?"

"A month."

"Then give notice when you get home, and we'll sort out a moving company to pack all your things and move them."

Her eyes search mine as if she's trying to see if I'm kidding, but I'm not. I don't give a crap about anything else right now. It scares me that she's still living in the same town as Ash Harris, but more importantly, I want her with me so I can love her.

"You did say once you were gonna be bossy when it came to me." She grins.

"Too right I am. I'm sick of us being apart when there's no need for it. Anything you want, Hayley, it's yours. *I'm* yours."

Tears roll down her cheeks, and I hold her tight.

The woman behind the counter gives me a forced smile. "Here's your receipt, sir."

I take it with a laugh, because when I'm with Hayley, nothing else matters.

WITH A CAR FULL OF BAGS, we make our way back to her parents' place. Hayley spends the whole journey examining her ring finger, shifting the diamond so it sparkles. We'll need to have it adjusted, it's a little tight, but she didn't want to leave the store without it.

We pull into the driveway. A late-model, bright red Ferrari sits in front of the house, and we park behind it.

"Flash car."

Hayley flicks me a smile. "Welcome to my life. Wonder who it is. We'll take all this stuff in so I can sort it out. Some of the clothes can go in my suitcase."

I grab the bags from the boot of the car, as she shoves her engagement ring in my face. "Mum's going to go nuts."

"At least your dad is fine with it. In fact, he offered to help pay for it."

Her mouth drops open. "No."

"I told him no. You're my girl, and I take care of whatever it is you need."

She flings her arms around my neck and plants a tender kiss on my lips. My heart is so full right now.

We walk inside, and her father greets us with a big grin on his face. "Did a bit of shopping, did we?"

"Someone did." I laugh, nodding toward Hayley.

"Your mother's got some old friend of yours outside."

Hayley smiles. "I'll just get these upstairs and be back in a minute." She reaches for the bags, but I shake my head. "I'll take these up to your room."

"I'll come with you. There's something in there I want."

We mount the stairs together, Hayley with an arm hooked in mine, and her head on my shoulder. She's happy, and that's all that matters to me right now.

"Is there really something in these bags you want?" I ask.

"I just wanted to be with you. Facing Mum can wait."

"Are you that worried she'll be upset?"

Hayley pauses at her bedroom door. "She's a lot like your mother, I think. Hates that she can't control my life. I could bring home a famous movie star and she'd hate him because she didn't choose him."

I walk in and drop the bags on the bed.

She wraps her arms around my waist and nestles into my chest. "I choose you, and that's what matters. After everything we've been through together, there's nothing she can do to disrupt my mood."

"Why's that?" I feign innocence.

She raises her face to smile at me. "Because I made the right decision. I'm marrying the man I love."

I kiss the top of her head. "So you'll settle for a humble doctor instead of a movie star?"

"There's no one else I'd rather have."

For a moment, I close my eyes and hold her tight. I love her more than everything else in this whole world, and I don't know if I can let her go at all after this time together.

"Should we go and spoil my mother's weekend with the news?" She grins.

"Do you really think it's going to do that?"

Hayley shrugs. "I don't care. I'm marrying you, Drew Campbell, whether she likes it or not."

God, I love her.

We walk down the stairs, hand in hand. Her mother's waiting at the bottom.

"Mum, I've got something to tell you."

Sonya turns, a fake smile plastered all over her face that leaves my eyebrows rising. This can't be good. I know Hayley's determined not to be hurt by her, but I know what my mother did to her. I tighten my grip.

"Hayley, there's someone here to see you."

Sonya takes Hayley's hand, and Hayley shoots me a confused look, following her. I trail along behind as Sonya leads us out the back of the house into the bright sunshine.

"Do you remember our phone call when I told you Courtney Jackson's son had been asking after you?" Sonya speaks in a low voice, and I realise there's a blond man sitting at the outdoor table. It doesn't take much to click that he owns the Ferrari out front.

Hayley groans. "Mum …"

I catch her gaze and raise my eyebrows. She shrugs in return.

"When you told us you were coming home, I invited him around."

Her eyes are full of irritation. "I'm here with Drew."

"Yes, but it wouldn't hurt to see him. Maybe become reacquainted?"

When Sonya says that I know she's just like my mother. She even has the balls to be brazen about it.

"Drew's standing right there, and I need to talk to—"

"Jamie. Here's Hayley. She's just been out shopping with her … friend."

My anger's building, but I don't need to say anything. Jamie stands and walks around the table, extending his hand. "Hayley. It's been years." When I think he's about to shake her hand, he pulls her to him and kisses her cheek. I don't miss that his hand lingers holding hers as he lets her go.

"Yeah, I think that's enough," I say.

Sonya turns her gaze on me. "Jamie and Hayley knew each other a very long time ago. Hayley had such a crush on him when she was a little girl."

"Mum." Hayley's voice is louder than before, and even Jamie takes a step back. "Stop it."

Her mother raises her hand to her chest with faux offence. "Stop what?"

"You're incorrigible. I bring the man I love home and you try and set me up with someone else?" Hayley's shaking with anger, and I slip my arm around her shoulder. She waves her hand around under her mother's nose.

Sonya blanches. "You're engaged?"

"Yes. To be married, in case there is some way you could misinterpret that." Hayley spits the words at her mother. "That was the thing I had to tell you."

Sonya glares at me. "You didn't think you should maybe talk to us first?"

David steps out onto the decking.

"For Christ's sake, Sonya. The girl's twenty-eight years' old. Drew spoke to me about it this morning, and I said I was more than happy for the two of them." He comes up beside us and grips my shoulder. "They're in love, and they're happy. Isn't that what we always wanted for Hayley?"

Sonya looks down her nose at him. "I wanted to find her the right man."

"Stop being such a snob. Remember what it was like for us? We had nothing when Hayley was born, but we had each other."

"I just worry."

It makes me think of Mum and how she always thought she was doing what was best for us. It still pains me to think of what she put Adam and Lily through for no apparent reason.

"Drew's a good man. A doctor. And the best part of it all is that he loves our daughter. All I care about is that he'll cherish Hayley and take care of her. They'll take care of each other."

Sonya's shoulders slump as if she's been defeated.

"I can see that," she says quietly.

"So, what's the problem?"

"Mum, Drew's everything I ever wanted. And his family is awesome. He might be in Hamilton, but his brothers have been there for me when I needed them. You need to give him a chance."

She nods, giving us a small smile. "Well, if you're getting married, I guess we have a wedding to plan."

I smile as Hayley wraps her arms around my waist.

"I'm sorry, Drew. I never had a problem with you, I just know what it was like when David and I first got married.

We had no money, and it was such a struggle." Her tone suggests her hurt pride, and I can't hold this against her. She never meant Hayley any harm.

Nodding, I hold Hayley tighter. "I understand. Hayley will be well provided for. Though, she's done a good job of taking care of herself all this time."

Sonya lets out a sigh. "She's done so much with her life. I'm so proud of that."

Tears well in Hayley's eyes. This is everything she ever needed to hear. She holds her hand out to show her mother the ring we just bought.

Sonya's mouth drops. "That's beautiful, Hayley. How much did that ...?" She meets my eyes. "Sorry, old habits."

"Lots." Hayley lets out an audible breath. "Will you help me plan my wedding, Mum?"

"Do bears shit in the woods?"

That's the last thing I expect to hear out of Sonya's mouth, and I'm the first to laugh.

Sonya steps up and plants a kiss on my cheek. "Welcome to the family, Drew."

27

HAYLEY

LEAVING IS SURPRISINGLY DIFFICULT.

I look around my cottage. It's amazing how big it looks with nothing in it. Drew wanted me to leave the movers to do their work, but I want to make sure the house is in good order when I leave.

I'll miss this place. When I needed time alone and space, it was everything I needed.

Adam appears in the door. The whole family's here to say goodbye to me. Not Drew's mother—apparently, she's under the weather today—but Drew's father came. There are walls up in this family, distinct lines that aren't being crossed, but I'll be proud and happy to be a part of it. Drew's brothers already act as if they're my brothers.

"Ready?" he asks.

"I think so."

He smiles. "Just think of what's waiting for you at the

other end. I'm happy for you two, and I'm looking forward to this wedding."

I grin. Mum had a lot of ideas, but I was firm that I wanted the wedding to be held in Copper Creek. Drew's mum has enough to deal with having to travel for chemo, and besides, this is my home. In six months' time, I'll become Mrs Drew Campbell, surrounded by both families, and I can't wait. "I'm excited about the wedding, true. As much as I'm looking forward to moving in with Drew, saying goodbye isn't easy."

"It's not supposed to be."

As I grab my bag and walk toward the door, Adam hugs me. "Just promise me you two won't get so lost in each other you forget us in the meantime."

I laugh. "We'll try."

"Good on you, Hayley."

I take a deep breath, and step out to the front doorstep. Margaret stands just off to the side, and after Adam follows me out, I pull the door shut behind me and lock it.

I hand her the keys. She wraps her arms around me, and I grin.

"I'll miss you," she says. "You'd better come and visit me."

"Of course I will."

She nods toward the house. "I'll drop the keys off on Monday, and that's that."

Tears well as I nod in return. She helped me find my little house, and it became my refuge.

"I'm so proud of you," she says. "You went through so much, and you came out the other side so much stronger."

"Thank you."

"Be happy," she whispers. "Send me an invite to the wedding."

"You bet."

Lily embraces me next, and tears fall as I hug her back. It's because Lily and Adam expanded their family that I met the man who means more to me than anyone else in the world. I feel like I owe them everything.

"No doubt we'll talk soon," Lily says.

I nod. "I'll keep in touch. How else are you going to be my maid of honour?"

Her eyes widen. "Really?"

"We want to involve everyone. And I can't think of anyone I'd rather ask."

She smiles. "I'd love to. When Adam and I finally tie the knot, I want you involved, too."

"Not in a hurry?"

"We have a few things we want to work through first that are gonna cost us a bit of money. Then we'll get the wedding we always wanted."

I grasp her hands. "Anything I can do to help, let me know."

"We'll be sisters-in-law. You'll be stuck with me."

"I'm happy to be stuck with you."

Of course, I can't get past Owen and Corey, who each give me a farewell hug, and I'm battling tears as I step into my car.

Four years ago, when I arrived in Copper Creek, I never knew how much I'd grow to love this place. It'll always hold a special place in my heart.

With a final wave, I drive, leaving behind the town that

gave me so much, going toward the city where my future lies. A future I never dared to dream of.

I don't have a job yet, but I'll take my time and find something perfect, something that fits into the life I'll lead with Drew.

That's what's important.

After what feels like the longest drive of my life, I pull into the driveway. The moving truck should have been, and most of my clothes are packed away, so I grab my suitcase from the back seat. It's enough to keep me going for a couple of days.

Drew's standing at the door when I make my way up the path, his eyes full of love and a smile on his face. Knowing I'm here for good this time brings tears to my eyes all over again.

"Hey," he says softly.

"Hey, yourself."

He takes my suitcase from my hand and leans over to give me a kiss.

"Get inside and put your feet up. You must be tired after your drive."

I yawn. "I am. Could do with a sleep."

"Then go get one. Doctor's Orders."

Pressing my hand to his chest, I look up at him with all the love in the world.

I'm home.

BAKER'S DOZEN TEASER

Chapter One
Ginny

"Do you, Drew Jason Campbell, take Hayley Louise McCarthy to be your wife?"

Drew grins. "Oh yes, I do."

I chuckle, along with the rest of the congregation. Even though I've never met them before, I can feel there's so much love in this ceremony. It's probably the biggest wedding Copper Creek's ever seen.

"Do you, Hayley Louise McCarthy, take Drew Jason Campbell to be your husband?"

"I do."

Wiping my eyes, I look around. Max waves from his post on the groom's side. He's standing with his father, and the two of them have the biggest grins on their faces. It's a beautiful ceremony. I give him a small wave in return.

Next to them are the other three Campbell brothers: Owen, Corey, and James. Max has told me all about them at school, and I think I know far more of that family than I should.

I look a little too long, and Owen's eyes meet mine. Blushing, I look away. I can't help it. I've heard all about the reputation of the town baker, and I'm not interested in just a hookup, but he's still heartbreakingly hot.

I've been so pre-occupied looking around, watching the family I know so much about, I miss the rings being exchanged, but I don't miss the celebrant holding out her hands and smiling. "Go on, Drew, kiss the bride. We know you've been waiting."

Drew pulls Hayley into his arms, and my grin grows bigger watching him kiss her. Love is a beautiful thing, and when it radiates from two people like it does from them, it's something special.

When he leads her out and the wedding party follow, it's like Owen Campbell's noticed me for the first time, and maybe he has as he fixes his gaze on me while trailing along behind his brothers.

The bakery isn't a place I visit. Health issues keep me on a gluten free diet. It eases the symptoms. Doesn't mean I can't enjoy the view of the baker. Maybe I could eat a little.

I stand, and follow the rest of the congregation to the massive marquee that's been set up near the trees. The cove is a beautiful place for a wedding, and it's such a lovely sunny day with no wind. The conditions couldn't be better.

There are a lot of out-of-towners at this wedding, and the businesses in town have geared up for a big weekend. From what I've heard, Hayley's dad is some bigshot, and a chunk of Auckland has relocated to Copper Creek for the wedding.

When I find the little card with my name on it, I sit at the table. The bridal party are having photos down near the water, and I can see them posing from a distance. Laughter floats through the air from them, and it makes me smile.

The water glitters in the sunlight, and I take a deep breath. I come from a small town, but there's something special about this place.

I pick a glass of sparkling wine from a tray and take a look around. The table I'm at is all names I don't recognise, but I'm not far from the bridal table which makes me feel incredibly honoured.

Big social situations make me nervous. I might be a teacher and surrounded by kids all day, but they're easy to deal with compared to a lot of adults.

The chatter increases as the bridal party makes it into the marquee, and I smile as I catch sight of Max.

"Ginny, I'm so glad you could make it." Lily greets me as she approaches, the bride beside her. "I'm not sure if you two know each other. Ginny, this is Hayley. Hayley, this is Ginny. She used to be Max's teacher."

Hayley's eyes widen. "The famous Ginny who Max wanted desperately on the guest list?"

I laugh. "I guess so."

"We told him he could invite one person thinking he'd invite a school friend, but you were the only one he wanted. It's great to meet you."

"You too. It's been such a beautiful wedding."

She grins.

"There she is." Drew draws up beside her, wrapping his

arm around her waist. He gives Hayley a lingering kiss that makes me blush.

"Babe, this is Ginny. Max's teacher."

He raises his eyebrows. "*The* Ginny?"

Lily laughs. "Stop it you two. You'll give Ginny a complex."

"Oi. You lot. Time to get seated." Owen walks over and ushers Drew, Hayley, and Lily back to the main table. He shoots me a grin over his shoulder, and I swear I melt into a puddle.

"Miss Robinson." Max comes running over, and I can't help but smile at his infectious enthusiasm.

"Hey, Max. You did well today."

"Did you know there's chocolate cake?"

I laugh and shake my head. "I didn't, but I guess I do now."

"Max." Adam beckons his son.

"See ya." Max runs to him, and I watch as he's led to his seat, a huge grin on my face. He waves at me again, and I can't help waving back. Of all the kids I've taught, it's Max who makes me proudest.

Owen Campbell's looking at me again. I blush as I meet his gaze, but then it could be someone behind me he's smiling at. Among the congregation are some pretty gorgeous girls. I don't recognise any of them as being locals, but then again, I do tend to keep to myself.

Today I made an exception for an exceptional boy.

When the meal's nearly over but the wine's still flowing, Drew taps the side of his glass with a spoon. A hush falls over the tent, and I turn my chair to get a better view of the bridal table.

Drew smiles. "We're going to make this quick as I'm sure everyone wants to get back to the food and drink. I just want to thank my brothers for standing with me today, and Maxxy. You're the bomb."

I grin, and Max cheers.

"A special thanks to Owen for the wedding cake. Hayley knew exactly what she wanted, and you did such an amazing job."

The cake's wheeled in, and it's gorgeous. Intricate patterns in the icing make it way too pretty to eat, but given that it's chocolate, I might break my own rule and have a tiny piece.

"I want to thank Hayley's parents for this amazing day. I'm so proud and happy to be part of your family. And last, but most important of all …" He pauses, and looks down at his bride. "Meeting you is the best thing that's ever happened to me. My heart wasn't whole until now. I'm the luckiest man on the planet to be married to you, Hayley, and I promise to love you each and every day for the rest of our lives."

I pick up a paper napkin from the table and wipe my eyes.

"Now, get back to eating and drinking, and we'll start the music shortly."

At one end of the marquee is a temporary dance floor, and when the food's been eaten, we all make our way over to see the bride and groom's first dance.

The band plays something sweet and slow as Drew and Hayley lose themselves in each other. I'm a little envious of their locked gaze. Surely nothing and no one can break that, and although I don't really know them, I hope it continues the rest of their lives.

Slowly, the floor fills with other couples, and I find a seat nearby and sip my champagne.

I can't complain about being lonely when it's my choice, but seeing so much love in the room leaves my heart aching a little. Though, that could be the wine.

The music speeds up, and I close my eyes.

"Dance?"

I open them to see Drew standing over me, his hand extended.

"Me?"

He laughs. "Hayley's taking a break, and she spotted you here by yourself. Thought you might fancy a spin around the dance floor."

I grin. "Why not?"

Taking his hand to stand, I follow him to the centre of the dance floor. Adam and Lily are there, along with Drew's oldest brother. He's really tall and a bit scary, but he has a big grin and a gorgeous blonde hanging off his every word.

"Do you know everybody?" Drew asks.

"I know Lily and Adam."

He nods. "This is Corey, and …" Leaning over, he places his hand to cup his mouth. "I have no idea what her name is. I think he just picked her up."

I laugh.

"Having fun?" Lily takes my hand, and I nod.

We dance for a while before I excuse myself to get some

more wine. One more is my limit. Any after that I'll be walking home.

Hayley joins her husband again, and leads him to the cake. Another tap on a wine glass quietens everyone down.

"I just wanted to say thank you again to everyone for coming, and to Owen for this magnificent thing that Hayley doesn't want to cut," Drew says.

Laughter fills the large tent.

"Make sure you get some." I look up to see Owen walk past as he shoots me a wink. I nod, and laugh as he takes the knife from Drew's hand. "I'll cut the cake with you if Hayley doesn't want to."

Hayley laughs, slapping him on the arm.

He holds the knife up as if in surrender. "Okay. You do it. But I want a big piece."

After they make their slice and feed each other cake, Owen takes over and slices pieces from it, giving small plates to Max to deliver.

Max heads straight for me. "Owen said this piece is for you."

I nod. "Thank you, Max."

He beams before heading to the next person, and I get a better look at the icing. Tiny swirls form hearts all over it. It's so delicate and light, but exquisitely detailed. It's a work of art.

I take a tiny bite. The chocolate mud cake melts in my mouth, and I can't help but groan at the taste and sensation. This is a cake made with a lot of love and care. I eat it slowly, savouring each bite. I can't remember the last time I ate cake. It's not part of my strict diet, and I rarely break it. This is worth it.

The music starts back up, and I look over toward the cake. Owen's not standing beside it anymore, and all I'm left with is the hope I can tell him what an amazing job he's done.

Then I spot him.

My heart melts at the sight of Max and Owen in the middle of the dance floor. Max is full of life and laughter, and his uncle seems to have just as much energy.

Max's eyes light up when our gazes meet, and he makes a beeline for my table.

"Come and dance with us, Miss Robinson."

I grin. "I don't know, Max. Looks like you two are having a lot of fun already."

Owen comes up behind him. "What are you doing, Max? Abandoning me in the middle of a dance?" He shoots me a smile. "Hi."

"Hi. Max is just trying to convince me to dance with you guys."

"You totally should. Owen Campbell." He holds his hand out for me to shake.

"Ginny Robinson." I take hold of his hand, and he pulls me to my feet.

"Now you're standing, that's halfway to the dance floor."

Max giggles. "Come on."

"Okay." My hand is still in Owen's as he leads me back to the empty spot, and he reaches for Max's with the other.

Max resists taking Owen's hand, twisting and turning. His excitement is contagious, and I find myself sneaking peeks at Owen who's smiling just as much as Max is.

"Are you having fun?" Owen asks.

"It's been a lovely wedding. The cake was wonderful."

"Thank you."

"I invited her." Max pokes his tongue out.

"Did you? Am I holding hands with your date?"

Max laughs and shakes his head. "Miss Robinson was my teacher."

"Ohhh, so this is the *famous* Miss Robinson. Max talks about you all the time." I laugh, as Owen twirls me under his arm, and I swing one way and then back again.

"Max was one of my best students. Weren't you, Max?"

He nods. "Mum says Miss Robinson is the best teacher I've ever had. But she's not my teacher this year."

Max left me at the end of last year to go to high school. When I came to town three years ago, he was struggling, but I don't think anyone had dealt with a child like him before. Max was behind in his learning, and from what I could see of his school records he'd had difficulties all the way through.

From talking to Lily, he'd had a premature and difficult birth which had influenced that. I took Max under my wing, and we made more progress in two years than he had since he started school. I worried he'd slip at high school, but from the sound of it, he's showing everyone what he's made of.

"You two should get married," Max declares.

My mouth drops open, and all Owen does is chuckle.

"Why's that?" he asks.

"Because then Miss Robinson could be my auntie."

Owen's eyes sparkle, and my stomach flips. I didn't come to Copper Creek looking for a hookup. I kept to myself after a bad breakup. But maybe he could be the man to make me change my mind.

"That's not quite how it works, Max. Miss Robinson and I don't really know each other." He ruffles Max's hair.

"Thanks for looking out for me though. Maybe when you're older, you can be my wingman."

"What's that?" Max asks.

Owen grins. "Go ask your father."

Max disappears in an instant, and I gape at Owen. "Poor Adam."

He shrugs. "It comes with the territory. He's just lucky I don't explain sex to Max."

I laugh. "I'm pretty sure he's got some ideas about that. He is in high school."

"Sometimes I forget how old he is."

Owen's phone beeps and he pulls it out of his pocket. His eyebrows dip.

"Is everything okay?"

He shakes his head. "There's been an accident just outside of town. Car versus truck. I've got to go."

"Is it someone you know?"

Owen shrugs. "Not sure, but I'm a volunteer for the fire brigade. If they're paging us, it's got to be bad."

I nod. "Go."

"You owe me a dance, Miss Robinson." He takes a step back and turns before I can say anything further.

I'm left standing by myself on the dance floor, with people still dancing beside me.

I look around the room. How many women has Owen been with here? His reputation precedes him, and I'm not sure what to think about that.

If he really meant anything by his words.

ALSO BY WENDY SMITH

Coming Home

Doctor's Orders

Baker's Dozen

Hunter's Mark

Teacher's Pet

A Very Campbell Christmas

Fall and Rise Duet

Falling

Rising

Fall and Rise - The Complete Duet

The Aeon Series

Game On

Build a Nerd

Bar None

Coming 2022 Love on Site

Hollywood Kiwis Series

Common Ground

Even Ground

Under Ground

Coming soon Rocky Ground

Stand alones

For the Love of Chloe

Coming 2022 Lost and Found

The Friends Duet

Loving Rowan

Three Days

The Forever Series

Something Real

The Right One

Unexpected

Chances Series

Another Chance

Taking Chances

Lifetime Series

In a Lifetime

In an Instant

In a Heartbeat

In the End

At the Start